DEAD BRANCHES

BENJAMIN LANGLEY

Published by Crystal Lake Publishing—Tales from The Darkest Depths

Website: www.crystallakepub.com/

Copyright 2019 Benjamin Langley
Join the Crystal Lake community today
on our newsletter and Patreon!
Download our latest catalog here:
https://geni.us/CLPCatalog

All Rights Reserved

Cover art:
Don Noble—www.roosterrepublicpress.com

Layout:
Kenneth W. Cain—www.kennethwcain.com

This is a work of fiction. Names, characters, businesses, places, events and incidents are either the products of the authors' imagination or used in a fictitious manner. Any resemblance to actual persons, living or dead, or actual events is purely coincidental.

No part of this publication may be reproduced, stored in a retrieval system, or transmitted in any form or by any means, without the prior permission in writing of the publisher, nor be otherwise circulated in any form of binding or cover than that in which it is published and without a similar condition including this condition being imposed on the subsequent purchaser.

WELCOME
TO ANOTHER

CRYSTAL LAKE PUBLISHING
CREATION

Join today at www.crystallakepub.com & www.patreon.com/CLP

ACKNOWLEDGEMENTS

So many people have helped to make this book what it is. It's a product of many experiences over the years, since my youngest days. I'd like to thank my parents for making me believe that anything is possible, and for feeding my love of horror since the beginning. I mean, how old was I when I was terrified of 'Stop Boris', the game in which you had to shoot the giant spider with the laser gun? Was that an appropriate Christmas present? We loved it! Thanks for buying me 'Scream' comics, and of course, Horror Top Trumps.

I have fond memories of watching horror movies with my siblings and with my mum and my nan on Saturday nights throughout my childhood (starting with the Hammer House of Horror classics), and that spread to a love of reading horror. We should have known it would come to this!

I couldn't do this without the support of my wonderful wife, Lisa, and my two girls, Malibu and Georgia. We've had some great times together, and you always give me the time I need and the encouragement to develop my writing projects. Lisa, thanks for listening to my ideas, reading my drafts, and helping to make this dream a reality.

Huge thanks to my good friend Michelle Foster who gave me feedback on an earlier version of the novel. (Actually, she swore at me for what I did to one of the characters.) Our regular meetups kept me sane and being able to discuss and plot out ideas with you is so valuable.

Don Noble, thanks for the awesome cover.

An early draft of this novel was part of my MA in Creative writing, so I'd like to that the staff at Anglia Ruskin University, particularly Colette Paul and Una McCormack. Thanks for the great advice, and all the recommended reading. I'll get through them all one day.

The first words of the novel (long since entirely replaced) were written on a delightful writing retreat at Le Verger in France. David and Michele Lambert are excellent hosts, and the opportunity to write in such a pleasant location really got the wheels turning on this one.

I'd also like to thank everyone who has supported me in my writing and given me encouragement in the writing groups and workshops I've attended over the years.

Thank you to Joe and the team at Crystal Lake Publishing for giving this book another chance to find an audience. I appreciate it.

Finally, thanks to all the writers of stories out there that keep us filled with wonder, and all of the readers that are holding a copy of this book—I hope you enjoyed it.

- Benjamin Langley

*For the friends we make
when we're young and innocent*

He's dying.
I read the letter to be sure.
The doctor says he's only got days left.

"What's wrong, Dad?" Charlie's in front of me, already dressed for school.

"Hey, Charlie!" I pull him into one of my inescapable bear-hugs. Two months from turning ten, he's almost the age I was when I last saw my dad.

He squeezes free, proving my bear-hugs fallible, and looks at the letter on the table. "Who's it from?" he says, his inquisitive face scrunched up.

I won't say Charlie takes after me. I was naïve, and he's a smart lad. But it's a common misconception that children don't know what's going on. Some people forget how curious they were as youngsters and don't remember that answers like it's nothing or don't worry about it encourage curious children to seek their own conclusions. Sometimes the best answers are the ones you find yourself.

"It's from my mother. Your grandmother." I don't remember the last time I let her see Charlie. It was never her fault, and it's unfair to keep him from her, but she's linked to too many bad memories.

"Your granddad's dying."

Charlie nods, but he's not affected. Had I told him my dad was a bad man? I'm not one for stories—not anymore. Now Charlie's older, I have to tell him. If I don't, I'm worse than they were. Mum said they tried to protect us, but what harm would the truth have done? Not telling us was the easy option. And look at the damage it did.

It's a long time since I thought of that summer. It's a long time since I thought of Little Mosswick and its network of drove-ways and ditches that were our secret trails around the village. Don't believe the myth that Fenland folk are somehow special, that they have an affinity with the soil and share some kind of secret knowledge. Don't believe there's an inherent goodness in that place.

I found out that wasn't true in 1990. It should have been a magical summer. The World Cup had just started, and we

2 DEAD BRANCHES

were young and believed anything was possible. We never knew such terrible things could happen. I made the mistake of believing what my family told me. I made the mistake of believing they'd keep us safe. Do I want to relive that? Perhaps the biggest reason I'd find returning to my childhood home so difficult is that, despite years of running the events through my head, before I locked them away for my own sanity, I'm still not sure of how much of what happened was real. And now, as I study the words that suggest he's dying, I wonder, can a creature like that even die?

PART ONE

Tuesday, 12th June 1990

Did the silence strike me as odd? Before it all began, every day the chickens clucked so noisily that they could be heard across the yard. But not on that day. The flurry of feathers–soft, white under-feathers–stained red, and drifting on the breeze, alarmed me. Chicken wire jutted out of the henhouse at an ugly angle, twisted and torn away from the wood, and a strong smell, like a well-soiled cat litter tray left to fester in the sun, hung in the air.

Reaching for the door, I felt a lifeless coldness. Heat used to radiate from the coop; its absence chilled me. Turn and run. That was my instinct, back to the comfort of my room, but I'd have to face him, and I couldn't return empty-handed. Before grabbing the handle, I took a few deep breaths. I didn't have to open the door far before the remains of a chicken tumbled out, brushing by my leg and falling onto my foot. It appeared intact: head, wings, legs, all there, but then, a bloody chasm. Bits of bone and pink-purplish flesh, still wet, glistened in the early morning sun. I stared at it and felt my gut tighten. What could have caused such carnage? Part of me didn't want to know but fear more than curiosity made me look.

Inside, blood stained the wooden panels and a layer of chicken carcasses, gore, and feathers hid the straw. Despite the devastation, despite the decimation, it was only when I saw a broken shell and hardening yolk smeared on a nest box, that I panicked. What if I went back without any eggs? Dad's face, puffy and red, came into my mind and I imagined him muttering *useless boy*. Then he'd pull on his boots and stamp off, swearing about me under his breath. I needed to find an egg. I swept dismembered birds aside, searching the corner where they often laid. Sticky with half-set egg, shards of eggshell clung to the straw. In the other corner, beside a dead chicken with one wing torn off and no head, something egg-shaped remained. I pulled the mangled bird aside by a cold, hard leg and as suspected, as hoped, found a single, speckled egg. I gathered it and hurried to the house where the smell of melting lard, and the intense heat of the kitchen made my stomach turn.

"You got some?" asked Mum.

I held out the palm of my hand, the lone egg, the sole survivor, resting upon it.

Dad glared at me. He scratched at one of his sideburns. "One egg? What good is one fucking egg?" He sneered as he stared at me, no doubt looking for faults; as always, he found something. "What's that slarred up your top?"

I looked at one arm, saw nothing, and then at the other. Streaks of red scarred my school shirt.

"You've ruined your shirt, boy. You must think I farm money. You must think I pull it out of the earth."

"Something's happened," I said, my voice reduced to a whisper.

Mum dipped a tea towel in the sink and came over. She scrubbed at the blood, causing it to spread further along the sleeve. "Whatever is it?" she asked.

"They're dead," I said, shaking my arm away from Mum. As I did so, the egg shot out of my hand and smashed onto the tiled floor.

"What the hell are you playing at?" Dad said rising out of his chair. Seated, he resembled a hulking beast, standing, an absolute behemoth.

I had to make myself understood before I stoked his ire further. "They're dead!" I said again.

This time he heard. "Who are?" His brow furrowed and his eyebrows became one long hairy caterpillar.

"The chickens! They're all dead."

As expected, Dad went over to the door and pulled on his size thirteen boots. "Why didn't you say in the first place?"

"Go get a fresh shirt," Mum said. "I'll clean this mess."

We both gazed at the egg. The sight of the orange yolk, broken and diluting with the transparent white made me think of the stiff egg yolk in the henhouse and the gored bodies of the hens, and, feeling bile rising in my gut, I dashed through the door.

My older brother, Will, stood on the stairs. "What have you done now?" he asked with a grin.

I rushed past him, and he turned to follow me back upstairs.

With ragged breath and tears welling, I pulled open a drawer looking for a clean shirt.

Will put his arm around me and guided me to the bed. "What's up?"

The tears came with an angry grunt before I blurted out, "He'll say it's my fault."

"What's your fault?"

I sniffed and rubbed at my eyes. "The chickens." I took another deep breath as I tried to bring my sobbing under control. "They're all dead."

Will rubbed my back. "How can that be your fault? Doesn't matter what he says, you know it's not true, I know it's not true, and Dad knows it's not true, either. He says stuff like that without thinking."

I took in a deep breath.

"You can't let it get to you."

I wiped the last of my tears from my cheek.

Will moved over to the drawers, pulled out a shirt and tossed it to me. "Come on. We don't want to be late."

I swallowed hard, tasting the snot the sobbing had drawn up. It had passed. Will had done it again. He always knew when I needed him, and how to calm me down. He was eleven, the second oldest at Little Mosswick Primary School, and about the coolest kid I knew. As long as I had him to rely on, I figured I'd always be all right.

The heat had prickled me all day and left me agitated. With the stench of blood stuck in my nostrils, and the vision of carnage in my mind, concentration failed me at school. After school, nothing changed. I'd started my go on Super Mario Bros. when a knock on the door distracted me. I mistimed my jump and Mario landed in the open mouth of a piranha plant. Will laughed as Mario's death tune played and he reached for the joypad, but then several rapid bangs drew us out of our bedroom. When we reached the middle step, Mum called my name.

Dad sat at the kitchen table chasing gravy around his plate with a piece of Yorkshire pudding. As usual, a smear of mud remained on his left cheek and he looked grey with stubble. Mum stood near the door, and my friend John's mum, who always insisted that I call her Barbara rather than Mrs Glover, stepped inside. It felt weird calling adults by their first names. She looked out of place in our kitchen in her red and white supermarket uniform.

She came over to me. "Tom." She put her hand on my shoulder, the knuckles red. "Have you seen John?" A string of saliva hung between her lips.

I shook my head. "Not since school."

"Did he have any plans?" said Barbara.

I shrugged. Had John said anything? With the mood I'd been in, I couldn't remember. I'd gone home for tea with my cousin, Liam, who had dragged me out of the classroom at the end of the day, and hopped around outside his brother Andy's classroom, urging him to hurry. Our gang, the Crusaders, consisted of Will, Liam, Andy and me. We used to be called The Muskehounds, but we had argued over who should be Dogtanian, so we changed it. John had been hanging around with us so much that we'd had a secret meeting to discuss whether he should be allowed to be a full-time part of the gang. We'd decided that he could, but we hadn't told him yet.

"Did he leave school on his own?" Barbara said. The saliva string broke.

"I don't know. Sometimes he walks with Chris Jackson."

"I've been there." She took a huge breath as if she'd forgotten to breathe until that moment.

"Did he get home and go out again?" asked Dad, glancing up from his dinner plate. Before waiting for a response, he picked up a knife and cut himself a slab of bread.

Barbara's head dropped, and she stared at the tiles. She was never there when John got home. Her job in the new supermarket in Ely meant John got the house to himself for a couple of hours. He always asked one of us over to play to avoid being alone.

"I'm sure he'll turn up," Mum said. She placed a hand on Barbara's shoulder. "You know what boys are like."

I couldn't pinpoint the exact moment Mum was thinking of because we often spent evenings out, reinforcing a hideout or trying to get a raft to float on the river, and then wandered home at dark, but we'd never dare do it on a school night.

Mum gave Barbara a sympathetic nod, her hand lingering on her shoulder. I could never imagine the two of them as friends. Everything about them was different. Mum looked like a proper mum should, but John's mum looked and acted more like a mum off the TV, with red lipstick and hair that didn't move. They lived in one of Little Mosswick's new housing estates that Dad swore so much about when they were built.

"I should go," said Barbara. She stepped outside and then turned back at me.

"Is there anyone else I could ask?"

John didn't have many friends. He was smart, and he knew it, and people didn't like that. I shook my head, and she turned away, her shoulders low. As Mum put her hand on the door, I said, "Wait," and Barbara turned. "Maybe Daniel Richardson? They hang out together sometimes."

Daniel and John *were* friends, but they'd fallen out when John had lent his imported Nintendo Gameboy to me and not him. Perhaps they'd made up. Perhaps John was over at Daniel's house trading Panini World Cup stickers. Maybe John was swapping his sticker of the World Cup trophy with Daniel, the sticker I needed to complete my first page. More than anything, if it meant John was okay, I wanted Daniel to have that sticker even if I never completed my collection.

"Want us to have a look around? See if he turns up?" Dad said without looking up from his plate.

"No, I couldn't ask…"

"It's no trouble. I'll bring him straight home if we find him." Dad rose out of his seat. He wiped his hands on his jumper and I wondered how he could even wear one in the eternal furnace of our kitchen.

"If you don't mind… Thank you." She turned to me, "And this other boy, Daniel?"

I told Barbara where Daniel lived, and she smiled weakly before hurrying out.

"It's not right leaving kids that age on their own," Dad said, after pushing another piece of bread into his mouth which distorted his voice. "Mothers should be home with their children."

He swallowed noisily then reached for his boots and sunk back into the seat to pull them on. "Couldn't leave her in that state. Had to do something."

He stood up and called out, "Will!"

Will thudded down the stairs and peered around the door frame.

"Come walk with me up along the drove to the river bank."

"Okay," Will said and fetched his shoes.

"You, boy," he said, glaring at me, "have a wander around the back field. Take Chappie with you. He needs the exercise."

We named our dog after the brand of food we fed him. We thought we were being original by not calling him Spot or Patch or Rover. A border collie, he had a black coat with a ring of white around his neck and over his shoulders and a patch around his left eye. We got him from the animal shelter. He'd been abandoned, so we didn't know his age, but in the last year, he'd slowed down. He showed no excitement when I fetched his lead, and he struggled to get to his feet.

"Come on, Chappie," I said, trying to muster enthusiasm.

He shook after he stood, and then stared at me with his watery eyes as I put him on the lead.

Our house was a couple of hundred metres from the main road (called Main Street) which ran through Little Mosswick.

A series of droves linked the various fields that made up our farm. It had been so dry that the stiff mud on those old routes had cracked and looked like the skin of an ancient dinosaur. Granddad Norman could name all the droves, but I only knew where they led to, or the streets which they crossed. I scanned the drove that led to the river, the one Dad and Will headed down, but I could see no sign as they'd disappeared behind the row of elderberry bushes.

I gave Chappie's lead a tug. "It's me and you again."

He stopped to sniff the gate post.

"How come it's always Dad and Will, hey Chappie?" I dragged him along as I gazed into the ditches on either side that separated the field of oilseed rape, alive with yellow flowers swaying in the breeze, from the field planted with the potato crop. "I'd rather be with you, anyway."

I didn't know why I kept peering into the ditches. Those on the left were bone dry and had dying grass and a few bulrushes withering away in them. The other side contained hundreds of nettles, with a few dock leaves sprouting at the edges. At least if anyone fell in, they'd be able to ease the sting with a rub of the leaves. A rustle came from within the nettles, and I pictured the horrible toad-like creature from the cover of the Fighting Fantasy book I'd been playing: *Deathtrap Dungeon*. If anything planned to strike, it would have been when I was alone. But John was strong and smart; nothing like that could take him.

I wasn't scared, but I didn't want to walk along the ditches anymore. When we reached the entrance to the field, I decided to cut across it.

I let Chappie off his lead and he disappeared beneath the sea of green leaves, and I had to follow the quivering of the plants to tell where he was. Given the size of the plants, I figured it would almost be time to harvest them, but I couldn't be sure. Dad expected me to know that sort of thing, but I couldn't keep it in my head. "Too busy with silly games and books," he'd say.

14 DEAD BRANCHES

I headed towards the back end which was never planted. It was home to a rusting Ford tractor that hadn't moved in my lifetime. John liked to tinker with machinery, so I thought it worth checking in case he'd wandered over to it.

I kept my eyes on the tractor, avoiding the twisted, oak tree in the back corner. Dead, at some point it had been struck by lightning, perhaps more than once, which had split the top of the trunk in two. It also bore a scorch mark like a gaping mouth, and the wild branches above resembled the hair of an ancient creature or the snakes of Medusa, and where the low branches had been severed it looked like it had stumpy limbs. In recent years, ivy had grown around its base, giving the impression it had returned to life, back from the dead like a zombie.

I'd been scared of the tree ever since Granddad Norman put one of his glass eyes into a knot on the tree's trunk the day after he told us the story of how he lost his eye. Not long after they bought the land, which hadn't been farmed since the Miller boys (whoever they were) had been killed during the First World War, my great-granddad wanted that land in use. He gave Granddad Norman, (who was no older than thirteen at the time) and his older brother, Arthur, one day to clear it.

Once, sheds had stood there, but they'd long since collapsed and the beams were left half-buried in the ground. The best method Arthur and Granddad Norman could think of was to drag them out using chains attached to the tractor. They'd almost cleared the entire field, but then they set their sights on the old oak tree which already appeared to be dead. They thought they could pluck it from the ground as easily as those beams that had only been sunk a year or two. They didn't reckon on the ancient evil that held the cursed oak in place. The tree, smelling blood and relishing the opportunity to do harm, allowed Granddad Norman to tie the chain around its trunk. Arthur started the tractor. The engine roared and the chain dug into the trunk. Granddad swears it bowed and looked ready to tear out of the ground when he heard something ping. The last thing he saw with his left eye was the broken chain flying towards him.

It was for the best, claimed Granddad, because if the tree hadn't taken his eye, then he would have fought in the Second World War and, like Arthur, he might never have come home.

Wedging his glass eye into one of the tree's knotholes the day after he told us that story was his worst prank yet. He spied on us from behind the old Ford tractor and slapped the side of his legs, laughing as Andy ran off across the field screaming, and he kept laughing until he had to dab at his good eye with a handkerchief.

I couldn't face the tree in case it looked back and who knows what would have happened if I got caught in its evil glare, so I turned towards the new bypass. John knew better than to go there, not while they worked on it. We used to mess around there when it was a huge pile of sand and rubble and unattended for days at a time, but he was more sensible than to play in the path of a steamroller.

A rustle came from the edge of the potato plants. "Chappie," I called, and the plant stilled. Seconds later, from another part of the crop, Chappie emerged. I kept my eyes on the spot where I'd seen movement. "Come on, Chappie. Here, boy!" I needed him by my side. Flashes of the morning's dismembered birds passed through my mind. Whatever got them lurked a few feet away, perhaps ready to feed again.

Chappie ignored me and sniffed at the tractor wheels. He cocked his leg up at it and whined as he peed.

I backed away from the plants, keeping one eye on them and moved over the tractor. Darting my eyes to the ground, I spotted a flat stone. I ducked, grabbed it and threw it towards where the rustle had come from. Though I missed my target by a few feet, it caused a scurrying among the plants, and I could see them quivering as whatever had been watching me sped away.

I checked the tractor for signs of John's presence. A thin film of dust and dirt lay on the seat, and it was obvious no one had touched it for a while. I lifted a sheet of corrugated iron,

16 DEAD BRANCHES

and flipped it over, watching the worms wriggle underneath. There was a strong earthy smell, but nothing out of the ordinary. We walked close enough to the oak tree to check the ground for footprints in the soft earth around it, but I wouldn't get any closer than that. I needed to escape the field in case the creature had gathered reinforcements, so I put Chappie back on his lead, and despite his protests, we hurried across the field. I jumped the ditch while Chappie ran down and scrambled back up the other side. One of our old dens still stood near the path that led back to the farmhouse. This one we'd called Narnia, because, when we built it, I was obsessed with the TV series *The Lion the Witch and the Wardrobe* which had been on a few months earlier. Our current base was across the other side of the oilseed rape field, and we called that one Moon Base One (Liam named it). We also had a smaller one, up by the school, called The Broom Cupboard. Narnia was built where the ditch came to an end and a couple of elderberry bushes met and formed a natural shelter. We used to climb down the ditch and hide under the bushes. All that remained inside was a pile of sticks Will had sharpened with his penknife back in the days when we called ourselves The Muskehounds. When it rained, the ditch got wet at the bottom and Mum told us off for getting our school trousers muddy, so we abandoned it. John didn't know about this base, and there was no sign of anyone having been there, so we wandered back home, passing the chicken coop on the way. Something awful had happened there. I saw those mutilated chickens in my head again, and then John's face. What if the same creature that gored the chickens had attacked John too?

Dad's boots were by the door. I walked in and he sat at the table talking to Mum. His face was red, and his hair stood up as if he'd been running his hands through it. He broke off his conversation when he saw me and stared until I turned away.

"He'll be okay," Mum said. She patted me on the back, and I slipped off my shoes.

"Can I give his house a call?"

Mum turned away and picked up a tea towel to wipe a perfectly dry cup. "Better leave them alone," she said. "I'm sure he'll be at home, but his Mum and Dad will be having words with him."

Having words: adult speak for telling off.

With that, I mixed a glass of orange squash and took it up to my room. It was the room at the top of the stairs, with the spare room on the left (piled high with boxes) and the bathroom on the right. Mum and Dad's room was on the other side. We weren't allowed in there.

In our room, my bed was nearest the door which meant Will had to cross my side to get to his. He claimed he had the better half as it had more privacy. As the older brother, he deserved that.

On top of our shared set of drawers (top two for Will, bottom two for me) our shared TV sat—a 21-inch Philips colour TV with Teletext and a remote control. Attached to that was our Nintendo Entertainment System, a joint Christmas present six months earlier. Will had begun playing again.

I walked over to the window, glad our bedroom didn't overlook the rest of the village; I didn't want to see the school and the estate where John lived. But looking out over the field brought me no comfort either as my eyes always came to rest on the oak tree. I pulled the curtains closed.

John and I had played football together at lunch time. Some of the boys pretended to play for Cameroon as John had on Monday. Before Friday night the only thing we knew was a few names from the Panini sticker book and what was on the Top Trumps card–they'd played at one previous World Cup and had drawn all three games. But after they beat Argentina in the opening game of the Italia 90, their stickers became the hottest property on the playground. A few of us stuck to being England players despite their draw with Ireland. We had a

18 DEAD BRANCHES

mini-Peter Shilton in goal, a little Gary Lineker up front and John was Paul Gascoigne.

By afternoon break the temperature made playing football unbearable, so we sat under the shade of the conker tree at the bottom of the school playing field. We argued. Laura Matthews had walked past, and John had said she had buck teeth. I disagreed. It wasn't because I liked her; it was because it wasn't true. Laura had a nice smile. I thought of things about John I disliked. He always bragged that his Nintendo Entertainment System, imported from America, could play the latest games, while we didn't get them for yonks. John had finished Super Mario Bros. 3, while I still played the original. I'd been going over to John's house to play his games regularly, but that day I couldn't take any more of his showing off. But if I'd have gone, he'd be at home and he'd be okay. Instead, I went to Liam's because he was so excited about his new set of Top Trumps which we didn't even get around to playing.

Will switched off the Nintendo, plugged the aerial back in, and picked up the remote. He opened Ceefax and called out, 'Belgium two, South Korea nil.' The South Korean team had two players per sticker because no one knew their players. Will turned off Ceefax and switched the TV over for the Netherlands vs Egypt match and beckoned me over to his bed which had a better angle for viewing the TV. I'd been looking forward to seeing Ruud Gullit, Frank Rijkaard and Marco Van Basten play having never seen them in action before. I'd heard they were magicians. I'd seen clips of the wonder goal Van Basten scored in the European Championships two years ago—a perfect volley from an impossible angle. No way could a normal human do that. These guys were more than that. They were superhuman.

Midway through the first half, I found my attention wandering as the magic show I'd hoped to see failed to materialise. Every time a Dutch player tried to pull a rabbit from the hat, the Egyptian defence bopped it back down. Thinking of John, I kept glancing at the Gameboy—John's Gameboy—and decided I wanted one last go. I picked it up and realised that I'd placed it on top of *Deathtrap Dungeon*. I stared at the hideous toad creature, with its drool-covered fangs, and its multitude of eyes and then flipped over the book. Could such creatures be out there? Had one got into the henhouse? Had one been watching me from the potato plants? I shuddered and tried to erase it from my mind as I put the Tetris cartridge in the Gameboy and started a game. I cleared line after line and got my highest score ever, and then I turned it off and slipped it into my school bag, determined to return it to John in the morning.

Wednesday, 13th June 1990

I woke early. The machines roared on the bypass, but concern, not their low growl had woken me. I re-checked my bag for John's Gameboy which I'd wrapped in the red school sweater that the bright light pouring through the crack in the curtains suggested I wouldn't need.

I opened the curtains to let more of the morning sunshine in, ignoring Will's groans as he turned away from the light and pulled his duvet, which he must have kicked off during the night, back over himself. The morning haze hid the old pumping station where the Little Ouse met the Great Ouse, but not the bypass. The yellow machines—diggers, rollers and tipper trucks—chugged and I thought about how much closer they could have been.

A couple of years ago, a man from the Highways Agency came to discuss the purchase of some of Dad's land for the bypass. It would have taken a small chunk of the back field— the bit where nothing grew and that horrible tree stood. Dad could have put up a reasonable argument. He could have said he didn't want to sell because the further away the noise of the bypass was the better. He could have argued that he planned to clear up that bit of land and plant it up, and it would cost him his livelihood to sell it, but Dad didn't do reasoned argument.

Dad held a grudge against the parish council and as a result every type of council or Government official too. First, there had been a land dispute with Peter Dalby (Dad banned me from speaking to Ian Dalby at school) where they'd sided with the Dalby family. Then the council refused his planning application for a new barn to store crops in. Dad's view was not so much you scratch my back I'll scratch yours, but if I can't have it, you can't either. So instead of turning them down, he had them out to survey, waited for them to make an offer, sat on it for weeks, and then rejected it.

Dad wasn't in a good mood. I'd gone downstairs to get myself breakfast, and he was sitting at the table. He'd not shaved, so his face looked grey, and his eyes were puffy.

"Up early, boy," he said. "Shit the bed?"

He'd say this from time to time when in a better mood, but his low and flat voice suggested that wasn't the case.

"You want breakfast, Tom?" Mum said, getting up from the table and taking Dad's plate with her.

"I'll have cereal." I took the box of Rice Krispies from the cupboard.

"Don't speak to your dad then," Dad muttered. He got up and headed for the back door. "Ignorant little shit," he said.

I looked at Mum, and she smiled. "Any plans for after school today?"

"Probably hang out with Liam and Andy," I said as I turned away, not wanting her to see how Dad had upset me.

I didn't wait for Will because he meandered to school, chatting to people as if he had set himself a challenge to arrive as close to the bell as possible, and I wanted to catch John on the playground as he arrived to apologise for not going over to play.

When the bell rang, I was still waiting. I told myself that he might be late. But John was never late. As the last few pupils deserted the playground and entered the school, including Will who tapped me on the shoulder as he passed, I gazed at the gate, hoping for John to stroll through. My eyes fell upon a crisp packet that scuttled along on the gentle breeze and a lump, like a fistful of bubble gum, seemed to solidify in my stomach.

As I entered the class, late, I stared at John's seat. Empty—he hadn't used ninja skills to sneak past me. That lump in my gut grew.

"Sit down, Thomas," said Mrs Palmer. She'd been our teacher since September. She had dark brown hair with a ruler-straight fringe, wonky teeth, and always wore mustard-coloured cardigans. People said she smelled of cucumber, but I'd never noticed. She wasn't strict and on some days, she let us out at break time early. Also, she'd taken me off the reading scheme and made me a free reader, allowing me to read any book in the library. She even let me borrow her personal copies of *The Chronicles of Narnia*.

She read out the register, and when she got to *G* and called out John's name, everyone turned to face his seat. It was odd for him not to be there. It was odd for anyone to be absent and it usually led to stories spreading about the missing person having the squits, the squirts, or the runs, but no one said a word.

I felt sick. The lump in my stomach was breaking down and forcing bile to make its way back up my throat. I had to swallow hard to keep from vomiting, and I couldn't get the bitter taste out of my mouth.

"Can I go to the toilet, Mrs Palmer?" I asked.

She came over to check my work.

"Thomas, you've not done a single one of these sums," she said, poking at my exercise book with her finger.

I hadn't even realised we were doing maths. "I'm desperate," I said, swallowing hard again.

"Okay, off you go. But I expect much more effort when you get back, or you'll be staying in at break."

To get to the toilets, I had to go past the headmaster's office. Mr Inglehart sat at his desk, and a policeman sat opposite him. I couldn't loiter for two reasons: one, I was still about ninety per cent sure I would throw up, and two, because Mr Jenkins, the school caretaker, leant on his mop at the end of the corridor. An enthusiastic whistler, no one ever recognised any of the songs he whistled. His bushy beard hid the end of the mop handle. He had a habit of marching children he found hanging around the corridors to Mr Inglehart's office, and while that would have given me a better idea of the situation, I didn't much want to chuck my guts up in front of my headmaster and a policeman.

In the toilets, I splashed water on my face and took a few deep breaths. I went into one a cubicle and locked the door. After a few seconds, I remembered this was the toilet that John had dropped the red food colouring into, making the water go dark red. Then I'd waited in the cubicle next door and John in the one on the other side. We waited for someone to come in to see how they reacted. We could barely contain our laughter every time the toilet door opened. The first couple of visitors used the urinals, and we needed someone to visit the cubicle.

"The ideal scenario," John had said while plotting this prank, "would be for someone to come in, and not notice it before they do a dump. When they turn round, they'll think they've shit blood!" He'd laughed so hard that he couldn't breathe until I slapped his back.

It didn't work out like that, but the result was still hilarious. The door creaked open, and then, a few seconds later, a high-pitched scream sounded out and heavy footsteps followed as someone fled the toilets.

John and I tumbled out of our cubicles howling with laughter and dashed into the corridor to identify the screamer. It was a year-three boy in Andy's class called Jimmy Wilson.

A week later we got wind of a significant number of year three kids pretending to be Ghostbusters. We found Andy on the playground and he filled in the gaps.

"Jimmy saw a ghost in the toilets," he said, his eyes wide.

It turned out that Jimmy's older brother, Gavin, a college pupil, had been telling Jimmy for years that a ghost haunted the school toilets. Now Jimmy had proof.

"So, what did Jimmy do?" John asked, winking at me and recalling that high-pitched scream.

"He says he yelled at it, and it dissolved into goo in the toilet."

"Right," said John. He turned and winked and me and then faced Jimmy. "Can we play?"

Jimmy shrugged. "I guess you can be ghosts."

"No, I want to be a Ghostbuster. You be a ghost."

"But it's my game."

"I only want to play for a minute."

Jimmy sighed. He knew the rules. If a bigger kid wanted to join your game, then they dictated the rules. "Okay, I'm a ghost." He raised his hands, wiggled his fingers, and gave off a ghostly moan.

John threw his hands up in fake terror and gave out the longest highest-pitched scream, and ran off into the distance.

At first, Jimmy looked at him with a puzzled expression, but then the memory of his own reaction must have hit him and, to avoid eye contact, he stared at the ground.

I scanned the field and spotted John. He'd stopped screaming and had fallen to the ground.

Before I got close, I knew he'd be in another one of his giggling fits. I lay on the grass next to him, and his infectious laughter spread.

At some point, Liam came trudging over and sat down beside us. "What's so funny?" he asked.

"Stupid kids in year three," said John between bursts of giggles. "We played Ghostbusters."

A wrinkle formed on Liam's brow, his cheeks puffed out, and he pouted. "What's wrong with Ghostbusters?" he asked without making eye contact, instead choosing to pick a daisy and toss it at his feet.

"Nothing, but these kids reckon ghosts are real!" John burst out into laughter again.

"Don't you?" asked Liam, throwing a daisy at John.

John shook his head, and for some reason answered in a Cockney accent. "I don't believe in anything I can't witness with my own two eyes."

"What about you, Tom?" asked Liam.

I kept my mouth shut.

I guess I'd been out of the classroom a little too long as Mrs Palmer was peering out when I wandered back along the corridor.

"Are you okay, Thomas?" she asked.

I wanted to say something. Worry ate away at my gut. My brain screamed out horrendous possibilities. The last thing I wanted to do was burst into tears in front of my teacher though. Imagine the humiliation. Instead, I nodded, hurried back to my seat, and figured that I better get stuck into the maths to avoid losing my break.

It felt even stranger when we played football. John was one of the best players and a captain, and even though I was rubbish, he always picked me (he had to get some good players in first, but he'd never leave me until the end). Without John, I was down to the last two. I only got picked before Stu, who always toe-punted the ball and tripped over his feet, because Will insisted that Chris (the other captain) should pick me.

Chris assigned roles on the team. He told me I had to be Richard Witchge, the Dutch player who'd come on as a sub in the game last night. "I'm going to be Gazza," he said.

"No," I said, without thinking.

"What do you mean?" he said. "It's my team. I can be who I like."

"John's Paul Gascoigne," I said.

"Well, John's not here, is he?"

"But you can't take his player. Be someone else."

"Right, I'm swapping you out for Stu," he said, so I had to go onto the other team.

Everyone played as if everything was normal until Stu toe punted the ball into a group of girls (including Laura Matthews) who were making daisy chains and they ran off with the ball and told Mr Inglehart, who liked to patrol the field to make sure no one had too much fun and to keep an eye on how his favourite pupils (those who played for the school football team) were getting on. Wasn't he concerned about John? He patrolled the field as he would on a normal day. Maybe there was nothing to worry about. Maybe John was already back at home and he'd be back in school in a day or two, but something didn't feel right, and I didn't like it.

At the end of the school day, I waited with Liam for Will and Andy. Liam and I were in the same class, and despite me being six months older, he was bigger in every way: He had bigger feet, he had a bigger belly, and he had a much bigger head. There was one thing I suspected was smaller: his brain.

"Shall we walk round by John's house? Check if there's anything going on?" I said.

"Might as well. We'll have to walk past Shaky Jake's." Liam did his awful Shaky Jake impression, for which he clenched his fists and tensed up his muscles so his whole body shook until his face turned red.

"Think he'll shout at us again?" I asked.

Liam sniggered. "Maybe if you walk into his yard."

"No way." I held out my hands.

"Dare you." Liam shoved my shoulder with the palm of his hand and as I was about to grab him into an inescapable headlock, Will came wandering out of his classroom.

"Guess what?" Liam said to Will.

"What?"

"Tom's gonna do a knock-door-bunk on Shaky Jake." Liam hopped from one foot to another and grinned from ear to ear.

"Watch he doesn't touch you with those stuttery old hands and turn you into a freak." Will then did his (better) Shaky Jake impression, which involved shaking one hand but holding it up towards my face.

"I'm not," I said, batting Will's hand away. "I said we should walk round the long way. John might be home."

Liam clucked at me and flapped his arms, and then Andy jumped between the two of us and shouted, "Cowabunga."

Andy was in class three, so still an infant, and he acted like it too, but I was always glad to have Andy around as it meant I wasn't the shortest in our group.

With our rucksacks on our backs, together we walked along Main Street. We had to cross the road before we reached the Post Office to go by Shaky Jake's house on the corner of Downham Close and Main Street. While we waited for a gap in the traffic, a couple of heavy lorries thundered by, their gust almost knocking us onto our arses. Mum and Aunt Anne would have been angry with us for not crossing outside the school with Mrs Barnes, the lollipop lady, but that was for the little kids (Andy had us to watch him), and Mrs Barnes had crazy hair and wore so much perfume it made you retch.

Shaky Jake had the normal-looking bungalow on the corner. The front fence was a mess of warped and rotting posts with the horizontal rail only connected at one side. A rusting sheet of corrugated iron replaced a missing section of fence, and there was no gate, just a gap where one once hung. We'd often rile him by banging on the corrugated iron, and he'd run out of the house, sometimes holding a saucepan or a wooden spoon and he'd stand there on the spot and shake. He'd try to yell at us but he struggled to get the words out spittle flew everywhere while the strands of his greasy fringe flapped around his forehead. One time, some spit flew out and hit John on the hand and he tried to wipe it on us to give us the lurgy.

"Come on. Let's go to John's," I said.

"You're not getting out of this," Liam said. "Knock-door-bunk." He started to chant and Andy joined in.

The kitchen curtains twitched, and I thought he was about to come out, but then Will yelled, "Look."

A police car drove past us and turn into Downham Close–John's road. We broke into a half-run and then stopped to watch the car pull up outside John's house. Maybe they'd found him and were bringing him home. But only two policemen got out of the car. They knocked on John's door.

28 DEAD BRANCHES

We couldn't see who opened it, but seconds later they went inside.

Will walked into Downham Close.

"What are you doing?" I said.

"Investigating."

We followed. We slowed to a crawling pace as we got closer to the police car. I'd never been so close to one before. Will peered in first.

"Is he in there?" asked Liam.

Of course, he wasn't. If they'd found him, they would have taken him in.

"No," Will said.

"What is in there?"

"Nothing."

"What's in there?" Liam said again, his voice high.

"I told you: nothing."

Liam, Andy and I peered in at the same time, but Will was right.

"I guess they haven't found him," I said.

"So, what should we do?" Liam said.

"Why don't we go back to Moon Base One?" Will said.

"All right," Liam said. "We'll drop our bags home and then see you later."

As we were about to split up, John's door opened. We ducked behind a bush and watched the two police officers leave. They stopped by the car for a moment but didn't enter. Instead, they crossed the road and walked towards Main Street, forcing us to edge further around the bush out of their sight. Where were they going? They walked through the gap in Shaky Jake's fence, followed the path to his door and knocked, but, after a minute, as no one had answered, they left.

"Right," Will said, leaving the security of the bush, "Moon Base One, twenty minutes."

A ditch and elderberry bushes guarded Moon Base One, located in a little spinney out by the field farthest from our farmhouse. A couple of hundred metres from there, the new bypass intercepted the drove which led to Wissey Hill if followed far enough.

We'd used rocks to build a path across the ditch and rope to pull the elderberry bushes into position. The advantage of the elderberry was that we always had plenty of the tiny berries at our disposal if we ever came under attack. We'd dug holes inside Moon Base One and disguised them with interwoven branches, so we stored provisions in there without fear of them ever being found. Will and I had been in there about five minutes when Liam pushed in through the branches.

"Check these out." he held out a stack of cards.

"Horror Top Trumps? You've had them for ages," Will said.

"No, look," he said but as he tried to show us the cards, he dropped them onto the ground. An evil face with diseased yellow flesh stared at me. Its beard and hair were both tightly curled, similar to Dad's hair when he'd been working hard and got hot and sweaty. Sticking out from that nest of hair were two horns. He was surrounded by fire and had sharp fangs. The Fire Demon. I'd never seen this card before.

"Liam, what are these?" I asked as I glanced at the other cards.

"Series Two. Thirty-two new cards. Check this one out." Liam picked a card from the floor and held it up to us. Even though it wasn't dark, he pulled out a pocket torch, and shone it onto the card, emphasising its magnificence.

"Horror rating one hundred?" Will said.

Death had hideous long teeth and a finger pointing out of the card.

"No way," I said. "Only Dracula has a horror rating of one hundred."

"Not anymore," Liam said. "And check this one out." He held up a card called Alien Creature. "Who's that?"

It was a light-brown-coloured creature with twisted teeth and dark hair in a bowl cut.

Will laughed. "Bloody hell. It's Palmer!"

I couldn't see it myself. The Alien Creature was much uglier than Mrs Palmer, and it had only two fingers on each hand, although its fur matched the colour of her cardigans. "It looks nothing like her," I said.

"You would say that, wouldn't you?" Will said.

"What d'you mean?" Liam said.

"Didn't you know? Tom always gets crushes on his teachers."

Liam and Will rolled around with laughter. It wasn't true. I didn't *always* get crushes on my teachers. There was one time, with Miss Wishaw, who had long, red hair, and read poetry with her sweet, soothing voice, but no one else.

"Ooh! Mrs Palmer," Liam said. He pulled the card towards his face and puckered his lips. "I'm Tom, and I love you."

I let them laugh for a minute. "Where did you get them?"

"Mum bought them for us from the toy shop in Downham Market."

"Cool. We should have a game. Where's Andy?"

As soon as I said it, he jumped into the base. "Surprise attack," he shouted as he clung on to my back and squeezed hard.

"Get off," I yelled. He'd shocked me. For a second, I thought I was under attack, but it's not like I nearly turned my pants into a lemonade factory. I guess with the Top Trumps in front of me with those horrible pictures and all the possibilities running through my head, I was on edge. "Come on," Will said, collecting the rest of the cards. "Let's play."

We played a couple of rounds and I saw a few new cards. Some of these monsters I'd never heard of, like The Living Skull and Dr Syn, and others were gory like The Fiend and Venusian Death Cell.

"What we should do," Liam said as he handed his last card over to Will, "is combine the two sets and play an epic game with sixty-two cards."

"Sixty-four," I said.

Liam squinted at me, his lip curled in confusion.

"Two sets of thirty-two would be sixty-four."

"You're such a bighead." Liam took back the cards, and shuffled them, but ended up dropping half the deck on the ground.

"Deal them already, will you?" Will said, and he tossed a berry at Liam.

"Let me shuffle them first." Liam gathered up the cards and continued his slow shuffle.

"So, what do you think's going on with John?" I said.

Liam dealt out the cards. "Well, the police are involved. We know that."

"Maybe Shredder got him!" Andy said, his eyes wide.

"He might have run away from home," Will said. "He hated his dad."

"I don't know," I said. "I don't think he hated him." John and I had spoken about our dads a few times, and his father didn't seem as bad as mine.

"What's your big idea then, Tom?" Liam said.

I picked up my cards and pulled one out at random. The Sorcerer. Maybe something magical had happened to him. Maybe a great wizard had enlisted him to go on an amazing adventure where he was the hero like in one of my Fighting Fantasy books. Or maybe he'd uncovered a monster's lair, and it had captured him and taken him away. "I don't know," I said.

After a couple more games, Liam checked his watch and said they had to go home so they could be back in time for dinner and catch the end of Uruguay versus Spain. Will said he would walk back with them, and I said I'd walk around the long way across to the back field, just in case. They knew what I meant.

32 DEAD BRANCHES

When I got near the end of the field at the bypass end, something rustled in the ditch. It was overgrown with stinging nettles. They moved. Over the sound of the heavy machinery levelling the verges at the side of the bypass, I thought I heard something else, perhaps a groan. Maybe John had come for a walk around here if he had no one to play with at home. I edged towards the ditch and the nettles quivered again. The slight breeze didn't seem strong enough to swirl the nettles that way. I peered in but could see nothing through the thickness of the vegetation. The grass was not trampled and none of the nettles were squished or broken as they would have been if something had fallen in. The machinery stopped and I could hear slow breathing. "John?" I said, and the breathing sound changed into a low growl. I thought back to our game of Top Trumps. One card flashed into my mind: the Fiend with its sharp talons slicing through its victim's neck.

I jumped as the machines coughed back to life. Was their sound disguising a louder growl? The nettles seemed to part as if the thing was coming towards me, so I ran down into the field of oilseed rape. Whatever it was, the movement of the plants suggested it was bigger than the one from the previous day. I could hear my feet, heavy against the ground, and over the snarl of the machines, another sound pounded the ground behind me. If it caught me, it would tear my head off. It may have done the same to John. I ran faster. Barely able to breathe, and with my face burning, I made it across the field, jumped the ditch and clambered up the other side onto the narrow drove which led home. I did not dare look over my shoulder because I didn't know the creature's powers. If it captured me in its gaze, I might have been put under its spell and forced to halt, and I'd be powerless to stop it removing my head and feasting on my tender neck flesh. As much as I didn't want to turn my head, a squeal, like the excited laughter of a toddler, made me turn my head before I could stop myself. I caught sight of that damned oak tree, my foot struck something, and I crashed to the ground. I tried to listen for the approaching beast, but all I could hear was my pulse, the blood racing thickly through my veins. Glancing awkwardly over my right shoulder, I could see the tree. Its crooked grin was wider than ever and the way it shook its branches made it appear to be laughing. The breeze ruffled my clothes and cooled my back, wet with sweat. Every second that passed, I thought would be my last, but the end never came.

Pensive, I rolled onto my back, certain that the creature would be waiting for me, mocking me, wanting to peer into my eyes before he stole my life (and potentially my ever-living soul too—as I said, I didn't know The Fiend's powers). Nothing. I looked back along the drove to where I'd fallen and stared at the tree root in the ground which I'd caught my foot on. It was almost black and covered in wet soil. It wasn't dull and grey and hard like the rest of the earth on the droveway. The nearest tree was a good twenty metres away. The oak was even farther away, but when I saw its warped face, I was sure that was where the root had come from. It had tripped me and wanted me to get eaten by The Fiend. But what had stopped it? Did I have magical protection? Was I the chosen one and destined to be a hero?

"Oi!"

I turned, and Dad marched down the drove towards me.

"What d'you think you're playing at lying in the middle of the drove like you're dead?"

Why did he always appear at the worst time?

"There's a young lad missing, could be dead for all you know, and you make out you're a dead body. What are you, simple?"

"I tripped," I said as I got up.

"And look at the state of your bloody trousers."

My kneecap had burst through a tear in the material.

"You think we're made of money? You think we can replace your trousers and shirts every time you act like a daft bugger?"

My face was hot and I couldn't talk. I swallowed and concentrated on my breathing as I marched past him.

"What are you doing playing out in your school clothes?"

34 DEAD BRANCHES

It was an ongoing battle to keep the tears at bay with Dad. If he saw them, he could call me a sissy, or a baby, and that meant he won. If I could make it home without crying, he still won, but the defeat felt less humiliating. When protected from The Fiend by some kind of magical force, I thought it might be because I was destined to be the hero, but what kind of hero has to struggle so hard not to be a crybaby? Younger brothers are never the heroes. Look at *The Lion, The Witch and The Wardrobe*. Peter was no crybaby. I was more like Edmund, likely to betray my family and screw everything up for everyone.

After dinner, during which Dad kept going on about me ruining my school trousers, Will and I went to our room to watch Argentina play the Soviet Union. We'd all laughed at school when Argentina got beaten by Cameroon, because, as world champions, they were supposed to be amazing. They had one player, Maradona, who even thought he was God.

Since Argentina had beaten England in the previous World Cup (which I was too young to remember), people didn't like them, but they were playing the Soviet Union which was even worse. They were always the baddies in films, like Rocky IV, which John had a pirate copy of, so I was cheering for Argentina. Then, about ten minutes into the game, the USSR had an attack and the Argentinian goalkeeper, Pumpido, ran out to get the ball and crashed into this Soviet Union player built like Ivan Drago. Pumpido stayed down and waved wildly to the bench.

"What's wrong?" I said.

"Dunno. Must be injured."

They stopped play for a long time and on the replay, I watched his leg curve like a banana when he tried to stand up. Watching it made my dinner return to my mouth and I could taste a mix of bile and gravy for a long time. This wasn't right. This wasn't supposed to happen at the World Cup. Goalie's legs weren't supposed to snap. Beasts weren't supposed to chase kids across fields.

Best friends weren't supposed to disappear.

NOW

Of course, it's raining. We don't get those long, hot summers like we used to. The recent heatwave was a short-lived abnormality. It's another factor which makes the childhoods of my summer, and what I consider the last childhood of my summer, seem so unreal. I remember summers so hot that there was a constant haze, but now we get regional flooding and broken promises of barbeque summers. Summer rains, back then, surprised us. Not now. I stare at my reflection in a puddle. Charlie's boot catches the edge, and it sends a ripple, distorting the image, and I wonder if my own memories are also distorted.

It still feels so real. Despite gaining a great deal of knowledge over the years since, I can't understand the logic. The sensation of being chased along the drove was real. When I think back to that day, a dread grips me, my chest constricts, and the day's panic returns. The thud of footsteps following behind was real, and the aura of malevolence tangible. Now, I reason it could have been the product of a vivid imagination spurred by the fiction I was feeding on, and fuelled by a lack of facts from our parents. The images on the Top Trumps are still etched in my mind. Name a beast from either series one or two, and I could draw it. I'd wager that I'd make a decent guess at its stats, too.

That's why Charlie isn't exposed to anything like that.

I leave Charlie at the school gate. He doesn't mind he's one of only a handful of pupils in year five who get dropped off at school by a parent, and he knows why. I've told him of the dangers that await those who walk home alone, and he doesn't want to be the sexual plaything of a paedophile. Of course, I've explained how small the risk is as I don't want him cowering in fear every time he leaves the house, but I'd be a terrible parent if I didn't make him aware of the genuine risks.

On the way home, I drop my reply to Mum's letter in the mail, letting her know we'll be there at the weekend.

These days, I communicate with Mum solely by letter. I'd email, but they don't have a computer. I gave her three strict rules regarding the content of our communication:

1. Don't talk about Dad.
2. Don't talk about the past.
3. Don't tell me anything about Little Mosswick.

Mum sticks to these, so her letters are brief. They include questions about how we are and comments in response to the pictures I send her of Charlie.

When we meet, which I allow once a year near Christmas, I go over the rules again so she doesn't cross the line. When we speak, it is embedded in the present. Victoria's death made this somewhat easier, as she can ask me how I'm coping, and tell me what a wonderful job I'm doing with Charlie. Am I? She says that to keep me on-side, still unaware that all I ever desired from her, back then and every moment since, was honesty.

Could I have used her support when a reckless driver made me a widower and a single father before I was forty? Definitely. Did I take it? Not a chance. Showing emotional weakness may have opened a window to let him back in, and I wasn't going to allow that for all the world.

But when I go back, I cannot expect her to live by those rules. When I go back, I'll have to deal with my baggage. But if he's dying, then it must be safe.

If he's dying, I can go back.

Thursday 14th June 1990

I made it to school early hoping that the last couple of days of worry would prove to be a waste when John turned up. He wasn't in the first wave of pupils I expected to find him in, so I slipped into school, sneaking past Mr Inglehart who was chatting to a parent.

John's PE bag hung on its peg. With the corridor clear, I crept towards it. I didn't know what I'd find inside, but I hoped for a hint that he was in some way unhappy or something revealing a reason to run. I lifted out his boot bag and peered in at the football boots, still grubby with clumps of mud and bits of grass from last week's game. Next, I removed his World Cup Top Trumps, with the scuffed case despite him only having had them for a week. It held nothing else, no note, no ancient artefacts, no clues, not even his P.E. shorts or top.

"That's not your bag, Master Tilbrook."

Mr Jenkins came towards me, holding a spray bottle.

"No, it's John's," I said.

"I know it's John's, and that's why you shouldn't be snooping in it."

"Sorry, I was looking for clues."

"Ah!" said Mr Jenkins. He stopped moving and gave me a smile. "Friends of yours, is he?"

I nodded.

"You know you shouldn't be inside before the first bell."

"Sorry."

"And if the wrong person caught you doing what I did, they might think you were thieving."

"I wasn't!"

"I know that, but not everybody is such a good judge of character as me. So why don't you go back out onto the playground and we'll pretend none of this happened?"

Mr Jenkins followed me out and then sprayed the window beside the door. He took a rag from his pocket, wiped the glass, and started whistling. Attempting to identify Jenkins' song, I didn't notice Liam sneak up on me, and he had his wet finger in my earhole before I had a chance to stop him.

I was still trying to dry my ear when the bell rang. Mrs Palmer stood by her classroom door and greeted us as we entered rather than organising handouts at her desk or writing on the blackboard—her usual routines.

Liam jabbed me in the ribs as I stopped by my desk and whispered, "Alien creature." I didn't find it funny, even though she was wearing one of her mustard-coloured cardigans, but I smiled and faked a laugh that Liam no doubt thought real.

Mrs Palmer didn't read the register either, almost as if saying John's name would draw attention to the fact he wasn't there again. Normally, a two-day absence escalated the rumours from the previous day, leading to a diagnosis of the hyper-squirts, or in severe cases, the dynamite-shits. I turned to Liam, who always sat behind me, but he was staring into space. I made eye contact with Daniel; he turned his head towards John's seat and shrugged his shoulders.

A knock at the door drew Mrs Palmer's attention.

"Psst."

I turned around.

"What does transition mean?" Liam said in a loud whisper.

I looked at the worksheet that Mrs Palmer had left on our desks (odd, because PE was supposed to be first on a Thursday), but I couldn't see the word Liam had mentioned. Mrs Palmer stood at the door, talking to someone in the corridor.

"What does what mean?" I said.

Mrs Palmer turned and glared before turning back to her conversation.

"Transition."

"Dunno. Why?"

"Something I heard the teachers talking about. Might be a clue."

Mrs Palmer closed the door and turned her attention to us: time for quiet if we wanted to avoid sharpening pencils during break.

"Today," said Mrs Palmer, "we have a visitor. P.C. Wade will come in after break to speak to you."

I could tell that Liam had raised his hand. He always grunted when he put his hand up as if a question or answer had hit him with force. Without waiting for an invitation Liam said, "Is it about John, Miss?"

Mrs Palmer put a hand to her temple. "Liam, please don't speak until asked to do so."

I turned to see Liam shrink in his chair.

"But yes," continued Mrs Palmer, "some of you may be aware that John has not been seen since school on Tuesday. P.C. Wade would like to speak to each of you about John."

We knew P.C. Wade. He regularly visited the school. A fortnight ago he'd spoken to us about road safety. With the new bypass ready to open, the volume of traffic passing through the village would fall, but he assured us that our lollipop lady, Mrs Barnes, would still be there at the start and end of the school day to help us cross the road. Before that he'd spoken in an assembly about the danger of construction sites. I remember sharing sheepish looks with John who'd come with me to mess around on the huge piles of sand and stone set aside for the bypass. We'd wander around the unoccupied machinery, sit in the bucket of a JCB or try to throw stones over the top of the sand heap. One weekend we found a load of empty beer cans pushed into the mound of sand so we hadn't gone back. We didn't want to get caught messing around at the older kids' hangout.

We worked through the sheet until break which had a dull story to read, with questions to answer, and then you had to write the next chapter yourself. I liked creative writing, but I couldn't get into it.

When the bell rang, Liam flew out of his chair and stood in front of my desk. "Let's ask to borrow the dictionary," he said.

It was my job to ask. If Liam asked, Mrs Palmer would say no, but she seemed to like me. "Miss," I called out as I stood.

"Yes, Thomas?"

"Can I check the dictionary?"

"Okay, but I have a meeting in the staff room. I want you out of here before I get back."

I picked the big dictionary from the shelf by her desk and turned to the 'T' section. "Transition," I muttered as I flicked through the pages.

"Ooh!" Liam said and smudged his finger onto the word.

"Transition. The process, or a period, of changing from one state or condition to another."

"Oh." Liam scratched his head. "What's that got to do with anything?" he asked.

"Dunno." I looked at the mustard cardigan hanging on the back of Mrs Palmer's chair.

When we returned from break, Mrs Palmer didn't want us to talk either before or after our interview with Wade, so we had to sit and read. I stared at the same page for the whole morning, the words not sinking in, and from the lack of the sound of pages turning I guessed everyone else was doing the same. Every time the door opened, everyone glanced up to try to read something on the face of whoever came back in. Mrs Palmer hushed whispers with a glare. We went in by surname order. Liam was questioned before me because his surname is Carter. He returned with his face red; he embarrassed easily and didn't like to be questioned because he had this habit of always looking guilty whether he'd done anything or not.

I had to wait until near the end. When they summoned Daniel Richardson, I knew I'd be next. John's mum would have spoken to Daniel on Tuesday night, and I guess he hadn't seen John either. A few minutes later, Daniel returned. He walked back to his seat, sat, and sniffled.

"Thomas Tilbrook," called Wade.

Liam's cheeks were still pink when he arrived at Moon Base One after school. Once embarrassed, he stayed that way until the next morning. He plonked himself on the log we used as a bench. Will nodded at him.

"What did Wade ask you?" Liam said, turning first to Will, then to me.

Will shrugged and continued to scrape the bark from a four-foot-long stick with his penknife.

"When did I last see John? If we were friends. Stuff like that," I said.

"What did you say?"

"I said we were best friends, and I told them he didn't like being left home alone after school."

"Yeah, I said that, too."

"I told them we'd had an argument."

"Tom!" Liam's cheeks reddened further than I thought possible.

"What?"

"They'll think you're a suspect."

"No, they won't."

"They will. Haven't you seen *The Bill*?"

"Shut up, Liam." I hadn't seen *The Bill*. Dad would never let us watch that, and I don't reckon Liam had seen it either, but I knew what he was talking about.

"They'll say you've got a motive."

"Liam," Will said, pointing with the tip of his penknife. "Leave it. Did they ask either of you if you'd seen any weirdos hanging about the village?"

"Yeah," I said. "Something like that."

"Me too," Liam said.

"What did you say?"

"No." Liam and I said it at the exact same moment so I blurted out, "Jinx," stopping Liam from speaking until released from the curse.

As Liam waved around his arms, hoping that Will or I would say his full name, Andy jumped into the hideout. As usual, he wore his Teenage Mutant Ninja Turtle gear. He had a dustbin lid strapped to his back as a shell, and a piece of orange fabric with eye holes cut out for an eye mask.

"Hey, I got nun-chucks," Andy said. He pulled out his weapon made from two cardboard kitchen roll tubes tied together with blue string. He held one tube in each hand and left them far enough apart for the string to be slack, and he grimaced.

"Radical," Will said and rolled his eyes before going back to sharpening his stick.

Liam peered out of one of Moon Base One's viewing windows after pulling the branches of the elderberry bush back. "Shush!" he said and ducked.

Will punched him on the arm for breaking the conditions of the jinx.

"Stop," he said, with panic in his eyes as he pushed Will away.

"What's up?" asked Will.

"Someone's coming."

"Who?"

"Shaky Jake."

We hushed and crept into the corners of the base to spy out.

Jake darted from one side of the drove to the other, glancing into the ditches. I saw his mouth moving as he muttered something, but I couldn't make it out. He made the same nonsensical noises, over and over, like a chant. Maybe it was a spell, or worse, a curse.

We watched him pass and walk off into the distance, and once we could no longer hear him, we dared to move again.

Eventually, I broke the silence. "Did the policeman come into your class, Andy?" I asked.

"Yeah." He tucked his nun-chucks into the side of his shorts. "He said if we had any information, or any questions, we should speak to a grown-up."

"No one said anything?" I said.

Andy shook his head.

"What are we gonna do?" Liam said.

"We're the turtles!" Andy said, "We'll find him then go for pizza."

Will closed his penknife. "We're not turtles. We're The Crusaders."

Andy picked a berry from the bush and squished it between his fingers. "But if we were the Turtles, we could be heroes and save the day."

"We can still save the day," Will said. He picked up the sticks he'd prepared and handed us one each. "Come on," he said. "This is our village. We know it better than anyone. We'll find him."

"How?" I said. Excitement flowed through us. This was our moment. We would be heroes.

"We'll walk back down to school and follow the road along, check the ditches."

Will was cut out to be the hero. For all my good intentions, when it came to the crunch, I'd probably hide away in terror and, if I was lucky, I might avoid turning into a crybaby. I was The Incredible Hulk in reverse, shrinking to the size of an infant when wound up. I could have drowned my enemies in tears. Liam bent his stick with both hands then it slipped out of one and thwacked him in the side of the face. He'd never let anyone down, but he was no hero. Andy laughed and swung his nun-chucks. He was the comedy sidekick.

"Don't you think someone would've checked the ditches?" I said, and instantly regretted it, proving myself to be the wet blanket.

"They don't know them like we do," Will said, like any good hero should.

I took a stick and followed Will out of Moon Base One. Liam and Will grabbed the branches and pushed them back in place to hide the entrance. We'd flattened the tall grass around the outside and then collected rocks and branches to make an enclosure. Liam, Will and I stepped over the thick mud at the bottom of the ditch which never dried out no matter how many days passed without rain. We clambered up the other side and waited for Andy who first checked that his nunchucks were secure. He took a step backwards before running towards the ditch. He took off and shouted, "Cowabunga," in mid-air. Together, Will and I caught him to stop his momentum from carrying him over into the ditch on the other side. Then we started our walk back towards the school, prodding our sticks into the ditch and random bushes as we walked.

"What d'you think happened?" Liam said as we reached the school.

"A car might have knocked him into a ditch," Will said.

"But wouldn't the driver have stopped?" asked Liam.

"Didn't when it happened to me," I said. I reminded them of what had happened the previous summer. I'd been cycling from Granddad Norman's cottage to the farmhouse when a lorry sped past. It didn't hit me, but the gush of air caused me to lose my balance and fall into the ditch. I pulled the bike out, but the front wheel was buckled. I was a couple of doors from Granddad's and was half-pushing, half-carrying it back there, but Mrs Johnstone, who used to work as a dinner lady at the school before she had her accident, saw me heaving the bike out and rushed over. She made me go with her into her kitchen and put TCP on my knees and elbows even though they were barely grazed, and before I could tell her not to, she called home to say what had happened. When Dad turned up, he said, "Come on," and dragged me off the stool. The benefit of being dragged away so soon was that I only had to eat one of her soft, old-people biscuits. Dad nodded at Mrs Johnstone and picked up my bike and tossed it in the back of his Land Rover.

"Poor boy never would have been hurt if you hadn't messed the council around with the bypass," said Mrs Johnstone.

Dad didn't speak on the way home. I never got my bike back. When I asked Dad what happened to it, he said it was too badly damaged. I'm sure the wheel could have been replaced.

"Speaking of Mrs Johnstone..." Liam said. He shuffled through the Top Trump cards he'd pulled from his back pocket. "Zetan Priest."

We laughed. The character on the card had a mess of white hair, and a white face, like Mrs Johnstone's. But the thing that most resembled her was its pink coat. It was one of the least scary cards in the pack, but with a Horror Rating of 95, Killing Power of 91 and Physical Strength of 94 it was powerful. It goes to show that you can't judge someone by their appearance.

We continued poking our way along the side of the road, not paying much attention until I thrust my stick and felt something other than the side of the ditch.

"I've got something," I called and prodded again.

Will reacted first and came to my side in a second, and he probed with his own stick. The nettles swayed as whatever was down there was dislodged.

"Is it him?" I said to no one in particular.

"I don't think so," Will said, and he sat at the edge of the ditch. Liam and Andy approached and peered down, trying to figure out what it was through the thick mass of weeds. Whatever I'd prodded didn't have the bulk of a body, but could it be a clue?

Heroically, Will shuffled on his bottom into the ditch, using his feet to trample and kick away any stinging nettles that awaited the chance to attack. "Torch," he called.

Liam plunged his hand into his pocket, pulled out the torch, and crouched to pass it to Will.

"Hold them back!" Will called, as a loose nettle almost swished into his face.

Liam and I used our sticks to hold them at bay, and Andy leapt across the ditch to do the same from the other side.

Will switched on the torch, and then a revolted noise came from the pit of his belly. Within seconds he flew out of the ditch and if it wasn't for Liam grabbing him by the back of his jeans, he would have run onto the road, into the path of an oncoming car. Shocked, I gazed at the vehicle and realised Laura Matthews was sitting in the passenger seat. I could feel myself turning red.

"Was it him?" said Liam.

Will looked sick. "No," he said. "Dead badger." He shuddered.

We hadn't found a thing. I felt like Mario when he gets through a world only to be told, "Thank you, but our princess is in another castle." John would like that joke, apart from him being the princess. I was about to share it with the others, but their expressions told me that none of them would have laughed.

"What now?" asked Liam.

"Let's leave it for today," Will said.

"I had a thought," Liam said.

"What?" I asked.

"You know I heard them teachers talking about that transition thing?"

I nodded.

"And you know when we looked it up, it meant changing from one thing to another?"

I nodded again.

"And you know Mrs Palmer is an alien creature?"

"What are you going on about?" Will said, and gripped Liam's arm, threatening a skin burn.

"Don't," Liam said, shaking his head.

"Get on with it, "Will said, "and stop saying 'you know' all of the time."

"Okay," Liam said. "What if this transition is a plan to turn everyone into aliens, like her?"

But Mrs Palmer only *looked* like an alien, right?

"Think about it," Liam said, which sounded strange coming from him because he was often the last one to think about anything. "No one saw John leave school. He might still be there, locked away somewhere."

"Should we go back and check it out?" I asked.

48 DEAD BRANCHES

"Be realistic. It'll be locked by now," Will said. "Plus Cameroon are playing Romania. We've missed the first half."

I suppose a hero knows when to call time on a search.

When we got home, I volunteered to make drinks in light of Will's roadkill encounter. He took Andy and Liam upstairs to watch the football and left me at the sink. I poured cordial into each glass, and, after I topped up the third one with water, I heard a shout, "Quick, Tom!" I filled the last glass, put them on a tray and hurried up the stairs. One glass tipped over, but most of the liquid remained on the tray, with a trickle of blackcurrant squash landing on the carpet. As I got into the bedroom they were huddled around the TV.

"You missed it," Liam said. "Cameroon scored, and he did a dance at the corner flag."

"Who did?"

"The Cameroon player."

"What's the score?"

"One nil."

The Cameroon players poured forward and looked like they would score again, but I had to sort out the spilt squash. I kept imagining the sound of the front door going and Dad coming in and seeing the mess. Even though we'd seen him on his tractor, miles away, he could travel great distances in an instant to catch me out.

I was about to go to the bathroom to get some toilet paper to mop up my spill when Cameroon raced forward again and Roger Milla scored. This time I saw his dance in the corner flag.

I smiled the whole time I scrubbed at the stairs carpet, using a bar of soap and a few sheets of tissue. I'd made the squash weak, and it didn't stain. A few bits of torn tissue stuck in the carpet fibres, but the colour matched. A purple stain would have been much more noticeable. I returned to the bedroom as Romania scored. In fervour, we cheered on

Cameroon, hoping they could stop Romania from scoring an equalising goal. When the final whistle blew, with the score still 2-1, we whooped and high-fived each other. I got out my sticker album. We found Cameroon's page. They were another one of those teams that had two players per sticker as if no one expected them to be of any interest. I had all of the players, missing only the shiny Cameroon badge and the team sticker. But Roger Milla wasn't in there, and we figured that made him even more special because even Panini didn't know him, but he'd scored two goals at the World Cup finals, and if that didn't prove that magical things could happen, then nothing would.

"Boy!" Dad shouted from downstairs.

Will was already down there. He'd gone to fetch a snack, and I'd been wondering why he hadn't returned.

I started down the stairs, not realising I still had my notebook (an exercise book 'borrowed' from school) in my hand. What did he want? Maybe Will had dobbed me in for something, but nothing came to mind. I looked at the spot where I'd spilt the drink, but I'd done a good job of cleaning it. He couldn't know.

"Come on, boy!" he called again. "Your Uncle Rodney's here."

I stuttered down the stairs, my feet like blocks of concrete, my nostrils blocking themselves in advance of being invaded by his alcohol stink.

I pushed open the door to see him leaning forward on his chair, his backside barely touching it. His hands jerked as he finished telling his story, "So there I was, trousers around my ankles, and he says, 'No! I said show me you're willing!' Of course, I left as soon as I could."

Dad laughed, his cheeks about to burst, and a huge smile spread across his face.

I looked at Will, and he appeared as confused me.

Uncle Rodney turned to face me. His top lip had a scattering of grey whiskers and his eyes were half closed.

"Thomas, my dear boy!" He opened his arms to welcome me.

I glanced to see if Dad was watching. He wasn't, but if I hesitated too long, he'd notice. I walked over to Uncle Rodney, rolled up the exercise book, and tucked it into my back pocket.

"What have you got there?" he asked, his voice getting higher with each word.

"Nothing."

"Still working on that family tree project?"

I'd started to put one together some months ago but had forgotten about it when I tried to get information from Dad and he'd told me it was a waste of time. "No, I-"

"Remember, boy, that ours is a tree with many dead branches."

I shrugged. Was he quoting Shakespeare again?

Dad interrupted, "Your Uncle Rodney knows someone who's giving away some chickens, so we'll have the coop back up and running in no time."

Thinking back to the disgusting scene from a few days prior, I couldn't imagine ever opening the coop again without seeing the dismembered birds. I was so caught up in that grim vision I didn't notice Uncle Rodney move to slap me on the back in what he thought was a friendly manner, but for me, it was like being swatted by a mighty ogre; Rodney had enormous hands that looked comical at the end of his long, thin arms. I couldn't help but jerk forward, my hip crashing into the table. Teacups rippled before sloshing over the side and onto the tablecloth.

"You daft boy," Dad said. "Look what you've done."

"You always were a little unstable," laughed Rodney as I grabbed a tea towel to mop up the spillages.

Me? Unstable? He was one who fell off the stage every single year at the Mosswick Amateur Dramatic Society's summer performance. I never found out what became of Macbeth as he crashed headfirst off the stage and had to be rushed to hospital for stitches. If he wasn't the originator and chairman of the MAD society no one would ever have cast him. I'm sure people only turned up to his shows because they were sure that he was going to make a fool of himself.

Will narrowed his eyes at me from across the table, where he sat next to Uncle Rodney. He slurped from a straw stuck in a can of Coke. It had weird letters on it, like an O with a cross through it. Where'd he get it?

"Would you like a drink, my boy?" Rodney raised his eyebrows.

I saw the blue and white striped carrier bag by his feet and tried to glance inside. It bulged with colour. Uncle Rodney reached his hand inside and plucked out a can of Coke. It has the same strange lettering. He pulled the ring-pull and handed me the can. As I was about to raise it to my lips, he put a fusty finger on them to stop me. With his other hand, he reached into his coat pocket and grabbed a straw. He was like a clown, or a magician pulling a string of hankies from his pocket, except his hankies would be dirty and tainted. He dropped the discoloured red straw into the can and as it bobbed back up, I pushed it down with my fingers.

"Sit down, young man," said Rodney.

I looked across the table to the seat by Dad, but as I was about to move, Uncle Rodney's hands grabbed at my hips. Rodney picked me up, as if I weighed nothing, and plonked me onto his right leg.

Rodney's strength always surprised everyone; while he was the tallest man I'd ever seen, he was stick-thin, and his hair, a dyed-brown-with-a-hint-of-red tangle of wiry curls, only helped emphasise his clownish appearance.

"No need to go all the way round there when there's a perfectly good seat here!" he said, and then he continued his conversation with Dad about people I'd never heard of.

Uncle Rodney spoke in a strange posh voice, nothing like the way that Dad or Granddad spoke. He liked to tell stories, so he was similar to Granddad in that way, but Rodney's stories differed wildly; they were about the theatre and people with strange nicknames, like Bobbo, Wiggy, and Archer who he hung around with in the pub, The Merry Maidens, in the next village over, Great Mosswick (which was smaller than Little Mosswick).

Dad sat there taking it in, fascinated by Uncle Rodney's nonsense.

I couldn't help but stare at the way he moved his mouth when he spoke, pushing out each vowel with his cheeks. There were small scabs on his left cheek which caught the light every time he tipped his head back to drink his tea. He caught me looking at him and brushed the side of his face. "Bit of a scrape with a razor blade," he said. "Hey, why don't you pick up the bag and see what's inside?"

Uncle Rodney always had the oddest chocolate bars. I picked out an orange packet with a brown bear on the front. The lettering said Bamse Mums. I passed one to Will who tore off the corner with his teeth and bit straight into it.

I was more careful, unwrapping it slowly and letting its chocolate scent waft into my nostrils. It was shaped like a bear, and was soft, with melted chocolate clinging to the packet. Of course, it had melted in our kitchen which was again as hot as the flaming rivers of hell. I took a bite to discover marshmallow inside. Flakes of chocolate fell from the bear, and onto Rodney's trouser leg.

He tried to brush the flakes away but smeared the melted chocolate into his trousers among the myriad of other stains. His hand came to a rest on my leg, and he gave it a squeeze.

I looked again at Will. He's stripped the chocolate away from the marshmallow at the foot of the bear. I did the same, cupping my hand beneath it, ensuring that no more fell onto Uncle Rodney.

"Time for your bath, boys."

I hadn't noticed Mum standing at the door to the kitchen. She often found something else to do when Rodney was around.

Will sighed and slurped what was left of his Coke, but I was happy to escape.

How could one member of the family be so different? But then I looked across at Will, and Dad and saw how similar they were. I looked at Rodney, who was blinking as if he'd lost control of his eyelids, and I wondered if that was how I was destined to turn out.

Friday 15th June 1990

Friday morning was roasting, and by break time I'd removed my jumper and tied it around my waist which raised a chuckle from Liam. "No one does that anymore!" he'd proclaimed as he suffered in the heat. Once break started, however, Liam saw the year six pupils had their jumpers tied around their waists too. He quickly squirmed out of his jumper, and in doing so, the Top Trumps which had been tucked into the waistband of his elasticated trousers tumbled out.

I stifled a laugh as Liam picked up the cards. He flicked through the pack, put a card on the top of the pile and said, "Follow me."

During break, we weren't supposed to go into the school building unless we were going into the library, going to the toilet, or if we had a detention.

"Where are we going?" I said.

"You'll see."

We walked past the entrance to the library, past a couple of classrooms, and past the first set of toilets. As we approached Mr Jenkins' cupboard (the one with the CARETAKER sign on the door), Liam peered in. Jenkins was gazing into a box and whistling something unrecognisable.

"Look at this card," Liam whispered.

He held out the Ape Man for me to see, a mess of hair from a bushy beard and a mop on top of his head, a face red with anger, and rounded, primeval teeth.

"Hello Mr Jenkins," Liam said, causing the caretaker to turn around.

"You boys shouldn't be in here at break," he said then turned back to whatever he was doing.

It was lucky he did so because I struggled to contain my laughter. Same bushy beard, same thick eyebrows, same red face. Admittedly, Mr Jenkins's skin tone was more hot-and-flustered pink than uncontrollable-rage red, he wasn't wielding the bone of a prehistoric beast, and he wasn't wearing fur, but his caretaker outfit could have been a disguise. He was strong; we'd seen him shift equipment around the playground and lift huge storage boxes around the school. Perhaps that was why we recognised none of the songs he whistled–they were so old, they came from the Stone Age.

"So, what do you think?" Liam said as we hurried back outside.

"He looks just like him," I said. "Mr Jenkins is the Ape Man!"

"But what about... as a suspect?" Liam's eyes were huge.

Could the Ape Man have taken John? "We better tell Will," I said.

Will was playing football. Everyone wanted to play as Cameroon again. We didn't have to wait long for a goal, followed by a Roger Milla impression. When the bell rang, we waited for Will to leave the pitch.

Liam held out the Ape Man card. "Who does that look like?"

Will shrugged.

"Jenkins," Liam said, nodding his head.

Will laughed and grabbed the card.

"Oi, Chris." He showed him the card. "Jenkins."

Chris laughed and called over some other boys and shared the joke. One boy made monkey noises and shaped his arms, his hands curling towards his armpits.

Liam grabbed Will's arm and pulled him closer to whisper. Liam was rubbish at whispering; he was too loud and his heavy breath always left people with clammy ears.

"What if Jenkins has John?"

"Because he looks like the Ape Man, you think he might be involved?"

"He's a suspect, right?"

"Give me the cards." Will held out his hand.

Liam sighed and surrendered the cards.

Will flicked through them before pulling out Fu Manchu. "This one has a moustache. It's that bloke that works in the petrol station. Maybe he's got John locked up in the back of a car!" Will mocked shock, placing his hands on his cheeks, and letting his mouth hang open like a cavern.

Liam took a sharp intake of breath and Will dumped the cards back in his hands and walked off.

"Do you think he could be?"

"Nah," I said, then had another look at the card. "But it's a good match." And we snickered all the way back to the classroom.

At lunch time, we surveyed the cards seeking other matches. We wondered if we could find anyone for Mr Inglehart. When he first came to the school three years ago, people called him *The Demon Headmaster*. The book used to be in the school library, but then it disappeared. At first, we thought he'd had it removed to stop the rumours, but it turned out he wasn't strict, he told no one off without a good reason, and he trained the football team, so the rumours stopped, and everyone thought he was okay for a headmaster. The only card he resembled was Dracula, and as he was outside walking around the playground most lunch times, we figured he couldn't be a vampire.

Liam chuckled as he stopped on a card. He covered his mouth with his hand.

"What?" I said.

"See this one?" He held out The Mad Axeman. It had a greenish face and white hair. He had one eye open. "Shaky Jake."

I nodded and was scanning the rest of the cards when Laura walked by with Becky. Laura had her hair in pigtails, and, as always, she was smiling. Becky had a fringe that came down to the top of her glasses, making her face look tiny, and she was always moody.

"Hey Laura," I said, and she came over to us. I could tell that Becky was trying to stop her, but with a sigh of reluctance, she followed.

"Which of these three cards looks more like Shaky Jake?" I held out The Mad Axeman, Madman (yellow, lumpy face and receding, brown hair) and The Mad Magician (Long white hair, top hat, dark, creepy eyes and a weird smile).

"He hasn't got white hair, but his face is like the magician's. His hair is more like the madman's."

"So, a cross between The Mad Magician and Madman?"

"I suppose so," said Laura, and she turned to walk away.

"Have you ever seen him do any magic?"

"No," she said, looking back over her shoulder.

"Tell her about Jenkins," Liam said.

Laura returned, and I shuffled through the cards until I found Ape Man. "We reckon Jenkins could be the Ape Man."

"That's mean," said Becky. "Mr Jenkins is a nice man."

Becky walked off and Laura followed her.

I stared at Liam, and he shrugged.

"What?" he said.

"What did you have to tell her that?"

"It's funny."

"But you made her go away."

"So?" I could almost hear Liam's brain ticking. "You fancy her, don't you?"

"No!" I said. I did though.

"I suppose it's a step up from Mrs Palmer. We couldn't have you hooking up with an Alien Creature."

"I never fancied Mrs Palmer."

"I'm not surprised. She's an alien."

"Let's get back to work," I said and flicked through the cards again. "How about this one? The Gorgon is Mrs Barnes."

Liam nodded. "Yeah, she has hair like that. It's her."

"Okay, that's good." I picked up the next card. "What about The Freak?"

"You're The Freak."

"No, you're The Freak."

"Freak."

"I know you are, but what am I?"

We didn't get much further.

At afternoon break Liam and I sat under the shade of a tree. In the sunshine, it felt like our skin would burn and peel away in seconds. A flash of John's face came to my mind, and then another, but this time with his skin blackened and charred. I shuddered and watched as Liam yanked up blades of grass and then split them in two. After a minute or so, he stopped and said, "Do you remember when John showed us that programme he'd recorded off Sky?"

John had satellite TV. He got to watch these cool American TV shows, like *COPS* and *WWF Superstars*. Sometimes he'd tape them for us so we'd know who he was talking about when he mentioned Hulk Hogan, or the Ultimate Warrior, or Rowdy Roddy Piper, or Hacksaw Jim Duggan.

"Which one?" I said to Liam because there were a lot of times he'd taped shows for us.

"*Unsolved Mysteries*. Do you remember it?"

I thought for a second, and then the memory hit me, "Yeah," I said.

"Do you reckon we could get in touch with them and they'd help us investigate?"

"Hey, Liam," someone shouted.

We looked up as a football trickled towards us.

Will was trotting over to collect it, so Liam got up and passed him the ball.

"What are you talking about?" asked Will.

"*Unsolved Mysteries*," I said.

Will picked up the ball, drop-kicked it back onto the pitch, and sat with us.

"That was the show with the crop circles at the start, right?" Will said.

"There hasn't been anything like that round here, has there?" I said.

"Worth keeping an eye out for," Will said.

Again, the image of John's burnt face came into my mind. "Don't you remember–there was that bit about that lady who burst into flame–spontaneous human combustion?"

"How about if that happened to John?" Liam said, a concerned expression developing on his face. "He got really hot while we watched that, and, remember, he has a shell suit."

"So?"

"Tom! You're not thinking! Don't you remember anything? Like when Wade came into the school with the fireman and they did that demonstration of how easily shell suits catch fire? And that's why they got banned from school?"

"Liam, calm down." Will stood up and headed back towards the game.

"You're still not getting it!" Liam's face reddened. "What if he was wearing his shell suit, heated up, and then spontaneously combusted!" Liam stood up too.

"Where are you going?" I said.

"To tell Mr Inglehart, so he can pass it on to the police."

"No, Liam, I don't think that happened."

"But they have to investigate the possibility?"

"There would be some kind of evidence–scorch marks on the ground…"

"Good plan. After school, we can search for burn marks and crop circles."

That wasn't what I meant, but I nodded. "Ace," I said and thought I could look for something sensible while he was searching for patches of blackened earth.

Liam sat back down.

"You don't think he's gone forever, do you?" I said.

"I don't know, Tom."

"It's so weird. Nothing like this has ever happened before."

"How about when your dog went missing? He came back, didn't he?" Liam said.

"Chappie always used to wander off and come back," I said. But he'd not done it recently. He'd not done much at all recently.

"Yeah, but dogs are smart."

"John's smart too, Liam. He'll be okay."

After school, we talked over our plan for the afternoon. "We could follow the drove round the back of the school. He might have gone off that way," I said. As you pass behind the school, you can see into the staff room. We liked to mimic the teachers and make up their conversations.

We each picked up long sticks as we started our walk, except for Andy who plucked his nun-chucks from his rucksack. Not long after, Liam thrust his stick over my shoulder, millimetres from my ear into an elderberry bush. Its leaves lurched towards me. There was nowhere to go. The man-eating plant would wrap its branches around my limbs and pull me into its mouth. Instead, with the slap of wings against branches, a flurry of feathers flew out, and two huge pigeons set off for the sky, leaving me to tumble onto my backside.

Liam stifled a laugh. Andy didn't. Will gave them a look and then offered a hand to help me up. "Come on, guys," he said. "This is serious."

Liam leant on the end of his stick and huffed. "What if John is here, somewhere?" Liam said.

"If we find him? Good." Will said.

"But what if I poke him in the eye?"

"Didn't do Granddad Norman any harm."

"But what if we do find him, and he's *not* okay?" I said, still annoyed at having taken a tumble.

"What do you mean?" Andy said.

"Nothing," Will said.

Andy gazed at the ground. He poked at a branch with his foot.

"He didn't mean anything." Will put a hand on Andy's shoulder. "Those are cool nun-chucks."

Andy held onto one handle and used it to spin the other around.

"Let's keep going," said Will.

Around the corner, a group of older boys lurked, Jimmy Wilson's older brother, Gavin, among them.

"Watchya Bill," Gavin said.

One of the other boys was smoking.

Will nodded towards them.

"What are you doing around here?" Gavin said.

"Hanging out," said Will.

"With a bunch of little kids?"

"My brother and my cousins."

"Wanna ditch them and come with us? Drew's pinched some fags from his dad."

"Better not," said Will. "I'm looking after this lot."

The older boys walked on past us. Was that the only reason Will hung out with us? I suppose he was one of the cool kids, and I was pretty far from that status. I realised that next year, he wouldn't have the bind of being in the same school as us. He wouldn't hang out with us after school as he'd have his secondary school mates. This would be our last summer together. I tried to forget it and peered through the gaps in the hedges towards the school, trying to see if anything peculiar was going on, or if anyone unusual came in or out. It wasn't until we got around to the back of the school playing field that we found something interesting beyond the Broom Cupboard—our small storage area where we kept a few sharpened sticks, our bows, and our supply of arrows.

"Hey, what's this?" Andy said as he pushed aside some leaves. There were a couple of empty packets of Fishermen's Friend—sweets so gross that no child would ever eat them—and, covered by loose dirt and wedged under a protruding root, a magazine. On the cover a woman posed in her bra and knickers, her head partially covering the title, *Fiesta*. We took it with us as evidence.

A twig snapped behind us and we turned. Coming from the opposite direction was Shaky Jake. When he saw us, he turned and hurried back the way he'd come.

From a distance, we followed him. The drove curved back round onto Main Street, a couple of hundred metres past the school, and opposite Downham Close. Shaky Jake had already gone into his house, and we could see his curtain twitching.

"Do you think we should report him?" I said.

"What for?" Will said.

"That's twice we've seen him snooping around. Perhaps he knows something."

"We can't report him for that."

"Wade asked if we'd seen any weirdos hanging around. He's a weirdo," Liam said.

"Maybe he's worth keeping an eye on," Will said, and then he looked over Liam's shoulder. "Is that Dad's Land Rover?"

Dad sped towards us and then stopped dead. He wound down the window. "Where the bloody hell have you lot been? Your mothers have been worried sick."

"Hi, Uncle Trevor," Andy said.

"Get in, the bloody lot of you."

We all glared at the magazine which had somehow ended up in my hands.

"What you got there, boy?"

"Nothing." I moved it behind my back.

Dad threw the door open, climbed out and spun me around. He took the magazine from me and glared at it.

"Bloody filth." He tossed it into the front of the Land Rover. "Get in. Now."

We climbed into the Land Rover. The smell of cigarette smoke was thick, and it was hard not to cough. I'd never seen Dad smoke, although there were often packets of tobacco around the house.

Dad reversed into the drove and turned the Land Rover around. He dropped Andy and Liam off first.

Aunt Anne stood by her door. She put up her hand, but neither Will nor I dared move to wave back.

"Thanks, Uncle Trevor," Andy said, oblivious to the extent of his anger.

As he sped towards home, he glared at me. "We'll have to have a talk about your little magazine later." He kept staring, long after he finished speaking and I kept thinking watch the road, watch the road, watch the road, and when he did look back, he was halfway over to the other lane and he had to snatch at the steering wheel to jerk us back to the right road position.

Mum came out of the house to meet us. She must have heard Dad pull up. He rolled up the magazine and, when he put it in the glove box, I caught a glimpse of a bag of Fisherman's Friends. Mum hugged me first and then pulled Will in too.

"Go in and wash your hands ready for dinner," she said as she let us go. As we entered the kitchen, we saw Granddad Norman sitting at the dinner table holding a mug of tea. He wore his patch, so hadn't put in a glass eye.

"What have you lads been up to then?" he asked, and leaned towards us, using his cane for balance.

"We were out with Liam and Andy," Will said as he went over to the sink and turned the tap on.

"Your poor mum has been going out of her head," Granddad said.

Will had turned the tap up too high and water hit a spoon in the bottom of the sink and sploshed over his top.

"We were looking for John," I said.

"That missing boy? He'll turn up."

I turned towards the door, wondering why Mum and Dad hadn't come in yet. Maybe he was telling her about the magazine. I wish we'd had a proper look when we had the chance. It might have been an important piece of evidence.

"What do you think's happened to him?"

Granddad tilted his head to one side.

I looked up into the same corner to see what he was staring at, but there was nothing there.

"Probably ran away from home to teach his parents a lesson."

Will was wiping himself down with a tea towel.

"Your dad ran away from home once, you know. With Uncle Rodney."

Will turned towards us. "Really?"

"You know Uncle Rodney's always putting on plays with his drama group?"

"The MAD Society?" I said and chuckled to myself.

"Well, he's always been into that; God knows how as we never took him to see a show in his life. But when he was seventeen, he came out of his room with a suitcase and told us he was joining a travelling theatre. He never did want to work on the farm, no matter how much I encouraged him to help out. Your dad was the complete opposite. As soon as he could walk, he wanted to be out there. He'd ride with me on the tractor, and he could lift a bale of hay up over his head when he were six-year-old, so the last thing I expected was for him to follow Rodney out of the door."

Mum and Dad walked in. Granddad pointed. "And just like that, a couple of hours later he returned. He was pale white, like all the blood had run from his face. Reckoned he'd seen a shug monkey and had done a runner. Later on, he said he'd come home because he was hungry, and Rodney had made no plans for dinner. It was a few years before we saw Rodney again."

Dad wiped his hands. "That story's a load of nonsense."

"You didn't hear it. You were outside."

"Yes, but I know how you tell it. I never ran away, and I never saw a shug monkey neither. I walked with Rodney to the bus stop and then walked home again when he got on the bus."

"Then why were you carrying your rucksack?" Granddad looked at me and winked.

"Are you heading home for your dinner?" Dad said.

"Why? Don't you have enough grub for me here?"

"Of course, we do," Mum said and Dad's face turned sour. He gave her one of those looks that I thought were only reserved for me.

"Good. That's one reason why I came over. The other was to see if you boys fancied fishing on Sunday."

Will yelled, "Yes," and I was happy to have an excuse to be out of the house, too.

Later, after we'd eaten and Dad had gone back outside murmuring, "No rest for the wicked," I asked Granddad about the shug monkey.

"You've never heard of one?" he said, leaning back in surprise. "It's much like the black shuck in many ways." He must have seen the puzzlement on my face. "Don't tell me you've not heard of that either?"

I shook my head.

"You've heard of people seeing giant black dogs which disappear, right?"

There had been something about it on an episode of *Unsolved Mysteries* that I'd watched with John once.

"It's much like one of those, but crossed with a monkey."

"Have you ever seen one?" I asked.

Granddad leaned back and took a deep breath as if he were about to launch into one of his epic stories. "No," he said.

"Do you know anyone that has?"

"Only that your dad reckoned he'd seen one that time."

"Do you believe in them?"

"I believe what I've seen with my own eye first of all, but that don't mean that things I've not seen can't be true. I know there's a lot more out there than we can always make sense of, but what's to say that the shug monkey and the black shuck aren't the same type of thing?"

I thought back to what had chased me the other day. Could that have been one of these things? Maybe the makers of the cards had collected these types of beasts together under the name 'fiend' because there was such a range of different names for them, and if there were so many different accounts, there had to be some truth in it, didn't there? Or maybe a third series of cards was on the way with horrors I could only dream of.

Back in my room, I took my exercise book and started to write down everything I could think of, from Mr Jenkins the Ape Man to spontaneous human combustion, confident we'd be able to solve the mystery and get John back. Once I recorded all the information, I made another list on the back page and titled it *Horror Top Trumps: Series 3*. I put down the Black Dog and Shug Monkey and then began to wonder what their stats would be. I paced the room, running calculations through my head. At one point I glanced at the window and then hurried back to the book to scrawl down another entry: Demon Tree.

NOW

How easy I thought it would be–write everything down and the answer would appear as if by magic in front of me on the page. A quarter of a century later, I still can't work out the trick. As a child, I believed that, as I grew up, the gap between what I knew and what I thought I knew would shrink. It didn't. Returning to Little Mosswick gives me a chance to confirm some of what I believed to be true. Maybe then it will be easier to cope with.

It was easy to decide to return, but as I get closer, I realise that I'm not ready. I pull over in a layby on the A10 somewhere near Ely and gaze out across the fields.

"Why have we stopped?" Charlie asks.

"I'm not ready, yet," I say and switched off the engine.

"You can see for miles!" Charlie says, craning his neck for a better view. He's observant; he notices tiny details in a way I never do. He reads people much better than I can, too. Maybe it has something to do with the way I've brought him up, to search for the truth behind the words, to ask what it is people really want when they speak. What a strange species the human race is. We develop a complex and precise language and rarely use it to say what we mean.

Charlie's gazing across the checkerboard of fields. It's so open; it looks like there's nowhere to hide. It looks like you couldn't keep any secrets here. I know better, and as I scan the land I spot a silo, deep ditches that would allow you to cross this landscape unseen, and half a dozen dilapidated barns, the corrugated iron roofs curling away from rotting wooden beams. I know that not far from here is the river where there are more places to hide or to be hidden: under bridges, in drainage pipes, and at abandoned water works.

"Was it like this where you lived?" Charlie asks.

"Worse," I say, not turning to face him, still staring across the fields.

The car rocks and I hear a vehicle. I turn to see a police car speeding away, blue lights flashing, drawing my attention back to the road. It's time to go.

Saturday 16th June 1990

Will was still sleeping when I woke, so I left him. I opened the door at the bottom of the stairs to find Mum alone in the kitchen.

She lifted her head and smiled at me, but the smile looked false and her eyes were red and strained. A cup of tea sat on the table, long since gone cold and having formed a skin.

"Where's Dad?" I asked. I liked to know so I was ready to put my defences up, if necessary.

"Cutting hay," she said with mock enthusiasm. "He's got a busy day."

"Did he go out last night?" I asked.

"No, why?"

"Nothing, I thought I heard the door." I'd been waking several times during the night. Any sound such as the rattle of the window in the frame or a door closing lifted me out of my dreams, which, last night, had been about monkey-faced dog creatures chasing me around the droves while the tree looked on, shaking its branches and laughing at me.

"Why don't you go and wake your brother? Can't have him sleeping the day away."

"Can we go out to play?"

"Wake Will up, and I'll think about it."

Will slept with his mouth wide open. I was tempted to drop in a Mojo from the last of my stack of penny sweets, but he snorted as I approached, so I ate it myself.

"Mum says you've got to get up," I said as I shook him by the shoulder.

He opened his eyes and gave me a grumpy look. "What's the time?"

"Half-past eight."

He looked agitated. "It's Saturday."

"Mum says we can go out to play."

Will shuffled up the bed into a sitting position, "Really?"

"She said she'll think about it."

Will threw himself back down. "Don't you know I'll think about it is adult speak for no?"

"But we can ask. We might be able to do something."

"If we're not, I bagsy first go on Mario."

Will and I passed the ball to each other as we made our way along Main Street. As we approached Shaky Jake's house, he passed it in front of him for me to run on to, and I passed it back again, but Will, and I swear he did this on purpose, lifted his foot so that the ball ran between the gap in the fence and on to Shaky Jake's garden and came to a stop in a flowerbed.

"Who kicked the ball onto that poor man's lawn?" Mum asked.

"Tom!" Will said.

"You did it on purpose!"

"Tom, go and get it. If Jacob sees you, I expect you to apologise."

If Shaky Jake saw me, I'd have run.

With each step, I expected him to fly out of the house, no doubt wielding a knife or other kitchen utensil to murder me with (he'd do serious damage with a potato masher), but I reached the flowerbed without incident and plucked the ball from among the flowers.

Shaky Jake must have been out, I figured, maybe wandering the droves for whatever reason he had, perhaps seeking other boys to kidnap.

"Will," I called and drop-kicked the ball.

He trapped it under his foot and beckoned me out of the garden.

I had other ideas.

I crept towards Jake's window. The curtains were drawn, but a crack between them remained. To shield the reflection of the light, I cupped my hands onto the window and peered in.

"Come away," Mum yelled.

I ignored her and stared into Shaky Jake's living room. Inside a large, dark wood cabinet, polished to a shine, held dozens of framed photographs of people, but they were too far away for me to make out who they were. The only other thing in the living room was a sofa which still had a plastic wrapping over it and looked as if it had never been sat upon, and a coffee table covered in magazines, some like the one we'd found behind the school.

"Tom, I swear, if you don't come off that poor man's lawn this instant, you'll have your father to answer to," called Mum.

I started to pull myself away from the window, but a sound came from inside—a gurgle of some sort, followed by a low grumble.

"Tom," called Mum.

"Quick," Will shouted. "Shaky Jake's coming."

I turned, but my feet slipped out from under me and I fell face-first into the grass. I scrambled up and managed to keep my balance as I hurtled from his lawn and glanced with panic down the road in both directions.

Will was bent double with laughter. He pointed at me but was unable to speak over his fits of laughter.

A quick glance along the road both ways told me that Shaky Jake was nowhere nearby, but when I caught sight of Mum's face, I could tell she was furious and that it was time to move on.

At the playing field, an adult game was on with proper kits and a referee. The smaller pitch was being used by kids from our school that we knew. It was odd for a Saturday, because, even though there were some dads in the football team, a lot of people's mums were there, too. Mum sat down next to Steven Farley's mum. He was in my class and we got on okay, but we weren't friends outside of school.

There were about ten kids already playing.

"Can we play?" shouted Will.

Daniel Richardson, who was in goal, said, "It's Chris' ball, you'll have to ask him."

Chris was in Will's class. He was at the other end of the pitch, and we watched him score a goal. As they were making their way back to kick-off again, Will went over to him.

"I'm on Chris' team. We're England. You're Holland."

I'd forgotten that England were playing again tonight, and against Holland, one of the best sides in the world. I was sure it was going to be amazing.

"What's the score?" I said to Daniel.

"It's 4-3. We're losing."

After our game, I was looking forward to the real thing. I was expecting a close game, and goals too, but maybe not so many as in our game, which ended at 7-5 to England when Chris had to go home because his mum had to go to Downham Market to do some shopping. We did offer to sub in our ball to keep the game going but other people had to drift off with their parents, too. As there weren't enough of us left for a proper game, we played Wembley for a bit. After getting knocked out early in the game I sat with mum and had a sandwich, a pork pie, and some crisps.

"Why are there so many adults out today?" I said.

"What do you mean?"

"Normally there are only kids playing football, and a few people watching the game."

"Aren't we allowed out to watch our children play?"

"You can but… it's not normal."

"People are worried, that's all."

"Because of John?"

Mum mopped at her forehead with a napkin. "It's hot today. I hope your dad took plenty to drink with him." She opened the flask and poured some orange squash into one of our plastic beakers. "Have a drink. Don't want you getting dehydrated after running around for so long."

"Where is he, Mum?"

"That's for the police to investigate. Don't worry."

"But he's my friend."

Mum ruffled my hair. "Why don't you see if Will wants a drink?"

But Will was busy trying to get the ball past Daniel, so I left them to it.

After Will had finished winning his third straight game, and we'd finished the food, we packed up the picnic. I offered to carry the picnic basket and Will had the football.

"Can we walk back the long way?" I asked.

"Which way?"

"Up the drove at the end of Hereward Close."

"I don't see why not. Is that okay with you, Will?"

"S'pose."

Hereward Close was another one of those newer housing estates in the village. It came off Main Street and then curled around to the left, but you could join the old drove from the end of the road. It later joined another drove (which might have been called Long Drove, but I can never remember the names, not like Granddad can).

A little way along the drove, in a field overgrown with wildflowers, stood an old military pillbox.

"Can I go inside?"

Mum held out her hand to take the picnic basket.

"Are you coming, Will?"

Will shook his head and bounced the ball.

The pillbox was at the edge of a field full of oilseed rape which was tickling my legs as I made my way through. Inside, darkness filled the pillbox. I called out, but only my voice echoed back. I ducked my head inside and waited for my eyes to adjust. It smelled damp. Water must have come in when it rained and later evaporated, but not without leaving a stink. I could make out the corners and the line of sludge along the bottom, so there was nothing much in there. A sweet wrapper hid in the corner. I crouched down and reached out to grab it. A thin layer of slime covered it. I moved back towards the entrance to bring it into the light. Discoloured and torn, the Stratos wrapper—another one of those chocolate bars that I only ever saw when Uncle Rodney came over—looked like it had been there months. Maybe it was from one I'd eaten myself, and the wrapper had blown away and drifted here, or maybe Uncle Rodney had eaten one as he was wandering the droves. Either way, it wasn't much of a find.

I felt itchy when I came out, and for the rest of the journey home, I couldn't stop rubbing my eyes. They were so bad I didn't notice Will throw the ball towards me and it thunked off the side of my head and into the ditch.

"Will, what did you do that for?" Mum said.

"I said 'catch'" Will said, through a restrained giggle.

"No you didn't," I said and rubbed the side of my head.

"I did. You weren't listening. You didn't catch it; you have to get it."

I looked into the ditch full of stinging nettles. "You threw it; you have to get it."

Mum sighed. "I don't care who gets the blasted thing! Hurry up and let's get home."

"I'm not going down there," Will said, "I didn't head it into the ditch."

"Well, I'm not."

"Leave it then, for all I care," Mum said and started to walk away.

Will and I approached the ditch together. We could see where the ball had forced the nettles to part.

"Get a stick and we can drag it along," Will said.

I looked for one, but my eyes were watering, and I couldn't see well. My nose had started to run too, and the snot coming out was so thin it was almost water.

Will found a stick himself and thrashed at the nettles. Their tops flew off and cleared a path to allow us to get over the ditch to collect the ball. Will pushed the stick into the nettles, and the ball edged out.

"Go get it then," Will said.

"You get it."

"I'm holding the nettles."

So, I went down into the ditch and dragged the football back with my foot and then threw it out. Will moved the stick, and the nettles pinged towards me, but they stopped before touching my skin. While they moved, I could see something else among them.

"Give me the stick," I said.

"No," Will said.

"Come on!"

"Why?"

"I can see something."

"What?"

"I don't know. Clothes?"

"Will you boys stop messing about," Mum said. "You've got the ball; let's go."

"There's something else."

"Give him the stick, Will, so we can home," Mum said.

Will passed me the stick, and I reached into the nettles. I dragged the object closer and I could see purple. I took a step backwards and managed to get the stick under the purple thing and dragged it out. It was a square of material, perhaps once part of a t-shirt, but now full of rot holes and covered in thick black grease marks.

"It's a dirty, old rag," Mum said. "Leave it alone."

I lifted it out of the ditch with the stick and then climbed back out myself.

"How do you think it got there?"

"I imagine it's some rag used on a tractor and it blew off one day."

Will chuckled.

"What's wrong with you?" asked Mum.

"You said 'blew off'," Will said, his hands crossed over his belly as he giggled.

Mum rolled her eyes and kept walking.

"So you don't think it's important?" I said, with the rag hooked by the end of the stick.

"You still going on about that dirty, old thing?"

"So it couldn't be a clue about what happened to John?"

Mum opened her arms and urged me to come to her.

"I'm sorry, Tom," she said.

"He'll be okay?" I said, half-stating, half-asking and wiped at my eyes.

"I hope so," she said and then we made our way home and I didn't want to check ditches or fields anymore.

My eyes kept itching and my nose kept running all afternoon so I was in no fit state to play Mario. I did try, and I got through the first world without so much as losing a life, but then the sneezes started, and I ran into a Goomba because I couldn't see. Will thought this was hilarious and made out I was fake sneezing to hide how bad I was at the game. Mum had left us to play on our own most of the afternoon, and it wasn't until Dad came home that she called us down. She'd cooked a ham that we were going to have with salad and potatoes.

"What's up, boy?" Dad said as I rubbed my eyes at the dinner table, "Have you been crying?"

"No," I said and looked at my plate.

"I think he might have hay fever," Mum said.

"Hay fever? You daft sod. You better get over that quick as I'll need you to stack the bales up in a few weeks."

I cut my ham and tried not to listen to him. The thought of stacking bales filled me with dread. Will would be raising them onto the top of the stack without a problem while I'd struggle to get them higher than my waist.

"You hear me? What you should do is go out there and roll around in the fields."

"Trevor," Mum said.

"Roll about in the grass and the flowers; take in so much pollen and build up your immunity."

I had a mouthful of ham. It was juicy. I tried to focus on what it tasted like and its texture.

"Whoever heard of a farmer's son with hay fever? I bet you've been in your room all day playing them silly games. That's why you get hay fever."

"We have been out today, haven't we Mum?" Will said.

Relieved, I relaxed in my chair a little.

"Yes, we had a picnic at the park, and then took a long walk back up the drove," Mum said.

"All right for some! Long walks! Some of us have to work for a living."

"Shut up and eat your dinner," Mum said.

"Okay, okay, just teasing you. Miserable bloody lot you are."

Mum threw a tea towel at Dad and he let it rest on his face. He shovelled potato onto his fork and tried to put it into his mouth, pretending not to know the tea towel was in the way. I never knew what to expect from him, and didn't know if I preferred him grumpy or when he was trying to be funny because when he was acting funny, he would catch us off guard when he turned.

Dad seemed to be in a good mood, and it looked like it was going to stay that way. He even said we could put the football on downstairs instead of sending us up to our room. A car horn beeped from outside. "We have a job to do first," he said. He got up and Will followed quickly, with me a distant third.

Standing by his car, Uncle Rodney had one hand on his hip, and he was wearing a huge pair of gloves, the kind you normally only see at falconry displays.

Dad peered into the back of the car. "Where are they, then?"

"Ta-da!" said Uncle Rodney, and he opened the car boot to the sound of clucking. A sea of brown feathers rippled inside, and then heads emerged, seeking the source of light. One rose above the rest, squirming out to stand atop another chicken and clucked. It jumped, landed in the dust, and started strutting towards me.

"Grab 'er," Dad said.

I waited until she was close and then pounced, but she darted out of reach. Meanwhile, Uncle Rodney was grabbing chickens by a leg, turning them upside down, and passing them to Will and Dad in groups of three per hand.

After a couple of trips to the car they'd moved all of their chickens, and I'd managed to corner mine. I reached a hand towards her and she had nowhere to go. She froze, ducking low to the ground, and I was able to reach out with both hands and grab her by the body. Proudly, I held her out and walked towards the coop, but then she started to flap her wings and I had to hold her at arm's length.

"That's no way to hold a bird," Dad said, and I could feel her squirming away from me.

Uncle Rodney was beside me in an instant and it seemed to calm her down. He took her from me and tucked her under his arm. He placed her into the coop. "And that makes thirteen," he said as he closed the door.

"Can we go and watch the football?" asked Will.

"You can," Dad said. "As Tom was slacking off while we were doing all the work, I think he should help his uncle clear these feathers out of the back of his car."

I trudged towards it. The blue rope in the back was peppered with downy feathers, and a fair few splodges of poo, too. For some reason, there were also a couple of loose Panini World Cup football stickers, one of them was the shiny world cup trophy sticker.

"Let the boy watch his football," said Uncle Rodney, and he pushed the boot down with one of his massive hands. "I need to give the car a good clean out, anyway."

I wanted to ask for the sticker, but Dad said, "Go on then, boy," and I hurried inside.

I was worried that England would get thumped because the Dutch were the European Champions, and last time they played, they lost 3-1 and Van Basten got a hat-trick, but England played well. It was an even first half, but England got even better in the second half. They scored two goals, but both were ruled out. First Gary Lineker scored, but it didn't count because the ball had bounced up to hit his hand before he kicked it into the net. Then, in the last minute, England got a free kick and Stuart Pearce scored from it, but the referee said it didn't count either.

"Why doesn't it count?" I said.

"I don't bloody well know," Dad said.

"It was obstruction," Will said.

"What was obstruction?"

"The free kick. It was for obstruction, which means an indirect free kick."

"So?"

"So, if it's an indirect free kick you're not allowed to score from it. It has to touch another player first."

"Well, that's not fair."

"It's time you two went to bed," Dad said, and that was another thing we didn't think was fair either.

Half an hour later, Will was snoring, but I was sniffling and I had an itch in the back of my throat. I thought that I'd go downstairs to get a drink to see if that would ease it, but I got halfway down the stairs before Mum's and Dad's raised voices made me pause.

"That's not what I'm saying," Dad said.

Hearing the anger in his voice, I backed up the stairs, but not before Mum's reply. "I won't lie," she said.

The sound that came next, I can't describe. It was like nothing human. It was a growl, but not that of an animal, a roar, but like one I'd never heard before. I couldn't get caught on the stairs, not with him in that mood. I hurried back to bed, but it was no longer the sniffling and the itching that stopped me from sleeping.

NOW

The closer I get to Little Mosswick, the more familiar it becomes until I know every bend and dip in the road. As I round the corner, I see familiar farmhouses, but new housing estates block the view across the whole village. I'm relieved I can no longer see across the land to my old home. I need to approach it with caution.

As I exit the roundabout to head into Little Mosswick, I see another police car, or, who knows, it could be the same one. A police officer stands in the road, urging me pull over. After I stop, I roll down the window, ready for his approach. He's older than me by at least twenty years based upon the plethora of grey hairs in his beard. I don't recognise him, but wonder if he was around back in 1990. He crouched down to look into the car. "Good afternoon," he says. "What's your business in Little Mosswick?"

"Visiting family," I say, the word sticking in my throat.

The police officer pulls out a photograph and offers it to me. "Do you recognise the child?"

It's John. The dimple in the chin, those blue eyes, the cluster of three moles on the left cheek.

"Sir?" Says the police officer. "Do you recognise this girl?"

I look at the picture again. It's nothing like John. Yes she has the chin dimple and the moles, but she also has pigtails.

"Would you mind stepping out of the car?" the police officer says. He steps back and speaks into his walkie-talkie.

"Dad," Charlie says. "What's going on?"

I shrug. Glancing at the police officer, reading the strain on his face, I realise that I don't have time to waste. I hurry out of the car.

"Would you mind opening your boot?"

I speed around to the back of the car and open the boot revealing the two bags I'd packed for Charlie and me.

The police officer lifts the bags, one at a time, and feels underneath them.

"Where were you this morning between nine and eleven?"

"Miles away. We left our home in Oxfordshire at around ten o'clock."

"Can I take you name?"

"Thomas Tilbrook. What's this about?"

"We're looking for a young girl. The girl in the picture."

"Who is she?"

"Her name's Jessica. She's a resident of Little Mosswick. She was sent to the post office for milk and hasn't been seen since."

"Have you spoken to my dad?" I say, almost screaming. "Have you spoken to Trevor Tilbrook?"

Sunday 17th June

Our fishing trip would allow us to explore paths we'd not yet checked. Maybe John had gone fishing out of boredom because we'd abandoned him. We'd been fishing together a few times. He had to borrow one of Will's old rods the first time, but then his parents bought him a new carbon fibre one. He didn't enjoy fishing that much—he hated putting maggots on hooks, and one time when he caught a ruffe, he couldn't get the hook out of its mouth and pulled it too hard and blood flew everywhere.

One Monday morning, he came into school and told us he'd gone to the river with his dad, and they'd caught a massive pike. He claimed it was bigger than the one on the cover of *The Angling Times* we'd seen in the post office the previous week, but he'd never told us about anything he'd done with his dad before, so it made my chin itch. But maybe he went fishing alone. Maybe he'd still be there, stuck in time, casting his rod into the water again and again, waiting for someone to find him.

Granddad came round at eight, too early for a Sunday.

"Time for breakfast before you go, boys?" Mum asked.

"Only if you've got plenty for me too," Granddad said. His uncombed hair stood like a crazy white mane. When it was like that, he reminded me of Aslan. Granddad was wise and strong and full of wisdom, and I sometimes wondered if he could do magic.

After breakfast, we set off to collect Liam and Andy. They were eating their breakfast, and Granddad tucked away another bacon sandwich. We stopped back at Granddad's house to pick up the fishing rods from his garage which had this odour of sawdust and engine oil, and the windows were covered in a mossy film which made everything inside look distorted and other-worldly. A new smell overpowered the oil, an animal stink.

Will tugged on my sleeve and pointed behind me.

I turned to face three dead pheasants hanging from hooks through their beaks. After seeing them, their smell grew stronger, and I couldn't help but put a hand to my mouth.

"Don't you worry none about my pheasants," Granddad said. "Leave them to hang for a couple of three or four days and they'll be proper tasty." He wasn't paying attention as he picked his tackle box from a shelf, and a heavy chain snaked off behind it, clattered to the floor, and coiled there.

"I'll pick it up later," he muttered. Looking at the debris on the floor, 'later' was not going to be any time soon.

We walked towards the end of the village which wasn't the quickest way to the river, but I knew where we were going. Liam carried the rods, and even though they'd been taken apart so they weren't that long, he kept turning to look into the ditches and clobbering Andy on the side of the head.

"Tom should carry the rods," Andy said, rubbing his ear.

I was already struggling with Granddad's fold-up chair. "Why me?"

"Because they're like Donatello's staff, and he's Donatello."

"We're not the turtles, Andy," Will said. He had no trouble carrying the tackle box.

"We are the turtles," Andy said, pouting.

Granddad turned and stared at us. "Turtles? Whatever in merry hell are you blathering on about? Of course, you're not turtles."

"We're the Teenage Mutant Ninja Turtles."

"Well, that makes a whole lot more sense," Granddad said, scratching his head. "Anyway, I know you're not a turtle," he said as he ruffled Andy's hair.

"How come?"

"Because you're a money box." Granddad pulled a twenty-pence coin from behind Andy's ear.

Andy muttered, "I am a turtle," with his bottom lip jutting out.

"Well, I ain't never seen a turtle in the river, but there have been terrapins in there."

"Really?" I said. I could see Will shaking his head.

"Oh yeah, dozens of them. You boys aren't old enough to remember it, but I took your dad and your mum there when they were little. You know that big old house as you go round the bend on the approach to Ely?"

We all nodded and continued walking, eagerly listening apart from Will who overtook us and walked on ahead.

"The family that used to own that house, many years ago, they had a menagerie. Used to be the Duke of somewhere or other, I forget, who had the house and before my time they had lions and tigers and ostriches there. When I went, they only had a few of the smaller cats left: pumas, lynxes, a cougar. What they did still have though, was a tank full of terrapins. Only when they found out that the Duke's great grandson or great, great grandson had been diddling his taxes for years and had blown the family fortune they were going to lock him up. With no one to keep the animals, he let what was left of them go, and the terrapins bred in the waters."

"What about the cats?" asked Liam.

"That's a story for another day." He stopped outside the entrance to Barnham's farm.

Just inside the gate was the barn from which Mr Barnham ran his bait and tackle shop. Will had marched on fifty metres down the road and Granddad had to summon him back.

"What're we going in there for?" asked Andy.

Andy hadn't been fishing with us before, so he didn't know that this was the best place in the village to get bait.

As we wandered through the gates, the barn door, which had recently been painted black, swung open.

"Aye up, Teddy," Granddad said.

"Norm. Taking your lads for a spot of fishin'?" Teddy said. He must have been tall if he stood up straight as he was almost as tall as Granddad Norman with his back bent and buckled. His long and pointed nose cast a shadow over the loose and saggy skin on one side of his face. He led us into the barn and stood behind the counter upon which sat an ancient till, and several empty tubs. Shelves held various rods and reels, spools of wire, and multi-coloured floats. A revolting smell—a sweet sickliness like candyfloss mixed with rotting vegetables—hung in the air. The dust clung inside my nostrils but there was no way I was going to breathe through my mouth and inhale it.

"What's it to be then boys? Worms or maggots?" said Mr Barnham.

Andy's jaw dropped.

"Well, it's this little fella's first time," Granddad ruffled Andy's hair, "so I reckon I'd not me teachin' him right if we did take a pot of each."

"Worms and maggots? What a treat," Teddy said. "I normally do this out back, but as it's your first time..." Teddy opened the door behind him and grabbed a larger plastic container. He took off the lid and the sickly smell engulfed the room. He tilted the tub towards Andy so he could see the hundreds, maybe thousands, of tiny yellow maggots writhing around inside.

"Gross!" Andy said.

"You won't catch fish without bait," Teddy said. He dipped his long fingers into the container and picked up a handful of the maggots. He dropped most into one of the smaller containers but left a couple to wriggle out around on his hand to show Andy. "How'd you like to pick out the worms yourself, young man?" Teddy laughed with his mouth wide open, showing the enormous gaps between his teeth.

Andy shook his head. "Granddad," he said, his voice quavering, "can I wait outside?"

Granddad chuckled and nodded at us.

We left Granddad in there with Mr Barnham. Andy still had a sickened look on his face, but Liam grinned. "Hold these." He pushed the fishing rods into Andy's arms. He reached into his back pocket and pulled out his wad of Top Trumps cards, both sets collected together and bound with an elastic band. He flicked through them and picked out The

Sorcerer, an old man with long, pointed fingers, a huge nose and a cavernous mouth, almost devoid of teeth.

We were still chuckling about it when Granddad came out. "What are you boys laughing at?"

"Nothing," we said together.

"Come on then. These fish ain't gonna catch themselves, are they?"

"How big can maggots get, Granddad?" Liam said as he peered into the pot full of them.

"Not much longer than your thumbnail. They hatch out into flies, see."

Liam must have been thinking about The Maggot card from his Top Trumps. With a Fear Factor of only 66, it wasn't among the most frightening cards in the pack. The picture made it look huge. Its head was twice as big as the human head which it scratched with its claw. I peered into the pot and watched them writhing.

"They don't even have limbs, or faces, or anything," I said. The monster version probably wasn't a maggot at all.

"Did you know," Granddad said, before setting his rod down to take up a more comfortable position, "that they sometimes put maggots on wounds to help clean 'em."

"Urgh." Liam shivered.

Andy shrank into himself.

Will cast his line into the water.

"Why?" I asked (after overcoming a slight shudder).

"They eat the dead flesh, which helps the rest of the wound to heal quicker."

"That's gross," Liam said. "I wouldn't let them do that to me."

"Not even if it was the only way of saving your life? You might get blood poisoning without it."

But what if the maggot burrowed in too deep and got into your brain? Then you might turn out like The Maggot. I don't know if I'd want to live as a monster.

We'd only caught one fish (a small perch on Granddad's rod) when we stopped for lunch.

"After we've had a bite, how about we go a little further up the bank? Might have more luck there," Granddad said.

I looked at Liam and he nodded back. It would be a good opportunity to scope out a different area.

"I know what you boys are thinking," Granddad said.

"We ain't thinking nothing," Liam said and started to pinken.

"Your friend that went missing, or run away. He might have come this way?"

"There's no harm looking," I said.

Will tossed a rock into the water.

"Well, no one saw him walking along the main road. If he did come this way, no one much would have seen him. Old Teddy Barnham has his fields left fallow. His boy doesn't want to farm it."

"How do you know no one saw him on Main Street?" Will asked.

"Police came to my door and asked if I'd seen him. Showed me a picture."

"So how do you know one else hasn't seen him?"

"Do you think I don't talk to my neighbours? What do you think I do all day now your dad won't let me help on the farm?"

Dad had always said it was Granddad's choice to give up working, and he often complained about how hard he had to work on his own.

"Anyway, I'm not doing anything more until I get some grub in me. I'm famished."

After eating the sandwiches that Aunt Anne had prepared for us, we set off along the bank. Granddad told us the names of the droves and where they led.

"Would it be possible to track someone along here?" asked Liam.

"If you had the skills," Granddad said.

"Don't you have the skills?"

"Well, in the winter anyone can follow footprints in the mud. This time of the year it's dry and cracked. You might make something out in the dust, but chances are the wind would have blown it away."

"I saw this programme where they could tell from the way the grass was broken or flattened that animals had walked by."

"Well, why don't you keep an eye on the grass, and tell me what you figure out."

And that's what Liam did, staring at the ground until we arrived at a spot sheltered from the blazing sun by a pair of weeping willows. It was there that Liam beckoned us over to the water's edge.

"What's this, Granddad?" He pointed at a spot on the edge of the bank where the grass was flat. All the way down to the water the grass was parted as if something had gone in there or crawled out.

"Well, I can't see no footprints, hoof marks, or anything of the like," Granddad said.

"What caused it then?" Andy asked.

"I dunno. Small animal going down for a drink? Maybe someone rolled something down the bank?"

"Like what?" Will said.

"I'm not a psychic. How about we cast in here and have a ponder on it?"

We had more luck with the fish there, and Andy even got the hang of putting maggots on the hook—the worms continued to wriggle from his grasp, though.

Once we had our lines in the water, I spoke to Granddad. "Has anything like this ever happened before?"

"What, a handsome, old fella fishing with his four grandsons? I should think so."

"No, I mean, like John. A kid going missing."

"You hear about it from time to time on the news."

"And what happens?"

"Sometimes they turn up, and well, sometimes it's not so good news."

"But has it ever happened here?"

"What in Little Mosswick?"

"Yes."

"Lots have things have happened here."

"But to kids? How about when you were young?"

"I suppose there have been one or two accidents. My eye. Teddy Barnham's brother drowned in the old pit which has since been filled in, but he weren't exactly a kid at the time."

"But nothing like this?"

"I don't rightly remember. It's not my place to give you a history lesson, is it? Now keep an eye on your float or you might miss a bite."

After about an hour, with us having caught at least two fish each apart from Granddad who kept missing his float go under, Granddad got up and peered into the water again.

"Clamber down and have a look. See if anything has been dropped in there," he said.

"No way. I'll slip," Liam said.

"I'll do it!" Andy said, jumping up and dropping his rod to the floor.

"Needs to be one of the bigger boys," Granddad said. "Though you are awfully brave for volunteering."

"Let me," Will said.

I smiled, and pictured him as the hero, racing to volunteer for a dangerous duty.

"If we make a chain—Will at the front, then Liam, then Tom, then me, then Andy—we can keep a hold of Will and make sure he don't fall in. His Mum'll have my guts for garters if I bring him home soaked."

"Mum! What about Dad? What'll he say?" I said.

"He's not the one to be scared of; I can tell you that for nothing. He thinks he's the big man, but I remember when he was a little boy."

"Did you take him fishing?" asked Andy.

"Yes, but he never had the patience for it. Always thought sitting around was a waste of time."

That sounded about right; he was always going on about how sinful time-wasting was.

We formed our chain and Will headed down the bank side. Liam had his fingers in Will's belt loops, and I had hold of the back of Liam's pockets. Granddad had a firm hold on me, and Andy was somewhere behind. Will kept edging forward until he was close to the edge.

"Anything?" called Granddad.

"I can't see. It's too dirty."

"Okay, let's back up."

We took a couple of steps backwards when Will shouted, "Stop."

"What is it?"

"I found something."

"What?" we cried.

"Sweet wrapper."

"A sweet wrapper? That's not what we were looking for!" Granddad said. "Come on up." He continued to back up.

Will grabbed the wrapper and showed it to us when he got to the top. Fisherman's Friend.

"Bloody litterbugs," Granddad said.

I stared at Will, urging him to say something about the sweets we'd found before. I couldn't find a way to put it into words.

"Boys," Granddad said, "why don't you pack the rods away?"

"But it's still early!" Andy said.

"It's probably nothing, but the more I look at it, the more it looks like something was dumped in there. It's likely a load of old rubbish, but I want to report it, so they can check it out."

"I saw the police by the river the other day," I said.

"They've got divers and snorkels and other contraptions, so if there's anything of interest, they'll find it," Granddad said.

"Is it John? Could someone have chucked him in the river?" Liam said.

"No, nothing like that. He would have flattened the reeds. Probably a fisherman ditching broken tackle, but we have to keep our eyes peeled."

All the way home I thought about what might have happened. If John had gone by the river, what reason would he have to dump anything? He wouldn't get rid of his clothes or any of his possessions unless he'd done something bad and was trying to hide the evidence. And the sweet wrapper didn't add up there either. That wouldn't have been John's. I remember we tried some once, and they made us gag. I don't remember where he got them from, he always had loads of sweets given to him, so we were going to share them, but they were so disgusting—like pebbles that dripped acid on your tongue. We spat them out in the bushes then ran to his house and downed a pint of water. If they were the kind of sweets that adults bought, it explained why they didn't eat as many sweets as kids.

I thought about what had emerged from the ditch and chased me along the drove. Could that have been some kind of amphibious creature that mostly lived in water, but could also survive in the ditches? "Liam, can I borrow your cards?"

He got them out of his pocket and handed them over. I was sure there was nothing in the original set, but I didn't know the new ones well yet. There were a couple which caught my eye: Terror of the Deep with Killing Power of 72 and a three-pronged trident, Creature from the Black Lagoon with Killing Power of 73 and clawed fingers on webbed hands, and

The Slime Creature with Killing Power of 68 and a spear and a weird trunk. None of them filled me with fear like The Fiend had.

Granddad flung the fishing equipment in his garage and then said we'd be okay making our own way home. We stopped a little distance from Liam and Andy's house.

"What do you reckon?" Liam said as I gave the cards back to him.

"There are underwater monsters, but I'm not sure."

"Add them into your book."

"There's no point going on about monsters," Will said. "John probably ran away. He might even have already come home."

"What about the sweet wrapper?" Liam said.

"It doesn't mean it was the same person who ate the ones near the school."

"But not many people can like them. They're disgusting. It's got to be some kind of evidence."

"Evidence of what?"

"That someone spied on the school, and kidnapped John," Liam said. His face changed as he understood the implications of what he was saying.

"That's why it's stupid talking about monsters. Monsters don't eat cough sweets, even gross ones."

"But what about aliens?" said Liam.

"Where's your Granddad?" Dad said, calling from the barn as we approached the house. He wore a boiler suit, buttoned all the way up despite the heat.

"Home," Will said.

"What, he left you to walk back here by yourself?"

"We've done it thousands of times, Dad."

"You might have done, but that was before."

"Before what?

"I'm going to have to have a word with that daft, old sod," he pulled the keys to his Land Rover out of his pocket, hurried across the yard, got in and revved the engine hard. He barely gave us a chance to get out of the way before he flew past and off towards Granddad's.

All the noise brought Mum out. "You're back early boys," she said. "Where'd your dad go in such a hurry?"

We told her what we'd seen and what Granddad was doing.

"Oh, I know what I was going to give to you!" Mum said, urging us to follow her. From the cabinet under the sink, she pulled out a paper bag. She handed us a book each. As soon as I saw the familiar green spine of the Fighting Fantasy series, I smiled. I'd played through all the books I had so many times the pages were worn, especially where I'd written, rubbed out and rewritten my stats. Will took hold of *Battleblade Warrior*, which had a lizard monster riding a pterodactyl on the cover, and Mum handed me *The Secret of the Scythe*. Will wasn't as keen on the books as I was, and he cheated, skipping the fights and using bookmarks to alter his choices.

I dashed up to the bedroom and studied the book in more detail. The cover featured a dark-hooded skeleton holding a huge scythe that dripped blood. It looked more like the Top Trumps' Devil Priest than Death, but I knew it was supposed to be the Grim Reaper from reading the back cover:

94 DEAD BRANCHES

> *Dare YOU travel to the other side?*
>
> *Only the desperate would travel the perilous paths into the Underworld to confront the Grim Reaper. Yet it is there that you must go if you are to unlock the secrets of the scythe and bring back your master, the great wizard Hexor, from the brink of death.*
>
> *Can you defeat the Grim Reaper and his dastardly puzzles, or will the dead-eyed wanderers of the Underworld devour your very soul?*
>
> *Part story, part game, this is a book in which YOU become the hero! Two dice, a pencil and an eraser are all you need. YOU decide which routes to take, which dangers to risk and which foes to fight!*

I looked at the cover again. The Reaper stood in a dark forest. Only the tree trunks were visible, each of which had a glaring pair of red eyes. Off to the left was an orange glow, a hint of fire.

I grabbed a pencil and then had to search for dice. As usual, they turned up under my bed. That's what you get for playing Fighting Fantasy in bed. I also found another set of Top Trumps I'd lost. Tractors. I'd never played them.

I rolled the dice onto the book and scored terribly—nine skill, eight luck and only seventeen stamina.

With those stats, I didn't expect to get far, and I was right. I encountered a goblin after a poor luck roll meant he spotted me hiding in a bush. Though I beat him, he got a few hits in, leaving me with thirteen stamina points. I came across a cottage on the road and decided to rest there to recover after being invited in by a 'kindly, old lady'. I should have paid more attention to the witch-hazel shrubs growing up beside her house; that was a hint that I shouldn't trust her. She poisoned me, and I fell into a deep sleep where I was confronted by a nightmare demon which I almost beat, but a run of bad dice rolls meant that I lost. I'd never been beaten by a Fighting Fantasy book so early. At least this one would be a challenge.

Will had already lost interest in his (though I spotted several torn pieces of paper on his bed that he'd used for bookmarking) and had switched on the TV to watch the build-up to Egypt versus the Republic of Ireland, which was in England's group. Every match in the group so far had been a draw, so if either team won they would be top of the table and probably go through to the next round. It wasn't a good game and before half-time, I'd picked up *The Secret of the Scythe* again.

Will interrupted me at some point during the second half. "Granddad was acting weird today."

"How?"

"Normally when you ask him a question, there's a crazy story to go with it."

"Granddad's stories aren't crazy."

"That's not what I meant. Over the top. Exaggerated."

"Like the story about the terrapins?"

"Exactly. There were probably one or two which were thrown into the water, but not *hundreds*."

"Don't you believe him?"

"It's not that. Sometimes he likes to make them more exciting."

"So?"

"Don't you think it was odd when you asked if any other kids had gone missing?"

"What about it?"

"There was no amazing story."

"Maybe there was nothing to tell?"

"Or they don't want us to know."

"They?"

"The adults. Can't you see they're not telling us what's going on?"

"With John?"

"With everything. They tell us it's wrong to lie, but they do it to us all the time."

I could see that Will was upset. Tears were welling up in his eyes and he kept rubbing his forehead as he was talking.

"But I heard them last night," I said. "Mum said she wouldn't lie!"

"Try them, then!" Will said, spitting out the words. "Let's go downstairs and ask them if there's any news," he said, shuffling off the end of his bed. He waited by my bed for me to move, but I could imagine Dad getting angry if we asked questions.

"See?" Will said as if reading my mind. "There's no point. They won't tell us anything. They'll change the subject."

"We should ask at school. See what our teachers say."

"They'll do the same thing, I bet."

Monday 18th June 1990

Will was right.

"The police are still investigating," Mrs Palmer said when Liam and I approached her at break. "I'm sure they're doing what they can."

"Do you think he's okay?" Liam asked.

"You boys get some fresh air. When there's news to tell, you'll be among the first to know."

"Don't you want us to stay in and tidy your cupboard?" Liam nodded towards the locked door.

A wrinkle appeared on Mrs Palmer's brow. "Why would you want to spend your time doing that?"

"To be helpful," I cut in as Liam struggled for words.

"That's very kind, but it's square and tidy. Off you go."

"She's hiding something," Liam said when we were out in the corridor.

I wasn't so sure. Mrs Palmer seemed way too nice to be an alien.

We stopped off in the toilets, and on the way to the playground, we had to pass Mr Inglehart's office. Creeping by, we overheard teachers talking. "We have to prepare the pupils for transition." Then a shuffling of feet suggested someone was moving towards the door so we dashed outside.

"See," Liam said. "They're still moving ahead with their plans."

"What can we do about it?"

"We need to search the staff room. They must keep their secrets there."

"Maybe it's not an alien invasion plan. Maybe it's innocent," I said, thinking about how much Mrs Palmer had helped me.

"It makes sense, Tom. Remember last year when Ian Dalby was off for ages, and they told us he was sick? And since then he never plays and doesn't talk to anyone? Maybe they turned him into an alien."

"What about John?"

"They've got him. He's going through the... transition... and he'll come back, but he won't be the same."

"But what would be the point in turning kids into aliens?"

"We won't see it coming, Tom." Liam's eyes grew large and he leant so close we almost butted heads. "When they launch the invasion, it will be through us kids."

At lunch, Liam and I met up with Will to decide on our plan for our search after school. We planned to walk up to the River Wissey and follow the bank the other way from where we'd gone fishing, past the new bypass. It granted a good view of the cornfields, and while I didn't like Liam's alien idea, I didn't want to rule out anything.

As we chatted, Becky Reid barged into our circle. "Tom, I need to speak to you," she said. Ignoring her was not an option.

I followed her to the step by the infant entrance where we could have privacy. "Laura daren't ask you herself, so I'm asking for her."

I felt panicky. Was Becky going to ask if I liked Laura? What would I say if she did? The only person I'd told was John. What if I said I did like her, and she didn't like me back? But what if I lied and said I didn't, and she did like me? What if I hurt her feelings?

"Laura wanted to know if you'd heard from John," Becky said.

"No," I said, and the panic disappeared, replaced by disappointment. "No one knows where he is."

"Okay. Thanks," Becky said before turning around and marching off.

"What was that about?" asked Will when I returned.

"Did she ask you out?" Liam said.

"Did she want to snog you?" said Andy, and he gave the back of his hand a sloppy kiss.

"No. Yuck. Nothing like that. She asked about John."

"You two would make a good couple," Liam said. "You're both bigheads!" Liam laughed at his own joke and looked from me to Will, waiting for a reaction.

I ignored him and went to line up, looking down the line to Laura, to see how she took the news from Becky. For once, she wasn't smiling.

At the end of the school day, Aunt Anne was waiting at the school gate.

"Have we got another appointment?" asked Liam with a groan.

"I'm taking you straight home. Tom, you too, I'm giving you a ride."

"But why, Mum?" asked Liam.

"Because I say so, that's why."

"But we have to continue our search for John," Liam said. He glared at me, wanting me to take over the argument.

"I don't need a lift, Auntie, I can walk."

"Your dad asked me to bring you straight home, so as soon as Will and Andy are out, that's what we're doing."

Andy's class came out next. Andy handed his mum a sealed envelope. She put it in her handbag to read later.

Will was last, trudging out the main doors with his hands in his pockets, chatting to some girl. When he saw us waiting, he trotted away from her.

"Who's your girlfriend?" Andy said and over-exaggerated a laugh.

"Leave him alone," Aunt Anne said and beckoned us towards her car.

It was unusual for anyone to pick us up from school since we were infants, and even then, someone only drove to pick us up if we had to go somewhere straight after school. It seemed strange to drive within the village, but, looking out of the car window, there were far fewer children walking home alone. Children pushed the cycles they would have otherwise ridden

100 DEAD BRANCHES

while walking beside their mothers. Adults herded children, urging them to stay close and take caution when crossing the road. Maybe the aliens had landed after all.

Aunt Anne said Liam and Andy could stop over for a while to give her a chance to have a cup of tea with mum and a natter, but they didn't speak while we made squash. As soon as we left the kitchen, one of them pushed the door closed behind us. I could hear chairs scraping across the tiles as they moved closer, no doubt to talk about us. We might have been in trouble for some reason. It's not like we don't often play out after school and go wandering where we want, so I didn't know why they were so serious about it all of a sudden. Will thought they were worried about what happened to John, but it wasn't like we were planning on running away.

We put the television on and checked BBC and ITV, but there was no football on. That wasn't right: there had been a four o'clock game every day since it started.

Will knelt on his bed and checked the World Cup wall chart. "No games until later. Argentina play Romania and Cameroon play the Soviet Union, but both are at eight." He switched the TV back to BBC, where Andi Peters was deep in conversation with Edd the Duck about the spate of quack circles which had appeared in the studio. Whatever was happening on screen wasn't sinking in. I blocked out Andi Peters singing the theme tunes and found my gaze drawn to the window. I looked across the fields at the old oak tree. Its branches hung lower as if it were hiding something. I tried to see the river, to where the police cars had been parked, but it was too far away to tell.

Teenage Mutant Ninja Turtles finished. I hadn't even realised it was on.

"Do you wanna play football?" Andy said.

"Or we could say we're going to play, but then explore," Liam said.

I nodded and Will headed for the door. We bundled down the stairs and Mum and Aunt Anne gasped as we crashed into the kitchen.

"Can we go play football?" Will said.

"Only out in the yard," Mum said.

"Can't we go down the rec?" Will said.

"No. You'll stay in the yard or not go out at all."

Outside, I dragged the football from under a hedge then we passed it to each other as we jogged towards the barn.

"Who's going in goal?" Liam said.

"Tom," Will said.

"Andy," I said, knowing I'd have a better chance of scoring against Andy as he was almost a foot shorter than the rest of us.

"No," Andy said, "That's not fair."

"We'll dib for it," Will said, taking charge when we needed someone to.

Will did the ip-dip-dog-shit song, and Andy had to start in goal. He didn't mind, because the rhyme had chosen him fairly. He enthusiastically dived for the ball as first Will banged one into the corner of the goal we'd marked on the shed, and then Liam put one over his head. There was a debate over whether it might have hit the crossbar as it was hard to tell where the crossbar was. Then I had a shot, and the ball sliced off my foot and off across the yard. I chased it and found a black splodge on it. I traced the path of the ball back across the yard to where it had picked up its stain. A black patch marked the ground. Was it a burn spot? The grass was dead around it, and some of that was black too—but it didn't look singed. I must have been staring a long time because Will had trotted over, followed by Liam, and then Andy. Liam gasped and pointed, and I knew what he was thinking: What if John had exploded on that spot? But there were always some remains, like a stray limb or a shoe.

"Oil," Will said.

"It's burn," Liam said.

"Nah, definitely oil. Touch it."

Liam looked at me. I reached forward...

"What the bloody hell are you lot doing?" Dad marched over to us. "Don't touch that; it'll get everywhere."

"What is it, Uncle Trevor?" Andy said, peering up at Dad like an ant looking at a grizzly bear.

"Tractor's leaking oil. You should know better than that, Tom. Are you soft in the head?"

"We were playing football," Will said.

"Playing football in a pool of oil. Daft bloody kids."

"No, by the barn."

"You'll have to stop. I've got to move the combine. Go on, get out of here."

I picked up the ball, forgetting about the oil until it covered my hands.

We returned to the house to find Mum and Aunt Anne drinking tea in silence. Will, Liam and Andy went back upstairs, and I tried to wash my hands in the sink, but I couldn't get all the oil off. The soap didn't seem to touch it unless I scratched my skin, then Liam shouted, "Tom, quick!" so I wiped my hands on a tea towel, leaving a dirty black stain.

I ran up the stairs to see them gathered around watching Newsround. There was a story about crop circles.

"There's been more of them!" Liam said, then, whispering to me, "The aliens are coming."

Mum served a beef stew with dumplings and mashed potatoes for dinner.

Dad rubbed his hands, said, "Lovely grub," like he always did, and picked up his knife and fork.

"So," Will said, holding his fork close to his mash, "how come we weren't allowed out after school today."

"Never mind that. Eat your dinner," Dad said, his words distorted as he kept a piece of beef in his mouth by wedging it between his tongue and his teeth.

"But it's not fair," Will said.

"I'll tell you what's not fair. That poor boy that's gone missing," Dad said.

"Trevor," Mum said, and Dad shovelled more food into his mouth.

"How about," Will said, ignoring Mum's glare, "if we visit Granddad after school tomorrow? Liam and Andy too? We'll go straight there."

"I don't know," Mum said. "I'd prefer you to come straight home."

"Go straight there, and call home the second you arrive," Dad said. "And I'll pick you up from your granddad's at dinner."

"We can walk back. It's only five minutes."

"Don't argue, or you won't be allowed to go at all," Mum said.

"But..." Will said.

Dad jerked his arm out, pointing at Will with his knife. A lump of mashed potato flew from the end of the knife, across the table, and landed on my lip. I brought my hand up to wipe it away.

"What's that on your hand?"

I looked at the black smears of the oil I couldn't get off.

"I thought I told you not to play in that bloody oil."

"It got on the football," I said. "I didn't see it."

Dad wasn't listening. In an instant he was out of his chair, leaning across the table, grabbing my hand and yanking me off my chair and around the kitchen.

"You're bloody filthy." He shoved me towards the sink. "Your mum's cooked you a lovely meal and you come to the table in that state."

My lip started to quiver. I hated it when it did that. I didn't know what to do.

"Wash your hands."

I turned on the tap, grabbed the soap and rubbed my hands together. It wasn't coming off. Then I sniffed, and I heard his chair scraping.

"Wash your bloody hands, boy." He grabbed my hands and pulled them under the water.

"Sit down, and eat your dinner," Mum said.

"Water's not even hot. Cold water won't do nothing." He turned the hot tap on more and turned off the cold. "Now wash them properly."

I put my hands back under the water for a second then picked up the soap again to lather up my hands. When I put my hands back under the water it was so hot, I pulled them back out again so fast that I caught Dad in the stomach with my elbow.

"Wash the fuckers." He grabbed both wrists and forced my hands back under the steaming water.

"Will you two stop messing about and eat your dinner," Mum said.

The water was so hot I couldn't hold back any longer and I cried out. Dad let go, and I pulled my throbbing hands away. They were pink.

"Sit down," he said.

By the time I got to the other side of the table, he was already shovelling food into his mouth again. Will ate slowly and without looking up from his plate.

When I tried to bend my fingers to pick up my knife and fork, they hurt too much, and I had to put them down again. Dad stared at me, swallowed his mouthful of food, and said, "If you're not going to eat, you can go to bed."

I got up. The chair scraped so loudly that I thought it would make my head explode. I didn't look back as I opened the door, my hands burning as I gripped the handle, and headed towards the stairs.

"Well, the boy's got no respect," I heard him say, "coming to the table like that. He must be doo-bloody-lally."

When Will came up later, I was in bed. I'd wrapped my hands in a flannel I'd soaked in the upstairs bathroom to try to stop them throbbing.

"Hey," he said, in a whisper, and perched on the end of my bed, "Wanna sit with me and watch the football?"

I shook my head. I didn't want him to see my hands.

"Do you mind if I put it on?"

"That's okay."

"I snuck you up this." From his pocket, he pulled an Orange Club biscuit. "I thought you might be hungry."

"Thanks," I said, and he put it down on the set of drawers by my bed, put the TV on, and sat on his own bed.

"Still nil-nil."

Will sat and watched the rest of the match and I watched him as the sun set and, as the room got darker, he started to glow green from the light of the television.

At the end of the match, Will shook his head. The Soviet Union had beaten Cameroon four-nil. What had happened to Roger Milla? Cameroon had been beaten by the biggest villains of all. How was that even possible?

"Does that mean they're out?" I muttered.

"No, they got enough points from the first two games."

So, the magic was still alive, but with my hands throbbing it felt like evil was winning.

Tuesday 19th June 1990

When I woke, I found my face cold from where I'd accidentally slept on a wet patch left by the flannel I'd fallen asleep clutching. One of my hands was pink and on the palm were a couple of small blisters. Every time I moved my hand, I winced. I couldn't get away with wearing gloves in June, so I spent most of the school day trying to hide my hands under the desk when in class, and in my pockets during break, grimacing whenever I slid them into hiding. No one noticed which was good because I wouldn't have known what to say. I couldn't say Dad was being horrible because he only wanted me to wash my hands, and he probably didn't realise the water was so hot.

During break, I didn't want to play football because I couldn't run around with one hand in my pocket. I said I felt sick and watched from the side of the pitch. Every goal was celebrated with a Roger-Milla-style dance and people laughed and joked. It was like everyone had forgotten about John, even though he first imitated a Cameroonian player copying when he shouted, "Omam-Biyik," when he scored the first goal at break eight days ago. Then he turned to Brian Harper, who was in goal, and copied Barry Davies (the BBC commentator) and said, "It will go down as goalkeeper error."

Uneasy, I left the field, returning to the classroom early.

Mrs Palmer was setting up a Bunsen burner on her desk and had already got out some beakers. "Hi Tom, the bell hasn't gone."

"Miss, how come no one talks about John?"

Mrs Palmer took a step towards me, "There's not much to say."

"Everyone's forgotten about him."

"Mr Inglehart is in touch with the police every day, and as soon as there's news they can share, we will get together and decide how best to do that."

She was willing to say more to me alone than she had to me and Liam. This made me think Liam was wrong, and that she wasn't an alien.

"Normally when someone's off sick or on holiday you ask someone to make notes for them, but you haven't done that for John," I said.

"You seem like the ideal person for the job."

The bell rang.

"Okay Mrs Palmer, I will."

"Tom, what have you done to your hand?"

I hadn't realised I'd let it slip out of my pocket for her to see and put it behind my back with the subtlety of a tap-dancing hippopotamus. "It's a… heat rash. It's too hot."

"Let me see."

She bent down and took hold of my hand as Daniel Richardson walked in. "Tom and Mrs Palmer sitting in a tree," he said in a singsong voice as he stared at us.

"K. I. S. S. I. N. G.," said Brain Harper, who followed behind him.

"Daniel, Brian, you've earned yourself a detention at afternoon break."

"Ah, but Miss…" said Daniel.

Mrs Palmer urged us to sit as she was going to show us an experiment, and we had to log the results. She gave me an extra sheet of paper so I could make a second copy for John, and it felt like everything might be okay again.

"So why were you and Mrs Palmer holding hands at break?" Liam said as we wandered onto the field at the start of our lunch break.

"We weren't."

"You were. Daniel saw you. He told me."

"She was looking at my hand."

"Why, what did you do?"

"Scalded on a hot tap."

"That was stupid."

"Yeah," I said as I saw Andy come out.

He had a huge smile on his face. He kept trying to say something, but he broke down with laughter before he could get his words out. After taking several breaths to compose himself, he said, "So, Tom, I hear you've got a new girlfriend." He laughed so hard he bent over double.

"What's this?" Will said, who arrived as Andy was practically wetting himself.

"Nothing," I said.

"People saw Mrs Palmer and Tom holding hands," Liam said.

"Tom, that's gross," Will said.

"She was looking at my hand."

Will's eyes grew large. "You told her what happened?"

"No! I told her it was a heat rash."

"Why lie?"

"You're a poet, and you didn't know it," added Liam.

Will glared at him.

"I don't know; it was the first thing that came into my head," I said.

"You know what, Tom," Liam said, "You can be really weird sometimes." This set Andy off into another bout of laughter.

"What's wrong with him?" Laura Matthews appeared at the edge of our circle, with Becky Reid lingering behind her.

"Nothing!" I blurted out. I didn't want her to hear about Mrs Palmer and me. Not that there was anything between Mrs Palmer and me.

She nuzzled her way into the circle, "What have you done to your hand?" she asked.

I couldn't say "nothing" again, I'd sound like an idiot, so I held it towards her.

She held the back of my hand and examined it. "That looks painful. Does it hurt?"

"A little," I said.

"How did you do it?"

"Scalded with hot water."

"I hope it gets better soon."

Liam edged her out of the circle. "We're having a private conversation," he said, emphasising the word private.

Laura looked hurt. She turned around to chat with Becky.

"Liam, that was rude," I said.

"Just 'cause you fancy her," he said.

"I don't," I said, mortified. Laura was still close. What if she'd heard?

"You do something stupid like scald your hand, and the prettiest girl in the class starts cooing over you," said Liam, going red.

"Maybe Tom's not the only one who fancies Laura," said Will. "Come on, let's play football."

We didn't have to cross any roads to get to Granddad's; we figured that was why our parents let us go by ourselves.

"Thinking about going to Granddad's makes me wonder," Liam said, "What if John got one of those brain parasites, and it sent him crazy and he went running off into the wild?"

"It's possible," I said. We knew about brain parasites from Granddad Norman because he once had one. He said it was on his fortieth birthday. He was ploughing a field when he felt a bump. He thought perhaps a beam had snapped, or a mouldboard had come off or got twisted, so he stopped the tractor. Sure enough, one of the mouldboards was bent. On the ground, there was a big bit of bog oak. He picked it up and carried it over to the end of the field by that old oak tree, and when he threw it to the ground something flew up and hit him where his left eye used to be. He reckons there was an awful squirming sensation. He says it was like when you let a worm wriggle around on the palm of your hand, only inside his head. He couldn't stop scratching so he ran home. This was when Granddad still lived in the farmhouse, and he tells us that if

110 DEAD BRANCHES

our Nanna was still alive, she would have confirmed the story, but he was speaking fluent French. I don't know if Nanna could speak any French or not, but he says it's true. The only way he could get rid of it was to stick his head in water. Apparently, parasites don't like the cold. So, Nanna fetched his pipe so he could breathe then filled the sink with water. Granddad thrust his head into the water and held it there for well over an hour until he could feel the parasite wriggling its way out of his ear. When he felt it slip out, he pulled his head out of the water. The trouble was that he'd had his head under the water for so long he'd washed the colour out of his hair. From that day, it was pure white despite Granddad never having had a single grey hair in his life before. He showed us the parasite once. He keeps it in a jar in his garage. It looks like a dried-out slug.

As we arrived at Granddad's house, we saw Uncle Rodney driving off. He gave us a wave with one of his enormous hands. At first, I didn't recognise the car; it was unusual to see him in a vehicle that wasn't thick with grime. We let ourselves in to Granddad's house and found him at the kitchen table staring at the newspaper. He'd got his glasses on the tip of his nose. There was no lens on the left-hand side. He reckoned he didn't need that as he only had the one good eye. I couldn't see the point of taking the glass out, but he said one day he might find a use for it. I doubt he'd ever find it again if it was in one of the tin cans or boxes that crowded his garage.

When he heard us, he said, "Yello, boys. Uncle Rodney's dropped me in the paper," he said, holding it up to show us before turning it over and putting it under a stack of mail.

Before he hid it, I caught a glimpse of part of the headline, seeing the words, 'CONCERN GROWS' and the outline of a picture which I was pretty sure was John.

"No school today?" Granddad asked.

"We're finished. It's half three," Will said.

"Half three?" he said. "Finished school? In my day you'd stay at school until gone five then go home and do a full day's work in the fields. You boys have got it easy..."

We joined in with the end of the sentence, "you don't even know you're born."

"You didn't really have to stay at school until five o'clock, did you Granddad?" asked Andy.

"Truth is I don't even remember. I know I went, but that's it. Got a nasty bang on my head one time and can't remember a thing from the first ten to fifteen years of my life."

"What happened?" Liam said.

"Well, you can't see the scar, because it's under my hair, but you can still feel the bump."

We took turns. He guided our fingers through his thick white hair to feel the ridge on the top of his head.

"If my brain had been any smaller, chances are it would have fallen out."

"But what happened?" Liam said.

"Patience, young man, I'm coming to that."

"Was it the tree?" I said.

"Was it heck! As if I'd give that old thing another chance to do me in. No, I was working on the combine harvester, you know, the red one, opening up one of the sides to clear out a blockage when the unloader swung down and cracked me on the head. Blood everywhere there was." Granddad paused and looked at us. "Not impressed?"

Liam said, "I thought it might have been an evil spirit, not the combine."

"Who's to say it wasn't an evil spirit knocking the unloader pipe, trying to bump your dear ol' granddad off, hey? Did you stop to think about that before you called my story boring?"

"We didn't say boring," Will said.

Andy had his hands on the table, his fingernails digging into the varnish. "Evil spirits can do that?" he said.

"I never said it was, or it wasn't. I'll leave that up to you to decide. Anyway, you boys don't want to be cooped up in here with me all afternoon. What are you up to?"

"What happened after you called the police?" Will said.

"I assume they investigated. They rarely report back. I did see them head that way with sniffer dogs, and one of their Land Rovers followed them not long after that."

"No other news?"

"They might have found something; they might not. I'm as in the dark as you are. Is that why you came to see me today?"

"We wondered if you wanted to take a walk with us up to the river and along the bank a little way," Will said.

"Ah, so that's it. Up to a little more snooping."

"Oh, no, Granddad," I said, "We thought it might be nice to get some fresh air, what with it being such a lovely day."

"Such a lovely day," mimicked Liam.

I ignored him.

"You think I was born yesterday? As it happens, I could do with getting up off my rear end; my old bones get so stiff if I sit for too long, and what harm did a little snooping ever do anybody?"

"Would you mind calling Mum first though," said Will. "Let her know you're walking us home."

Once Granddad was off the phone, we walked from his cottage along Main Street, past the village sign.

"Well, if we head up Wissey Drove, then back along Catchwater Drove that'll bring us to Long Drove and we can follow that back to the farmhouse," Granddad said. I took his word for it.

"How do you know all of this, Granddad?" I asked.

"When you've been about as long as me, not much passes you by. Besides, we used to drive cattle down these droves, when there was money in keeping cattle."

We turned onto Wissey Drove. I'd felt irritated all day, but as soon as we headed down this path the itching intensified. I kept scraping my tongue with my teeth.

"Whatever are you doing?" Granddad said.

Liam saw me pulling a face as I scratched my tongue, and he covered his mouth to hide a laugh.

"Itchy tongue," I said to Granddad.

"Well, you know what they say about getting an itchy tongue?"

"No?"

"Means you're about to find some luck."

My heart raced. Was today the day we were going to find John?

"Come 'ere," Granddad said.

I walked over to him, thinking that he was going to give us a great idea.

"You got something in your hair." He reached towards me. He brushed the hair beside my head, then in the flat of his hand held out an old coin.

"Was that in your hair?" cried Andy.

No. It wasn't. Granddad's favourite trick normally made me laugh, but what that coin represented was a spark of hope fading away.

"Aren't you going to take it?" Granddad said.

I forced a smile. "Thanks." I popped it in my pocket and gave my eyes a rub.

The grass soon gave way to a grey mud path with two deep grooves running along it with tractor tyre marks in odd places where the ground was a little softer. Mostly it was dry and cracked where we hadn't had any rain in so long. I looked down at the ground and then up at the wrinkles on Granddad's face and wondered if Granddad was older than the Earth itself.

We stopped where the drove met the river. There was a wooden bridge across it. Andy ran onto the bridge.

"We don't wanna go that way, Andy," Granddad said. "You'll end up at Twelve Mile Bank and we'll have to trace our steps all the way back."

Andy jumped, listening to the sound of his feet as he landed on the wooden bridge.

"See that building by the river there," Granddad said, pointing to a ruined, brick building that spread, somehow, halfway over the river. "That's an old pumping station. I had a cousin who worked there and looked after the drain."

Andy wasn't listening. He went back to the drove and pulled up a handful of blades of grass from a clump and took them back to the bridge. He dropped them over the side and watched as they drifted under. He turned to the other side of the bridge and waited.

"Why isn't it coming?"

"Probably sunk," Liam said.

"Or it got stuck," Will said.

Liam headed for the bridge too, but instead of crossing onto it, he clambered down the bank to peer under it.

"For Christ's sakes, don't fall in, Liam. Your mother will string me up by my delicate bits if I bring you back soaked to the skin and covered in bog slime."

Liam crouched to peer under the bridge.

"Well?" Will said.

"It's dark, but it looks like there's something," Liam said.

"What?"

"I don't know—have you got a stick?"

"Andy, go get a stick," Will said.

Andy ran to the trees across the bridge and scanned the ground.

"There aren't any."

"Break one off." Andy bent a low branch down. He jumped to put more of his weight on it, but it only bowed further without breaking.

"Can I borrow your knife, Will?"

"Or you could use this one," Granddad said. He pulled the thickest Swiss Army Knife out of his pocket that must have had about a zillion different tools. He pulled one out. "Try the saw."

Andy took it. His eyes wide, he almost tripped over my legs as he made his way back across the bridge. He pulled the branch again and started sawing at it. Within a few seconds he'd sawed it through and the part still attached to the tree bounced up and thwacked him in the face. Unperturbed, he grabbed the severed branch and dragged it along to Liam.

"Go back onto the bridge and watch what comes out," Liam said. I could hear him grunting as he pushed the branch into the water. There was a slurping sound, like when you get a welly stuck in mud.

"What is it?" shouted Liam.

"A log," Andy said. He stared at his shoe and toed a leaf off the bridge, but didn't bother watching it drift into the water and float off.

Will and Liam joined him on the bridge and watched it bob away down the river. I stood by the side pinching my nose which had started to run, and I had no tissue left to mop it up.

"He could have fallen in somewhere else," Liam said.

I looked along the river. If that was the case no one would ever find him.

"What do you think happened, Granddad?" asked Liam.

"I don't rightly know. Police are doing their best, and that's a good thing."

"But shouldn't they have some clues?"

"Truth is they probably do, but they're not ready to release the information."

"Which way should we go?"

"Keep going up this drove, as I said before." Granddad rolled up the sleeves of his cardigan and we continued. Andy walked up high on the river bank, and Liam followed behind him, looking across the fields in all directions. We reached the point where we could see the bypass cross the river.

"What used to run along there was called Dark Fen Drove," Granddad said, pointing along the path of the bypass. "See, these council folk they know the old roads had the best paths through the fen, that's why they followed it along this way. Of course, they did want to cut across our land to save a bob or two and keep it straight, like a Roman road, but the lay of the land don't always allow for that."

Granddad swatted a bug off his forearm, and I noticed a scar there I hadn't seen before.

"How'd you get that one, Granddad?" I asked.

"I've told you that one before, I'm sure I have."

We shook our heads.

"What, I've never told you about the time I got mauled by a Fen Tiger?"

Andy gasped, and we closed round Granddad.

"Maybe this'll make up for that boring old story I told you about cracking my head open." He leant forward on his stick, so his face was no more than a foot away from any of ours. "We'd had a few bad storms and a lot of trees had come down over the winter, and with the east wind sweeping through, ferocious, it blew most of the debris off the land and into the ditches. Well, the second we got some rain the fields got waterlogged. The ditches up by Catchwater Drove were too full of junk to function properly so the water came back up onto the land. We couldn't have that; they would have been unplantable for the season and what with us having two little ones and another on the way there was no way we would be able to make ends meet without being at full capacity. Only thing I could do was clear the ditches and make sure the water could run off. And that's what I was doing when it happened. I pulled out all of these branches—bigger than the one Andy had off that tree—but there was something else in the bottom. As I got closer, I could hear purring—not like you'd hear from a cat, much, much deeper." Granddad stopped his tale to mimic the sound, a low, menacing rumble, before he blurted out the next part, making us jump. "Then its eyes were shining out of the mud and I scrambled back, fell in a heap onto a bunch of the branches that I'd yet to haul out. I tried to climb out but my trousers were snagged on something, and this shape in the mud, it started to grow. The eyes closed in on me, and it sniffed. Well, I put up this arm to protect myself, and it claws at me and tears into my arm. I shouted and tried to struggle away, but only succeeded in snapping some of the branches I was lying against. Don't ask me how but I kind of fell into them. They were all around me like a cage—but it was protecting me because the creature couldn't get through. I don't know how long I was in there, but at some point later something scared it off—a gunshot from a couple of fields over, probably Carter's farm—your great granddad on your dad's side," Granddad nodded towards Liam and Andy, "He was always out shooting. Liked to catch himself a pheasant. There was a time or two he'd bring one over to us and we'd have it off him in exchange for something. Anyway, the beast was scared, and it ran off. Well, I knew what it was because I'd heard stories about the Fen Tiger, but I didn't believe them until that day I was almost eaten by it. You see, Fen Tigers was the name given to the folks who resisted the drainage around here. But they had to have got the name from somewhere, didn't they? And they took the name from that cat-like beast that patrols these lands."

Fen Tigers, black shucks and shug monkeys, were they real? Where did they come from? Where did they hide?

"How did you escape the cage?" Liam asked.

"Well once that thing was gone, I picked it apart, one branch at a time. Tore my trousers to shreds getting out of there. When your grandmother saw me, she didn't know what to say. A right state I was. Of course, I had to go back to finish the job, but let's say I didn't jump into another ditch without checking there wasn't something down there waiting for me." Granddad smiled at us, then laughed as he stood back up straight again.

"You know you told us about the Duke and his little zoo," Andy said.

"Yes."

"Is that where the Fen Tiger came from? One of the escaped pumas?"

"You know what, young man, I think you may well be right. That may have been the case with this one."

That didn't sound right to me. There was something much darker at work than that.

Granddad must have seen me frown, for he continued. "Or it could be a much more evil, much more sinister creature." He pointed with his stick, "We'd better get a move on, or your mothers will carve me up for dinner, and this old flesh won't be good eating."

118   DEAD BRANCHES

Granddad turned down what must have been Catchwater Drove with Andy following close behind him. Liam nodded at me.

"What?"

"Something else to add to the list."

"What list?"

"Tom! Don't you pay any attention? About what might have happened to John. Fen Tiger attack."

Liam trotted off to catch up with Andy.

"I've asked Granddad about that scar before," Will said.

"And?"

"He never said anything about a tiger. He said he couldn't remember."

I didn't like the way Will questioned Granddad's stories. You never saw Peter question Aslan.

"Well... maybe he remembered," I said.

"It's not the kind of thing you'd forget." And Will set off to catch up with the others.

A few minutes later we turned onto Long Drove and the farmhouse was in sight. I was trying to avoid looking at the oak tree, so kept my eyes on the ditches as we walked. The tree always made me feel weird when I was with Granddad because I couldn't stop thinking about what it had done to him. I kept seeing his eye go flying out of his skull, and no matter how hard I tried not to think about it, the eye always ends up going into the tree's mouth, where it gets chewed up as the tree laughs.

As I gazed down, I didn't see who was walking towards us. Liam had to drop away from Granddad's side to poke me in the ribs.

"It's the crazy man, Shaky Jake!" he said, "Think if we go 'Boo' he'll fall into the ditch?"

Jake was paying about as little attention to us as I had been to him. He was glaring into the ditches on the other side and muttering.

"How do?" Granddad said as he got closer.

Jake looked up. He was blinking a lot, and he licked his lips with his tongue darting in and out, lizard-like, He nodded his head in a deliberate way which couldn't be confused for one of his twitches.

"What did you speak to him for?" Liam said when we were a little way clear of Shaky Jake.

"Why shouldn't I say 'ello?" Granddad said.

"He's crazy. He comes out of his house and chases us down the road."

"And what do you do to make him chase you? I know how you boys go looking for sport."

"But this one time," Andy said, "he had this knife, and it was bloody and if he caught us, he might have stabbed us to death."

"Don't be daft."

"It's true," Liam said.

"Will? Were you there?"

"It's true. Sort of," Will said. "We were standing by his kitchen window, and I saw him cutting meat."

"And why did he chase you?"

"Tom was pulling faces at him."

"You were too!" I said.

"Have you ever stopped to think that if you didn't deliberately wind him up, he wouldn't react the way he does, and then everyone wouldn't say he was crazy?"

Granddad stopped walking and leant on his stick. "Now you boys run on ahead, and I'll catch up with you in a minute or two."

And we left him there. We took a slight detour off the path to head to Moon Base One for a quick meeting.

"So, what have we got on John so far?" I asked.

"Nothing. We've got nothing," Will said.

"No. Not true," Liam said, "We've got loads of people from the Top Trumps, and we keep hearing the teachers talk about transition."

"Rubbish. We've seen no sign of him. The police are probably doing better than us, and this is *our* village."

Liam put his hands on his hips. "But what about the stuff Granddad was talking about today?"

"Like what?"

"Bog slime. What if something pulled him into the river? There are cards which show water monsters." Liam counted on his fingers. "What about evil spirits attacking him? What about the Fen Tiger?"

"You can waste your time on that crap if you like," Will said, "But I'm going home before Granddad beats us back because then we'll be in real trouble."

Andy dashed to the base entrance and peered out, "I can't see him. What if he's already back?"

We jumped across the bank and ran down the drove and back alongside the field. We were sure Granddad had dashed for the farmhouse and dropped us in it until we looked back down the path and realised he hadn't moved since we left him. We went into the house. I could hear the television on in the living room, which was odd because Mum never put the TV on during the day. I made some squash which we downed straight away, so I made some more. Mum must have heard the tap running because the TV went quiet, and then she came into the kitchen. She stuffed a tissue into her sleeve.

"What were you watching?" Will said.

"Anglia News."

"Why?"

"Oh, no reason. Someone I know was going to be on there, that's all."

"Someone you know is on TV? Who?"

"No one you know. Don't worry about that. Do you boys want a drink?"

Surely, she could see the drinks in our hands?

"Whatever's wrong with your eyes?" she said.

They felt like they were burning. My tongue was also sore from where I'd scratched it so much, and even the inside of my ears tingled.

"They've been itchy all day."

"Hay fever," she said. "I must make you an appointment with the doctor, get you some medicine."

Dad wandered in with Granddad behind him. He must have heard her.

"Is he still whimpering about having bloody hay fever?"

"I wasn't," I muttered.

"Ain't no good living round here having hay fever. You better shake that off quick-sharp."

There was nothing I could say. My eyes were welling up. It was the hay fever.

"Liam, Andy—make sure you've got everything and I'll run you home."

I waited until they were gone until I snuck upstairs to the bathroom where I stared at myself in the mirror, leaning in close so that the only thing I could see were my eyes. My lower eyelids were puffy and bloated, and the whites of my eyes were almost yellow as if a thin layer of pollen had coated them. Thick red veins zigzagged towards my iris. In the corner of my eye, the side by the nose, was a load of gunk. I dabbed at it with the toilet tissue. This was the itchiest part. If only I could pluck that part out, it might get rid of the itching. It might get rid of my hay fever. It might stop me from being a stupid, little crybaby. There was a pair of nail scissors on the windowsill. I could stick them in there, and pop that bit of the eye out with no problem. I picked up the scissors and slipped my thumb and finger through the holes. With the back of my other hand, I wiped at my eyes again. I scrunched my knuckle into the left eye and could feel it pulsing inside, trying to push back, but I didn't care as it had stopped the itching. I was going to do it. Cut the bad part out and live a better life. I took my fist away from my hand, and everything through that eye seemed dull and unreal. I moved the scissors towards the eye, but my vision hadn't cleared enough.

"Tom." Will knocked on the bathroom door.

"What?" I said, annoyed.

"Come on. You've been in there ages. I need a piss."

"Go downstairs," I called through the door. The scissors started to feel awkward in my hand, the finger holes too tight around my fingers.

"I can't."

"Why not?"

"It stinks. Dad must have been in there."

I laughed. There was no way he'd dare say that if Dad was home. I had to let him in after that. I put the scissors back on the windowsill and opened the door.

I took out my exercise book, and added a page on the Fen Tiger, which I put after the shug monkey and black shuck. Flicking back through, I read the headings. RUN AWAY, HIT BY LORRY, ABDUCTED BY ALIENS IN SCHOOL, SPONTANEOUS HUMAN COMBUSTION. Underneath each, I'd written EVIDENCE, but there was nothing but speculation. On another page was a separate section to record evidence that we couldn't put against a possible cause. The only thing I'd noted on there was FIESTA and FISHERMEN'S FRIEND, but they could have been there for ages so we couldn't confirm that they were connected.

West Germany versus Colombia was on in the background. It ended 1-1 to the Germans, but I didn't see either of the goals except for in the replays at the end of the match. I was too distracted by my book and trying to make sense of it. Each of the Top Trumps creatures we'd talked about had a page, and some were linked to people in the village. Then there were the new Top Trumps I planned to create for the other possibilities.

"What do you think about John?" I said to Will after he turned off the TV.

"He probably ran away."

"But don't you think he would have said something to us before?"

"Do you tell your friends every time something bad happens at home?"

I glanced at my hand, which was almost back to its normal colour, but the skin was peeling off in some places around where the blisters had burst.

"What about some of these other ideas?"

"What? Aliens? Fen Tigers? It's bullshit."

"Isn't."

"Yes, it is, Tom."

"But Granddad said…"

"Don't believe everything Granddad tells you."

"Why not?"

"Do you think that if he had a parasite in his brain, it would turn his hair white?"

"What should we do then?"

"Keep a look out. Listen."

Then the door creaked open, and we both stopped talking. It made me think of the way Aunt Anne and Mum stopped talking the other day every time we entered the kitchen. Mum stood at the door.

"Bedtime, boys," she said and stood staring at us for a minute. "And don't forget to brush your teeth."

She spoke to us like we were five and six again. I can't remember when she last reminded us to brush our teeth. But she even watched us do it and then tucked us into bed.

A little while after she left, and after Will had fallen asleep, I heard the front door open. It was probably Dad going out to check something on the farm or maybe to let Chappie out for a wee. What else could it be?

Wednesday 20th June 1990

I woke early and took Chappie for a walk. Mum insisted on keeping an eye on me and said I had to stay in view of the house. It had rained overnight, and it felt much cooler. As I trudged around the field with Chappie, we encountered several clusters of horrible brown slugs. Mustard-coloured, they reminded me of Mrs Palmer's cardigans, and, since Liam was obsessed with the idea, alien creatures too. Why weren't they black? Were they alien slugs? Chappie stopped to sniff at one, and, surprisingly, chose not to eat it. He'd eat anything, but maybe he drew the line at alien servants. The alien theory sounded most likely at this point, given that nothing else we'd come up with made any sense.

Somehow, I'd not spotted him before, but Dad was standing at the back of the field. With a spanner, he whacked at the body of the old tractor and cried out something unintelligible. His hair stood on end, pasted with sweat, and his red face shone. He'd not seen me, and I had no intention of changing that. I took a shortcut across the field and picked up my pace, forcing Chappie to reluctantly match me.

I could see someone walking along the back drove. They must have come from Hereward Close. I squinted and, looking at the way the man fidgeted as he walked, I was sure it was Shaky Jake.

"What's he doing here?" I said to Mum when I got back, pointing at the tiny figure almost out of view on the drove.

"Who dear?"

"Shaky Jake."

"Don't call him that, Thomas. It's not nice to call people names."

"But why's he walking around like that?"

"He can walk where he likes. The droves aren't private property."

Mum wasn't getting what I was saying. "Don't you think we should be keeping a better eye on people like him though? What if he knows something about John?"

Mum stared at me, and half a minute passed before she spoke. "Hadn't you better be getting ready for school?"

At school, we were spending the morning at the church to sing hymns and learn a little about the history of the building, which meant that we'd have to spend the morning with the vicar, Reverend Lloyd Meath. He came into school from time to time and brought his guitar with him and told stories about Jesus. He had a habit of closing his eyes for a long time while talking, and his hand gestures were over the top. Everyone took the mickey out of him, and he knew it, but he didn't care. If we imitated him, then he'd reached us. That's what he claimed. We often saw him after school outside the vicarage where he spent a long time tending to his garden. We didn't like to get caught in conversation with him because he was too serious, so if we saw that he was outside, we'd cross the road to avoid him. This usually led to a brief rendition of the line from the hymn: *cross over the road, my friend.*

The whole class had to walk together to the church, with Mrs Palmer leading the way and Mr Inglehart following us. It seemed excessive considering we didn't have to cross any major roads.

Liam and I were towards the back. I told him about seeing Shaky Jake acting weird this morning, and he said we should investigate him more. I agreed, but couldn't think how we'd go about that. As we walked through the gates, I held back to read the dates on the gravestones.

"Look," I said to Liam. "There's a girl there that was only nine or ten when she died." I pointed to the gravestone and felt a hand on my shoulder.

"Keep moving boys," Mr Inglehart said, urging us into the church.

Liam and I managed to get on pews towards the back for the hymn-singing part, so we were able to mouth the words and continue our conversation. "1952–1962 it said. Surely Granddad would have remembered that."

"What was the..." began Liam.

Mrs Palmer scowled at us. A fraction of a second later we joined in with the hymn too until her attention was elsewhere.

"The name?" Liam said.

"Don't know. Ingehart stopped me reading the rest."

After listening to the vicar tell us the tale of the Good Samaritan and advise us all to take care of each other, we did some rubbings on various bits of stone inside the building.

"Can we do a rubbing on the graves?" asked Liam.

Mrs Palmer moved him to one side where Reverend Meath couldn't hear. "No, you can't do a rubbing on a grave! How is that showing respect to the dead?"

"Sorry," he murmured, with his cheeks reddening.

"Could we do some from outside the building though?" I asked.

"I don't see why that would be a problem. Do not step on any of the graves!"

"Of course, she said yes to you. She loves you," said Liam, and stuck his tongue out.

We slinked around the churchyard, pretending to take rubbings at appropriate spots.

"Look," I called to Liam, "Ernest Barnham. Must be Teddy's brother that Granddad was talking about."

"How old was he?"

"Fifteen."

"I thought Granddad said he wasn't a child?"

"I guess Granddad was wrong."

We continued to work our way around the graves, reading those that hadn't worn away too badly.

"There's Nanna's," I said. Then one a couple of spaces away caught my eye. "Liam," I said, "Who was Enid Tilbrook?"

He shrugged.

"June 1931–May 1952. She would have been only twenty when she died."

"Was she Granddad's sister?"

Liam jutted out his lower lip. "Never heard him mention her."

But Granddad always spoke about family. Why had this relative been forgotten?

After school, Mum was waiting by the gates. Despite the playground being rammed full of parents, it was oddly quiet when we came out. I'd updated Will at lunch time when we were back at school, and he said there was no point asking Mum. I ignored his advice. "Mum. Who was Enid Tilbrook?"

"I don't know, dear. Why?"

"We saw a gravestone with her name on it."

"She's probably some distant relative."

"Can we go see Granddad?"

"You're not going to bombard him with questions?"

"No, it would be nice to see him, that's all."

"You saw him yesterday."

"And it would be good to see him again today."

"I suppose, but not for long. I've got to get dinner on."

But when we got to Granddad's house, he wasn't there.

"I suppose we ought to go home then," Mum said.

"He might have gone for a walk. Can we follow the path that goes round the back of his house and comes out the end of the village?"

Will gave me a puzzled look.

"Go on then," Mum said, and the five of us set off on a diversion. The path led us behind Teddy Barnham's house and farmyard. The shed where he bred maggots wasn't painted quite so well out the back. As we moved on a little farther, we saw why. Teddy was only halfway through painting the side. Standing on a small set of step ladders, he held a tin of creosote in one hand and a brush in the other.

"Poor old chap. He doesn't have a single family member good enough to help him out, and he has to struggle on by himself," Mum said.

He didn't look like he was struggling. He stood straight up instead of bent and crooked like we'd seen him at the weekend and the job didn't seem to be bothering him at all.

"Hello Mr Barnham!" shouted Andy.

He turned and gave us a wave. "Back for more maggots, young fella?" he shouted.

"Not today," Andy said.

"Have you seen Granddad?" shouted Liam.

"I can't say that I have."

We gave him a wave and continued on our way without coming across Granddad before we were back on Main Street.

At dinner, after he'd finished eating but before he got down from the table, Will said, "Tom saw something interesting at the church today, didn't you, Tom?"

"What's that?" Dad said.

I didn't want to ask him in case he turned funny, but now if I didn't, it would be equally bad. "We saw a gravestone for Enid Tilbrook. We wanted to ask Granddad who it was."

"I'll tell you," Dad said. "She was your granddad's cousin."

"She was twenty when she died," I said.

"Is that so?"

"Do you know what happened to her?"

"Can't say I do. Are those plates gonna wash themselves?"

Will washed, and I dried. My hands were still sensitive in water, so I was doing all I could to avoid that. After we'd finished, I had another go at *The Secret of the Scythe*. My rolls for skill and luck were much better this time, but a couple of bad stamina rolls left me weak. I stayed on the road and beat the goblin without hiding which meant I got the first hit in, and I didn't go into the witch's house at all. There was an option to snoop around, but I thought it was best avoided. Not far beyond the house was the entrance to the Underworld. You had to go through the mouth of an enormous dead tree. As you approached, you were attacked by tree roots. I put the book down and stared out of the window at the tree in the field. Could it be a gateway to hell? And if it was the gateway to hell could something have emerged from there and taken John?

<u>NOW</u>

Last year, Charlie had a piece of homework in which he had to produce a family tree. I was powerless to avoid thinking about my family, and the names I'd have to put on there. I wanted Charlie to succeed, but I couldn't help.

For the first time since I asked for his daughter's hand in marriage, I gave Victoria's dad a call. They hadn't seen Charlie lately (my fault—I didn't have anything against them; I'd forgotten about them) so they were more than happy to take him for the weekend and work with him on their part of the family tree.

When he came back home, Charlie was quiet. At first, I thought he'd had a bad weekend which made me think I should keep him from his mother's side of the family too, but when he showed me the piece of work he'd produced with his grandparents, I thought it was fantastic. They'd taken Charlie back generations and halfway across the world with their family tree and presented their history beautifully. I hadn't been honest about my reason for sending Charlie away to work on this project, and, thinking they were being considerate, they'd left plenty of room on one side of the tree for Charlie to trace his family on my side.

"Maybe I could make it up?" Charlie said, staring at the blank side of the paper after listening to my outburst about my family.

"We don't make things up," I told him.

"What can we do then?"

I took out a pair of scissors, excising the space where we could have put my side, and emailed his teacher, explaining that I didn't have anything to do with my family, and didn't want Charlie getting involved. I thought that would make it okay. When Charlie got the homework back, the teacher had praised it. When Charlie brought it home, he put it in the bin.

Family is the last thing I want to think about as I drive through the village, but there are memories all around me. I pass the playing field where I spent so much time kicking around a football without ever developing any level of skill. But there are so many new houses I don't recognise, row after row of identical homes. I've never been a fan of massive housing developments where each house is identical and without character, and they seem out of place here in Little Mosswick.

I pass a new building on my right and am surprised to see it labelled Little Mosswick Primary School. What happened to my old school? I didn't think I'd feel anything when I returned, but this made me feel slighted.

As I approach the post office, I see another police car parked outside. I also notice the post office has grown an extension—a Chinese takeaway that also sits askew to my memories of the village.

Continuing through the village, I witness nothing else that causes distress, leaving the Little Mosswick that I remember. There are numerous sale signs outside rundown properties. It feels as if the old Little Mosswick has been abandoned, as if they've tried to move the heart of the village to one end, but all they've done is turned Little Mosswick into a Frankenstein village, held together with the ugly stitches of new roads. Maybe the whole place should have been left to die. I'm glad I was taken away in 1990. I'm glad I didn't come back sooner. Maybe I've returned too soon?

Thursday 21ˢᵗ June 1990

England versus Egypt. Evening kick off. A win would put England through to the next round, and defeat would boot them out of the tournament. Wherever John was, I knew he'd be excited for this one too. At break, everyone was talking about it. Egypt had drawn with the Netherlands and the Republic of Ireland so they wouldn't be easy to beat. Through the excitement, mind kept returning to John.

I turned to Liam and asked, "Do you think John will be allowed to watch the football, wherever he is?"

"If they can get a clear picture on the spaceship."

"John could convince them to let him," I said. I felt a tear trickle down my face.

"He could talk them into anything."

"Do you remember when he persuaded Inglehart to let the whole class watch the match against Hilgay?"

"That was ace. We cheered every pass and every tackle!"

"Hilgay were terrified."

"No wonder he didn't let us do it for the next game."

"What's it going to be like next year?" I asked.

"What do you mean?"

"Will and his class will have gone to secondary school. We'll be in the top class."

"It'll be different," Liam looked at the floor and kicked at a loose stone.

"I always imagined John would be with us. The three of us would be the kings of the school." In truth, I'd imagined John and me as the kings of the school and hadn't thought about Liam in this little fantasy.

"John'll come back. He's got to," Liam said.

"Should we be doing more?"

"Like what?"

"Like get inside the staff room to see what the teachers are hiding."

"Now?"

"No, we'll do it at lunch."

We sat and watched the others play for a while and when the ball came rolling our way after Chris had hit a shot a mile wide (he was no Gazza) we decided to join the game.

When Mrs Palmer let us in after break, she told us we'd be doing a science experiment. She went into her cupboard to get out the equipment, and Liam jumped up and followed her.

"Do sit down, Liam Carter," she said.

"Thought you could use a hand, Miss," Liam said, holding his arms out to take whatever she had to hand out.

"That's very kind of you." She sent him into the cupboard, and he came out carrying a stack of beakers.

After handing them out, Liam approached. "It's clear."

Together, we made a mess of the experiment. We measured out the wrong volumes, adding too little of the substance so nothing happened. That was a better outcome than Daniel and Brian's, who put too much in and had their mixture bubble and foam over the top and onto their textbooks. While muddling through, we formulated a plan, and when Mrs Palmer let us out for lunch instead of rushing for the canteen, we dashed around the back of the school.

From the field, we could see through the staffroom window. This allowed us to scope out where we needed to search if we were able to get in. There was a small area that we couldn't see which would be our starting point. Otherwise, the staffroom was full of nothing other than comfy chairs and bits of paper pinned to the wall.

"If the plan's on one of those," I said, "we'll never find it."

"But it's empty at the moment," Liam said. "If we don't go now, we won't get another chance."

We entered the school through the side door, so we were quite sure that no one had gone into the staff room as we made our way to the entrance. I tried the handle and was surprised to find it unlocked. Before I stepped inside, I glanced again at the sign on the front.

STAFF ROOM. NO ADMITTANCE TO PUPILS.

I gulped as I stepped inside, and Liam followed. It smelled of coffee, and there were newspapers strewn on the tables.

"I want a go on one of those seats," said Liam, gazing at the cushioned chairs.

"We don't have time to mess about."

"But they look so cosy."

I walked over to the part of the room we couldn't see from outside and discovered a bunch of pigeon holes, half of which were crammed full of paper, and another door. "Where do you think that leads?" I asked. It couldn't go anywhere–there wasn't room. It was on the external wall, and it couldn't lead outside. Was this the portal to the alien base? I looked around, waiting for Liam's response, but saw him sitting in one of those chairs with a serious expression on his face.

"Liam, this is important."

"So's this."

I turned around expecting to see him pretending to be asleep. Instead, he held a newspaper and pointed at the headline: NO NEW LEADS IN MISSING BOY CASE.

"What's it say?"

"Not much more than the headline. It's been nine days..."

I heard a laugh from outside. It sounded deep. Maybe Mr Inglehart.

"Quick," I said. "Hide." There was only one place to go: through the door. I waited until Liam was beside me, and then pulled it open, half expecting to see John in there attached to a bunch of machines and wires, or to see stars and planets, but instead, it was stacked with exercise books and textbooks going back decades. We bundled in and pulled the door closed and were stuck with the smell of mouldy books for the rest of our lunch break.

We overheard the teachers' conversations, but they were uninteresting. When the conversation stopped, and we heard the door close, we crept out of the cupboard, and out of the staffroom.

"Why don't you come over to mine to watch the game?" said Liam. "Bring everything we've got and we'll come up with a plan."

"And hide that newspaper somewhere," I said.

I think he'd forgotten that he was holding it. He stuffed it into his P.E. bag, and we went back to class.

Mum and Dad were more than happy for us to spend the evening at Aunt Anne and Uncle Alan's house. After dinner, which included ice cream topped with the magic chocolate sauce which hardened so you had to crack it with your spoon, we went up to Liam's room. Will stayed downstairs with Andy. He didn't feel like talking about it.

I got out my exercise book and flicked through the pages. "We said that he might have run away. What evidence do we have for that?"

"Nothing," Liam said.

"Well, not nothing. We know he wasn't happy about being left at home on his own, but is that enough to make you run away?"

"No. I'd love it if Mum left me alone once in a while."

"But if it was every day?"

"True."

"What evidence have we got against him running away?"

"He never told us. I think he would have done."

"Also, if the police thought he'd run away, they'd have questioned us more about that."

"Okay, so he might have run away, but there's no evidence. What's next."

"Hit by a massive lorry. That's out. Surely if that was the case, they would have found him. We've walked up and down the village and not seen a thing."

"What else?"

"Kidnapped."

"By aliens."

"Aliens is one of the possibilities for kidnappers. But a non-alien could have taken him."

"We have motives for aliens. Remember, *transition*."

"Plus I saw a bunch of weird alien slugs."

"But what else can we do? We've checked the staff room. Where else is there?"

"We have to keep our eyes open and listen for possibilities. What else have we got?"

Liam got out the Top Trumps and spread them on the floor. He pulled out the Alien Creature and put it to one side. "Oh, and remember, Mrs Johnstone is the Zetan Priest."

"But we don't have a motive for that."

"Do Zetan Priests need a motive?"

"You don't even know what a Zetan Priest is."

"So, neither do you."

"Well if we're going on lookalikes Teddy Barnham looked like The Sorcerer, and I swear he has to have some kind of powers to paint that whole barn by himself, plus he has to put up with the smell of the maggots."

"That's another motive there. Granddad said maggots can feed on dead flesh."

"You don't think John's dead, do you?"

We were both quiet for a while. Liam was eyeballing the cards. "Hey," he said, pointing at The Hangman (Horror Rating 88), "he looks like your dad."

I grabbed the card and examined it. "He doesn't look anything like that."

"He has the same hair."

Liam was right; he did have the same hair. I picked up The Cannibal (Physical Strength 93), who was bald. "Well if we're going on hair, this one looks like your dad."

We both laughed; then another card caught my eye. I pointed at the Beast card. For some reason, the hairy, green creature was on a stage. "Reminds me of Uncle Rodney."

Liam laughed. "Uncle Rodney's never on stage long before he falls off!"

"You know who's been wandering about the village a lot?"

"Who?"

"Shaky Jake." I picked up The Madman card (Killing Power 69). His mouth was tight and his eyes were closed like Shaky's when he's wound up, and his hair was similar too: brown, receding, and sticking up in random tufts.

"He might even be an alien."

It would explain his weirdness.

I don't remember watching the first half of the football because I was still thinking about the cards. Liam had left them in his room when I wanted nothing more than to study them again. But by the time the second half started and England had missed their first chance I was interested. Only a win would mean they progressed to the next round, so we worried every time they lost the ball. Mark Wright scored with a header for England from a Gazza cross when there was still half an hour to go. We were cheering for England to score more goals; they didn't, but that was good enough. At the end of the game, they showed us the table and, because Ireland and Holland had drawn, England finished top of the group. Because the games from group E were played earlier in the day, we knew that England would play Belgium in the next round.

Mum came in shortly after it finished. "Are you ready?"

"Where's Dad?" Will said.

"Chatting with your uncle. Come on, it's late and you've got school in the morning."

We went outside. Uncle Alan was leaning in and talking to Dad through the Land Rover window.

"Well, thanks for the update," said Uncle Alan, "I'll catch you later." As we passed him on our way to the Land Rover he said, "See you later boys," and then started chanting, "Engerlund, Engerlund, Engerlund."

If England had gone out of the tournament, I don't think I could have taken it. The fact that they had got through, that they had survived the group stage, made me think that John was okay too. All England had to do was win the tournament and everything would work out fine.

NOW

Having watched England in numerous tournaments since, I've learned not to depend upon them too much. For a period of time, things look to be going well, but an implosion is rarely far away.

As I drive through the part of Little Mosswick I remember, I see it's as sick as ever. But if he's dying, if he's really dying, then maybe the village will heal. If I don't see him go, then I'll always think he's out there. Maybe I need to see Dad die before I can heal.

Driving by Downham Close I slow down to look at Shaky Jake's house. It's gone. The plot has been grassed over, but while the green looks like a pleasant place to sit or play, no one does. Beyond it, on the road where John used to live, I see more For Sale signs. People have given up on this area.

A little further down the road, I come to a stop outside the old school building. The gates are closed, long since chained together, but behind it, the building still stands.

"My old school," I say to Charlie.

"What was it like?"

"Until year five, great. I liked the teachers. I worked hard. I had good friends."

"Then what?"

"Everything changed. I didn't go back."

"Why'd they close the school?"

"I guess that there were too many ghosts wandering the corridors."

Charlie leans closer to the window, staring at the school.

"Not real ghosts. You know I don't mean real ghosts, right?"

"Yes Dad," says Charlie. He sighs.

"What is it, Pal?"

"You always do that."

"What?"

"You'll talk about a ghost or a monster or a skeleton in the closet and then insist on explaining that it's not a real ghost, or monster, or skeleton."

"I don't want you getting mixed up."

"They do teach us about metaphors and similes at school, Dad," says Charlie with a smile.

"They taught me too," I say. "Didn't stop me from getting confused."

I pull away from the school, and less than a minute later I turn onto the drove towards my old house. From the outside, it hasn't changed at all. The house had stood for a couple of hundred years without change, so why would my twenty-year absence make any difference?

As I pulled up around the back of the house and saw the field, I realised that there had been one enormous change: our fields were covered in solar panels.

Friday 22nd June 1990

I opened the kitchen door and Mum and Dad stopped talking. It was becoming a bad habit. They both clutched their mugs of tea and took a sip.

"What's up?" I said, and they looked at each other.

"You want some breakfast? I can do you some bacon," Mum said.

"No thanks. I'll have cereal."

"Your dog's missing," Dad said and Mum stared at him.

"What do you mean?"

"I let him out last night after we got home, but he didn't come back in."

"Where did he go?"

"How the fuck should I know?" He rose out of his chair.

"Did you look for him?"

"I gave him a shout this morning."

"Why don't you go wake your brother? He's got a big day today."

Ignoring her, I grabbed my trainers and pulled them on.

"We'll look for him later," Dad said as he sat down again.

Mum stood at the stove cooking bacon. "You've got school. Eat your breakfast."

The hot fat turned my stomach and the sizzling and crackling from the frying pan felt like it was happening inside my head. "No," I said. How could they be so calm? Didn't they care about anything?

Though early, it was already warm, but it wasn't only the warmth I felt; as soon as I was in the open, I could feel my eyes itch and the scratchiness in the back of my throat returned. Even the inside of my ears needed a good itch. I tried to get the itchiness out of my head by thinking of the places Chappie would normally lead me to when I took him for a walk. We had a few usual routes, but it had been a couple of years since he'd bounded off seeking adventure. Fearing the worst, I walked out towards Main Street. There was a little traffic going through the village, but it wasn't heavy, and no new road kill decorated the tarmac.

I walked back past the house as Dad was coming out.

"Any sign?" he said.

I shook my head, "Not yet."

"I'll check the barn, and you take a walk across the field."

What if the tree got him? I looked across at it. The branches were shaking even though there was next to no wind. I turned away but knew I had to take another look. I stared at the ground, counted to ten, and then looked up. There was something near the tree. I hurried up the drove, but before I got to the entrance to the field, I heard a whimper. I listened. It came from the ditch on the left–it sounded like the noises Chappie made when he slept. I looked down and could see him curled up at the bottom of the ditch with flattened nettles around him.

"Chappie!" I called, and he raised his head. He tried to struggle onto his feet, and after a few seconds, he shuffled into an upright position. I slid down into the ditch beside him, flattening more nettles so they didn't sneak up my trouser legs and cover me in stings. He was breathing heavily, but he was comforted when I stroked the top of his head. He licked at my wrist, and when he seemed more comfortable, I put my arms underneath him and lifted him up. He felt so light, and it was easy to plonk him down out of the ditch. I didn't even notice that my hands had been in stinging nettles until I glanced down and saw how blotchy they were.

Chappie was okay walking back to the house although slower than usual.

"Found him then?" Dad said from the barn. He had his overalls on and had already started work on one of the farm vehicles. So much for helping me. I didn't expect him to, but he followed us back to the house.

"There he is!" Mum said as we walked in, and it annoyed me, as she acted as if he'd wandered back himself and she was the first to notice. He plodded straight to his bed and curled into a ball.

"Is he all right?" I said, looking at Mum, then Dad, not knowing if either would give me an answer.

"He's getting old," Dad said.

"Let him have a rest and we'll see how he is later," Mum said. Then she must have caught sight of my hands, "Oh look at you! You must have got stung. Let me put some lotion on it."

She took this purplish bottle of liquid out of the cupboard and a bag of cotton wool balls and insisted on covering my hands in the goop.

"Oh dear," she said. "It must be a bad sting. The skin's peeling."

Dad had already gone back out again by this point, but I didn't feel like telling her that the skin was peeling because Dad had scalded it as I got the feeling she'd tell me not to be daft even though she was there and saw him do it.

When I arrived at school, Liam was hopping from foot to foot.

"What's up with you?" I said.

"You know you said we should keep our ears open?"

"Yes."

"Guess what I heard Mr Inglehart talking about in his office."

"What were you doing in his office?"

Will wandered over. He was slightly earlier than usual and kept glancing over his shoulder.

"Nothing, I was crouching outside the window. Guess what I heard him talking about?"

"Who was he talking to?"

"I don't know. Guess what I heard them talking about!"

"Why were you crouched under his window?" Will asked, suddenly catching up with the conversation.

"Tom! Will! Guess!" Liam was flapping his arms so wildly he looked about ready for take-off.

"I don't know. A school trip?"

"No."

"I give up."

"No, guess."

"Mrs Palmer's stick insects."

"Now you're being silly. Guess properly."

"I don't know, Liam. Tell me."

Liam stopped hopping from side to side, leaned in close, and whispered, "Transition."

Will rolled his eyes and walked away, calling, "See you losers later."

"I'm not a loser. You're a loser!" cried Liam, triumphantly, and then turned his attention back to me. "What shall we do?"

"What did you hear?"

"I don't remember everything they said."

"What did they say, roughly?"

"Something about having to move on with the next stage of transition before it was too late, and how they couldn't let the current situation stop them from moving forward with year six."

"Will's in year six."

"We've got to warn him."

"Why didn't you say something before he left?"

"He called me a loser! I got confused!"

"Come on. Let's go."

Mr Inglehart appeared at the door and called pupils in for the start of the school day.

"What are we gonna do now?" asked Liam.

"If we run to his classroom, we might be able to get to him in time."

Liam sped off first, and I followed behind. We were in the corridor and heading for Will's classroom when the door to the caretaker's cupboard swung open. Liam had to swerve out of the way, and his legs collided with mine. We fell in a heap.

"That's why we tell you not to run in the corridors. We say it again, and again, but nobody listens until someone gets hurt." Mr Jenkins stood over us, holding his mop as a

Neanderthal might have held a spear. His eyebrows met in the middle, and his beard had grown thicker and more menacing.

I untangled my limbs from Liam's and scooted away from Mr Jenkins on my bottom.

"Go on," said Mr Jenkins. "Get up. Don't tell me you've broken something. That's the last thing we want to be dealing with."

Liam and I awkwardly stood and started to move away.

"Hold on a minute. Someone needs to give you two a serious talking-to. What if one of the infants had been in the corridor? You could have knocked them down, and they might have cracked their skull. We can't be having that, can we?"

"No, Mr Jenkins," Liam and I said in unison and started to walk away.

Again, Mr Jenkins stopped us, lifting the mop slightly as a barrier. "What else?"

"Sorry, Mr Jenkins."

"That's better. Off you go." He pointed with his mop. "And remember—your classroom's that way."

We had no choice but to take that path.

Mrs Palmer urged us in from the doorway to her classroom and gave us a telling-off for running late. She told us to sit down, did the register, and then told us to get our P.E. kits on.

"What are we gonna do?" asked Liam in one of his noisy whispers.

"Right," said Mrs Palmer. "Tom, you change in that corner." She pointed to the area by the sink, near the stick insects. "And Liam, you go to the book corner."

The class changed in silence, and soon we were out on the field placing cones to make lanes for a relay race. I had snuck back over to Liam, and we were dropping cones out together when I saw Will, and the rest of his class, heading across the playground and towards the school gates.

"Look," I said to Liam, and nodded towards them, with one eye on Mrs Palmer.

Liam was less discreet. "Will!" he shouted.

"I've had enough of you two already, today," cried Mrs Palmer. A vein bulged in her neck. She never got angry. "You're going to sit out this activity, and you'll be spending break with me too." She split us again, pointing out spots on either side of the field where we were to sit in silence, facing away from each other.

As I sat alone, watching the horses in the neighbouring field, I wondered why Mrs Palmer was so edgy. Maybe she was nervous about whatever plan the school had for year six. including Will. I tried not to think about what might be happening to them. Were they being beamed onto the spaceship, one at a time, ready to be strapped into the alien machines to have their brains wiped? But if Peter could defeat the White Witch's Secret Police, then Will could cope with a few aliens. Will would be too smart for them and would flee before they started the transition process. And if Will escaped, maybe he could sneak aboard the alien ship, and free the rest of the class. He could come face to face with the alien master and use his strength and wits to defeat him and save the entire planet. He had, after all, been sneaking his pen-knife to school since John went missing. I kept staring at the sky, waiting for the inevitable explosion, but perhaps defeating the aliens was more difficult in reality than in imagination.

Until break, Mrs Palmer had us working on long division. She had brought both Liam and me to the front, but on opposite ends of the row, so we couldn't talk to each other. While we worked, she kept looking at different documents on her desk and fiddling with her bead necklace.

Eventually, break came, and Mrs Palmer released the rest of the class. Once their noise had disappeared from the corridor, she asked us to approach her desk and then sighed. "What has got into you boys, today?"

Liam shifted his weight from one foot to the other and tugged on the loose skin by one of his fingers. I could tell that he was desperate to put it into his mouth and tear it free.

"I'm sorry, Mrs Palmer," I said, avoiding eye contact by staring at the desk.

"Sorry only works if you mean it. You can't have a chat mid-lesson whenever it takes your fancy."

"We were worried about Will, Miss," Liam said.

I didn't want to have this conversation. I didn't want Liam to expose what we already knew and put us at risk.

"Tom's brother?"

"Yes, Mrs Palmer," I said.

"What are you worried about? Is he not well?"

I looked up. "We saw his class go off somewhere, that's all." I looked over at Liam, but he was staring at Mrs Palmer.

"Where are you taking them?" he said in a voice which I think was supposed to be menacing, but it made him sound dumb.

"They're at Fenland Village College for an induction day. Didn't your brother tell you, Tom?"

"He must have forgotten," I said.

"In a month's time he'll be finished here, and then in September he'll be at Fenland, and you two will be year sixes, where we don't expect any chatter whatsoever."

I had one more question to ask. If she was ever likely to tear off her human flesh disguise and devour us both, this was the question that would prompt it. "What's transition?" I said and shuddered.

"Transition? As in transition from primary school to secondary? It's days like today when Will gets to visit the secondary school he'll be attending in September."

I nodded. Liam's face was screwed up and reddening.

"I'm not going to have you two sitting around while you're on detention," Mrs Palmer said as she stood. "Sharpen my pencils."

"How do we know she's telling the truth?" Liam said at lunch time while shoving the remainder of his sandwich into his mouth.

We sat under the shade of a tree on the edge of the field updating Andy on what had happened that morning. He'd been worried because he hadn't seen us at break and thought we might have been eaten by a teacher. He'd even peered into the window of our classroom, risking a telling off from Mr Inglehart to find out where we were.

"I used my Turtle Power to stay hidden," Andy said, with a smug grin. "So do you think Mrs Palmer was telling the truth?"

"We'll know when Will comes back."

"If he comes back."

"Don't say that, Liam; he's coming back."

"What makes you so sure?" Liam stood up. "We've been talking about what happened to John, and before, you agreed that aliens might have taken them away. We even found proof, so why do you believe Mrs Palmer and not me?"

Andy stood too and whispered in Liam's ear. He then broke down into a fit of giggles.

"Well, they were holding hands," Liam said, laughing with Andy. "That's why you believe her, and not me. Just you wait till I'm proved right. When none of them year sixes come back, maybe then you'll believe me."

"Don't say that," I said. I could feel myself getting hot and angry. I tried to get up, but while I was pushing myself up from the ground Liam shoved me back down and walked away with Andy.

At least I wasn't going to get into trouble for talking to Liam after lunch as I had no intention of talking to him. For a second, I thought I might have to because Mrs Palmer asked us to get into pairs for a junk-modelling project. Even worse, we were asked to make rocket ships. Normally I'd work with Liam on class art projects (our potato-printing artwork was awesome), but I couldn't imagine anything worse than having to stare at his podgy face. Plus, with us working on rocket ships he'd probably think they were for the alien fleet to attack with, or something else stupid.

"Liam, Tom," said Mrs Palmer, and I feared that she'd throw us together, but maybe she saw the way my face screwed up and took pity on me as she said, "I'm keeping you apart after this morning's performance. Liam, you work with Brian, Tom, work with Daniel."

I'd barely spoken to anyone else since John went missing, so it was a pleasant change to talk to Daniel Richardson. We kept on the subject of our junk model well, suggesting ideas to each other. It was nice to work on something together properly as Liam would normally go blundering ahead. I peeped over at him and laughed to myself when I saw that he'd managed to stick two of his fingers together.

Daniel had been casting glances at Mrs Palmer for a while, and when she was talking to some girls at the other side of the room he said, "So have you heard anything about John?"

I shook my head.

"I heard someone say he might have been abducted."

Not aliens again. Had Liam been spreading rumours around the school when it was supposed to be our own private investigation? "Did Liam tell you about his alien idea?" I asked.

"Aliens? What?" Daniel couldn't suppress his laughter, and he made Mrs Palmer glare at us, so we grabbed some junk and pretended we were making the body of our rocket.

"So you've not heard anything?" asked Daniel again.

I shrugged and tilted a fizzy pop bottle at an angle to see if we could use it in our model.

At the end of the day, Will was already waiting with Aunt Anne on the playground.

"See!" I said to Liam.

"Don't be such a bighead. You think you're so cool, but do you know what? You're not." And with that, he swung his elbow back and caught me in the gut, knocking the wind out of me. He turned and gave me a look that told me not to tell.

I couldn't if I wanted to. The rest of the journey, thankfully brief, passed in silence.

"How come you never told me you were going up to big school today?" I said to Will after Aunt Anne dropped us off.

"Big school? Babies call it that." Will laughed. "You're on drinks duty." He ran inside and straight upstairs, leaving me to get us some squash. First, I went to see if Chappie was okay. He was asleep. His drink bowl was empty, so I topped it up, and then I made squash.

Carrying the drinks upstairs, I thought about how angry Liam had been. Had I been unfair to him? I couldn't see how I had. His idea had been wrong. You'd think he'd be used to that. In the bedroom, Will had already put the N.E.S. on to play Punch Out. He was in no mood to talk, mashing at the joypad's button, and throwing punch after punch at Glass Joe without thought.

I glanced out of the window, feeling bad for hurting Liam's feelings, even though he'd been the one who elbowed me in the stomach. Maybe he felt as awful as I did. I looked around outside until my eyes fell on the tree. I'd forgotten about it until I saw the oak tree's branches swaying, but there had been something under the tree earlier, and if it wasn't Chappie, what was it?

"Hey Will," I said.

He stared at the screen and dodged to the left as he pressed the buttons on the joypad.

"Will," I said.

"I'm busy."

"Come check something out with me."

"No." He continued to hammer the buttons until Glass Joe fell to the canvass.

"Please," I said.

"Later," he said, continuing to pound the buttons as if it would stop his opponent from rising before the ten count.

I stood by the door until Little Mac was declared the winner, but then he started the next match without even looking at me. I was on my own.

"Where are you going?" asked Mum as I put my shoes on.

"I left something outside when I found Chappie this morning." I lied.

"What did you leave out there?"

"My goalkeeper gloves." I have no idea why I said that, it was the first thing that came into my head. Maybe it was because the football was sitting by the doormat, but couldn't say the football, because it was there, and she could see it.

"If you had your gloves, why did you take them off and get your hands stung, you daft little monkey?"

"Um… Chappie doesn't like me stroking him with gloves on." This was true.

"Okay, go fetch them and come straight back where I can keep an eye on you, and for Christ's sake don't go falling into the nettles. You're stung badly enough already. I should put more lotion on your hands."

"Can it wait until I come back?" I asked.

Mum nodded, and I sprinted out of the house.

It was probably going to be a load of rubbish; that's what I told myself as I entered the field. Maybe something the people working on the road had thrown over the ditch and it had come to rest by the tree. Maybe a polythene bag had blown from the yard across the field and clung to the tree trunk, and it just looked bigger because it had torn open. But the closer I got, the more I started to dismiss the boring possibilities. It was red, the same shade as our school jumper.

The closer I got, the more convinced I became that it was a jumper, until I reached a point where it could no longer be denied. It was torn in loads of places and there were patches of a much deeper red all over it, and mud smeared on the front. I picked it up without thinking that I should leave it as evidence. I had to know if it was his. I found the label inside, and sure enough, sewn on with red cotton was a name tag: 'John Glover'.

I scanned the ground by the tree. Footprints. I bent to examine them and got a waft of that maggoty smell that always permeated from the ground around the tree. The footprints pointed towards the tractor. I followed them. The corrugated iron I'd lifted the other day had a footprint on it too, and next to it a red, circular stain, with a small partner beside it. John had been here, and he was hurt. I searched around the tractor, but there was no further sign of him, so I kept walking in a straight line from the tree. I tried to imagine where he'd come from, but I couldn't make out a route. There was only one place he could have been heading: the farmhouse. He'd escaped from whatever beast had held him, fled across the field, and was running to our house for help.

But he didn't make it.

Had the beast caught up with him?

I followed the quickest path out of the field onto the track that led to the farmhouse.

Then I saw it. The gap in the tall nettles beside the ditch on the other side. He'd run, and he'd fallen in, and he needed my help.

I dashed over, his jumper still in my arms, and looked down.

It was him, John, lying on his side, his feet lost beneath a blanket of nettles. His face was down, but I knew that haircut. Mum wouldn't let me have mine shaved at the back like that.

"John," I said, in a whisper, like I was scared of waking him. I bent down and said "John," again but he still didn't react. It was too quiet. I couldn't hear any breathing. I couldn't hear the wind rushing through the grass anymore. Everything was still. I swear I could hear my blood flowing into my heart and pulsing through my body. I edged into the ditch, closer to John, and put a hand on his shoulder.

"John," I said. He was cold. I shook him in the way I do Will when sent to wake him, but there was no stirring. I tugged at his shoulder and his body twisted onto its back. His mouth fell open and his skin was white apart from a large wound on his forehead and around the neck, where it was purple and blotchy.

"John," I said. I tried again, only louder this time, and I kept saying it until I was shouting his name, but he couldn't hear me and he would never hear me no matter how loud I called.

I don't know at what point I clambered out of the ditch and ran, but that's what I did; I sprinted towards home, shouting John's name, and then Dad was shaking me and all I managed to do was point to where I'd found him.

Later there were police, but by then I was inside, and Mum had put a blanket around me even though it was hot and I was drinking tea that had about five sugars in it. I wanted to go back outside to see what was going on, but I couldn't move or tell Will what happened when he came down. Although he was asking me questions, I didn't know how to use my voice; I couldn't work my mouth to answer him. I didn't know how to tell him that my best friend was dead.

PART TWO

NOW

Charlie's used to death. He overcame the death of his mother with maturity. After the accident, when she lay in the hospital bed, unresponsive, I never told him everything would be all right.

I remember the horrified expression of the nurse as I explained to seven-year-old Charlie that his mum's brain was dead. That meant she wouldn't be waking up again. We were going to turn off the machine, and he'd have to deal with that.

Together, we cried, but I never told him it would be okay. I never gave him false hope. Hope is a castle on the sand, and it's only a matter of time until the tide turns.

Ridiculously, I hoped for a miracle. I clasped my hands together when they switched off the life support. So, when the heart-rate monitor flat-lined, when the castle collapsed, I broke all over again. That's what being brought up with lies does.

And don't think I gave him any of that crap about going to a better place either. The only place other than here is worse, much, much worse.

Friday 22nd June 1990–Evening

I don't know how I got into bed, but it felt much later. Will was sitting on his bed, reading, and as soon as he saw me move, he shouted, "Mum."

She must have floated upstairs because I didn't hear her feet on the steps and there were at least three that creaked. She sat on the side of my bed and stroked my hair. My forehead felt clammy and my hair sticky with sweat—that's what you get for lying under the duvet in the middle of a hot June day.

"Are you okay, Thomas?" she said, and I didn't know what to say.

"Do you want something to eat?"

I shook my head.

"You should have something. How about a nice ham sandwich?"

I shook my head again.

"What about a big bowl of chicken soup?" And that sounded like the best idea in the world.

While I sat at the table slurping soup from the spoon, Dad came in with P.C. Wade.

Dad put his hand on my shoulder and I jumped. "The policeman needs to ask you some questions."

I nodded and pushed the soup bowl away from me. I'd eaten about three-quarters without tasting it.

"So, Thomas, you know me from school," said P.C. Wade.

I nodded again.

"I need to ask you a few questions about... what you saw this afternoon."

"Yes," I said and he readied his notepad and pen.

"When you came in, your parents say you were holding a jumper. Where did you find that?"

"By the tree."

"Did you know it was John's?"

"I looked at the label."

"How did you find the body?"

"I saw blood nearby, and I followed it in a straight line."

"Did you disturb anything else?"

I couldn't think. I wanted to retrace my steps. I was struggling to believe that any of this was real. "Can I see him again?" I said.

"We've removed the body," said P.C. Wade.

"Oh," I said, and I stood up because I figured there wouldn't be any more questions. P.C. Wade left a few minutes later after having one of those whispered conversations with Mum and Dad outside the front door.

"Whatever did you want to see the body again for?" Mum said when she came back.

"Because I ran away and left him," I said. "It felt wrong."

Upstairs Will was sitting on his bed cheating at *Battleblade Warrior*.

"Good book?" I said.

"Not bad," he said and came over to my bed.

"What happened today?" I said.

"I don't know. They kept me out of the way."

"Didn't you see anything?"

"I watched out of the window, but I couldn't see much."

"Did you see them take the body away?"

"No. Mum kept giving me jobs to distract me. There were loads of police. They had cars on the bypass and police Land Rovers on the drove and on the field."

"Did they say what happened?"

"No. He's dead. That's all I know."

"I never thought that would be it." I could feel the tears gathering.

"Be what?"

"That he'd be dead. I always thought we'd find him, or he'd come home."

"Me too." Will put his arm around me. "John would have been pleased that you were the one to find him."

With that, the tears flowed.

"Thomas," called Mum from downstairs.

I opened the door and called back.

"Uncle Rodney's here. He wants to see that you're okay."

I sniffled, cleared my throat, and called back, "Tell him I'm fine."

He came creeping up the stairs a moment later. For a tall man, he was light on his feet. It must have been his acting experience. "My dear boy," he said as he saw me. He kept moving closer until he loomed over me. He bent down and wrapped his arms around me in an awkward hug. "What a terrible, terrible thing for one so delicate as you." He let me go, and I glanced at Will who had retreated back to his bed and peered at us over the top of his book.

"And the poor boy was dead when you found him?" asked Uncle Rodney.

I didn't want to talk to him about it. He didn't even know John. I nodded but said nothing.

"Such a tragedy. Life is a precious thing and a young life even more precious." He came forward to hug me again, and he held me for about half a minute without either of us saying a thing. When he let go, somehow, he had a chocolate bar in a blue wrapper in his hand. "For you." He handed me a Stratos bar and returned downstairs.

"Do you want it?" I said to Will.

"You don't?"

I shook my head and held it out to him.

Will took the chocolate bar and tore the end of the wrapper off. He took a bite, and before he finished swallowing, he said, "What did he look like?"

I couldn't answer right away, and it wasn't until after he'd taken another mouthful and then gulped it down, that I answered, "Like John... only... different."

"Different how?" His voice sounded like his mouth was gloopy with chocolate.

"You know the wax works we saw in Great Yarmouth, how they look almost like real people, but they're not?" We visited there the previous summer on holiday. The beach was nice, and there were some good rides in Joyland, but the waxworks were creepy, and half of them were of people I'd never even heard of.

"Yeah."

"It was like that, but not. He looked like a waxwork model, only he was real. It was like he wasn't actually there."

"I've never seen a dead body before," Will said.

For a while, I thought that made him very lucky.

Saturday 23rd June 1990

I was woken by the sound of someone shouting my name. I didn't recognise the voice. It wasn't Dad, or I would have been up straight away. It wasn't Mum's soft shout either. It was a sad, desperate shout that lured me out of bed.

On the stairs, I heard another shout, but this was Mum's voice, "You stay up there, Tom."

I stopped, not knowing what to do until I heard the original voice calling my name again. I had to see who called me in so desperate a manner. I came to the kitchen door and went to push it but someone was leaning against the other side.

"I'm sorry for what happened," I heard Mum say, and her voice sounded forceful in a way I'd not heard it before, "But you have to go."

"Tom," said the voice again. It was a woman's voice.

"Hello?" I said.

"Tom, it's me," said the voice. It didn't help.

"Mum, let me in," I said. "Who is it?"

"It's Barbara. Mrs Glover… John's mum."

I felt Mum's weight shift away from the door, so I opened it and entered the kitchen.

"I'm sorry," she said, looking at Mum and then at me, "but I had to come."

She looked so different. Her face was so white, and her eyes were so dark. I don't think she'd slept since John disappeared.

"Can you show me where you found him?" she said.

Mum came between us. "You don't have to if you don't want to."

"It's okay," I said. I understood why John's mum wanted to see where he was found and it felt right that I should show her.

Mrs Glover followed me out of the house. "I didn't get to see him until he was at the mortuary. We had to identify the body, even though we knew it would be him."

Together, we walked across the yard and onto the drove. Dad glared at us from the yard. I watched him march inside as we followed the track along the drove to the point in the ditch where I'd found John. Mrs Glover had heels on, and she put her hand out for support as she struggled across the mud, so I helped guide her between the rows of potato plants.

As we got closer, a gust of wind came from nowhere, and John's mum gasped.

I turned to face the wind and found myself glaring at the tree. I swear that its mouth—the big scorch mark shaped like a mouth—had changed, as if it had turned up at the corners into a laugh.

We couldn't get to the ditch as the police had put tape around the area, but we moved to the edge of the cordon.

"He was there." I pointed into the ditch.

John's mum raised a hand to cover her mouth. I tried not to look at her as she did that silent crying thing where the shoulders bob up and down. I didn't know what to say.

"Did he look... peaceful?" she said.

"He did," I said, and it was true. Yes, something terrible had happened to him, but there was no terror on his face; the only thing that was remarkable about it was the lack of emotion, and I guess that's what peace is.

"Why?" she said and buried her face in her hands. "What kind of monster could have done that?"

I hadn't heard him approach, but then Dad was there. He put a hand on my shoulder and then nodded towards the house, so I walked away.

I had an urgent need to beat Super Mario Bros. Will was on his bed cheating at his Fighting Fantasy book. He didn't notice as I ejected Punch Out and put in Mario. He didn't notice me speed through the first few worlds, or use the shortcut. He knew about the first one where you skipped from world 1-2 to world 4-1 by running across the top of the screen to get to the

Warp Zone, but he didn't know you could skip from 4-2 to 8-1. John had shown me this when he came over to play one day when Will was late back because he had a school trip to a museum in Cambridge. For the first time, I completed world 8-1 without losing a life. I lost a life on world 8-2, due to that stupid cloud that throws out the red spiky things. I'm sure I heard Will snort when he heard Mario's death tune, but when I turned around, his nose remained buried in the book with his fingers saving at least two other pages. Even though one of the red things got me, I was lucky not to get taken out by the big bullets that fly across the screen. They normally had me beat, and I'd only ever finished the level once before.

When I reached world 8-3 before, it was the Hammer Bros that killed me, but this time I ran straight under them. That was one of John's tips, telling me that I didn't have to beat every bad guy, just get to the end of each level. This time I succeeded and was onto the final level. At the start, I mispressed the D-pad and fell into the first pool of lava. I was down to my last life and never thought I'd do it. Somehow the flying fish kept launching directly underneath me and dying as they hit my feet when normally they'd fly at my head and kill me. Even the jellyfish swam away from me instead of towards me.

Then there was Bowser. He was throwing out so many hammers I didn't think it was possible. And when he jumped in the air, there surely wasn't time to run underneath him. The music changed, warning me that time was almost up, so I went for it. As he came forward, there was a gap in the hammer stream and I closed my eyes, pushed forward and jumped. I don't know how he missed me. I expected to hear the death jingle, but instead, it was the sound of the bridge falling away. Even as Mario walked into the next room, I expected the little mushroom guy to tell me that my princess was in another castle, but she wasn't, she was in front of me. THANK YOU MARIO! YOUR QUEST IS OVER. It said. I'd done it. I turned to get Will's attention, but he was already watching.

"Well done, bro," he said.

Later, Will put the football on, but neither of us was watching. It was Cameroon versus Colombia. When the score flashed on the screen at the thirty-minute mark, I realised I'd not taken a single bit of it in.

"Remember when John got us to play as Cameroon?" Will said.

I did. It was on the first Monday we were at school after the World Cup started, the day before he went missing. It was the last normal day we'd had. "He'd be cheering on Cameroon, wouldn't he?"

We started supporting Cameroon. We had to wait until extra time, but Will and I high-fived when Roger Milla put Cameroon in front. Then the funniest thing happened. The Colombian goalkeeper made a huge mistake. He was playing sweeper-keeper and hanging around halfway between the goal and the halfway line. When a player passed it back to him, he mis-controlled the ball and Roger Milla took the ball off him. As the keeper was miles out of goal, Milla dribbled up to the 18-yard line and scored with no one to stop him.

John would have loved that. A tear trickled down my cheek as they showed another replay.

Colombia scored to make it 2-1, but Cameroon held on till the end to progress to the quarter-finals. "If England beat Belgium on Tuesday," Will said, "they'll have to play Cameroon."

NOW

"Hullo!" I hear a shout from the barn as Charlie and I walk towards the back door of my old house. I turn to see a portly man dressed in the kind of clothes Dad used to wear, the kind of clothes you don't see outside of Fenland farms or Sunday evening TV dramas: a checked shirt and shapeless beige trousers held up with suspenders. As he approaches, he rubs his hands on his thighs, adding another layer of grime to them. A grin spreads across his familiar face, and his cheeks redden. Following behind him is a young boy, dressed identically.

"Liam!" I shout, "where's Dad?"

"Where he's been the last month. In bed."

"Are you sure?"

"Of course, Tom."

"Have the police been?"

Liam plonks his hand on my shoulder. "No. You're here now. You can relax. What's got you so wound up?"

I tell him about the police car and the missing girl, and the boy beside him looks up at us.

"That's Jessica Matthews," says the boy.

"Who's this?" I say, smiling at the child.

"This is my boy, Billy," says Liam. He ruffles Billy's hair.

"I didn't know you had a son."

"Yeah, was married for a bit, but that didn't work out. Billy comes to stay with me every other weekend. Ain't that right, my boy?" He slaps Billy on the back, and I realise how big his hands are. It must be a family trait, and I guess I should thank my mother's genes for missing out on that feature.

"What were you saying about the girl, Billy?" I ask.

Billy pulls a phone out of his pocket. It's newer and more expensive than mine. "Saw something on Facebook. Her mum was asking if anyone had seen her."

"No need to worry yourself about that son," says Liam.

"That's the kind of thing they said to us, remember?"

Liam looks at me, puzzled.

"When John was missing, our parents told us there was nothing to worry about. Only there was, wasn't there?"

Liam pulled Billy close to him. "You'll scare him," he says.

"Maybe he should be scared."

"Billy," says Liam, bending down to talk to the boy, "why don't you take…" he turns to my son, "Charlie, isn't it?" Charlie nods and Liam continues, "Why don't you take Charlie to see the tractor we've been working on?"

Billy jumps with excitement and grabs a less-enthusiastic Charlie by the hand. "If our Dads are cousins," says Billy, "are we cousins too?"

Once they're out of earshot, I lean towards Liam. "What did he say the name was, Matthews?"

"Yeah, Laura's girl. Do you remember Laura? She was in our class."

Of course, I remember. Even though I've not thought of her for the best part of three decades, hearing her name still hurts and her words ring around my head again. With it, comes a flood of memories. What if her girl is suffering the way John did? "Can't you see?" I say. "It's happening again, and we're making the same mistakes they did!"

Liam shakes his head. He takes a handkerchief from his pocket and mops the sweat from his brow. "What are you talking about?"

"Our parents used to send us away when they wanted to talk. Don't you remember the whispering? It drove us near crazy!"

"We got caught up in the excitement, that's all. That's what kids are supposed to do."

I stare into his eyes and try to make him see sense. "You can't keep lying to them."

"What would you do then, Tom, warn them of every possible danger out there, have them worried stiff all the bloody time?"

"Yes. It's what I do. Charlie knows the risks, and he knows the probabilities of them happening too."

Liam shrugs and turns towards the boys. "Some childhood that is."

"At least he'll have one," I say.

Liam shakes his head. "How come you never took any of my calls?" he asks.

"I'm sorry," I say. "I couldn't deal with anything to do with this place."

"We could have got your Dad's conviction squashed if you'd have said something."

Somehow, I resist the urge to correct him. Nothing I could have said would have made Dad look better, not after what I saw.

Sunday 24th June 1990

After breakfast, Dad dragged Will out to help stack the hay bales. While I was glad to avoid it, I also had this horrible feeling I'd not been asked to help because I wasn't good enough.

"Your dad and I think it'll be best if you rest today, and get ready to go back to school tomorrow," Mum said and urged me to go back to my room.

I took advantage of the time and picked up *The Secret of the Scythe* for another play-through. With reasonable dice rolls, I felt confident I'd be able to make my way through the game better than before. I avoided the witch's house, tackled the monsters on the way to the Underworld, and then found myself in front of a grotesque living tree. I had to roll a die to test my luck, and I was not lucky, which meant that the tree had tied my legs together with its roots. This meant that I took double damage every time it attacked me. I rolled the dice for a strong attack, but one of them hit the corner of the book, bounced off, and rolled under the bed.

As I hunted for the die, there was a knock on the door. I thought Mum was downstairs, but after a second impatient knock, I hurried downstairs, hoping it was Granddad. When I opened the door, I found a cheesy-looking man standing there with his hair swept over to one side. He had a camera hanging around his neck and, in one hand, he held a small tape recorder.

"Are you Thomas Tilbrook?" he said.

"Who are you?"

"I'm looking for Thomas Tilbrook. It's important that I talk to him."

"What about?"

"Are you Thomas Tilbrook?"

"Might be." There was something about his manner that made me reluctant to answer him.

"Listen, if you are Thomas Tilbrook, would you mind answering some questions for me?"

"Who are you?"

"My name is Joseph Price."

"What do you want?"

"I need to speak to Thomas Tilbrook. That's you, right?"

"What do you want?"

"I'm a journalist. I work for the Daily Report. Have you heard of us?"

I'd seen the paper in the Post Office but had never read it. Most of the headlines on the front page were stupid, and they often had a woman in a bra and knickers on the front too. Liam liked to point and laugh at it when we went in for penny sweets. "Yeah."

"Can I come in?"

"No."

"Will you answer a few questions about John Glover?"

"No."

"I can pay you."

"No."

"Surely an intelligent young man like you could think of something to do with one-hundred pounds."

I was tempted. I'd be able to buy my own horror Top Trumps, enough stickers to complete the World Cup sticker album, and a new game, too—maybe enough left over for the next Fighting Fantasy book, but I didn't want to talk about it.

"Go away," I said and tried to push the door closed, but he put his foot in the way.

"Mum," I called, panicked.

"Who's this?" I looked up and Dad was standing behind the reporter.

"He won't go away," I said.

"We'll see about that." Dad put one of his huge hands around the back of Price's neck, his sausage fingers curled around both sides.

"I need to speak to your son about what happened here, Mr Tilbrook."

Dad spun him around and released him, only to grab him again by the throat.

"There could be a significant sum of money in it for you, Sir," Price said, his voice strained.

"If I ever see you again, I will throttle you, understand?" Dad lifted him off the ground and threw him back.

He landed on his bum. He sat up and blew some dust off his camera. "I could sue you for that," he said in a croaky voice. He brought his hand up to his neck and gave it a rub.

"You better get off my land quick sharp, or you'll have a bloody lot more to sue me for."

Joseph was slowly getting to his feet until Dad jerked his body towards him. Then he scrambled up and set off into a run.

"What did you let him in for?" Dad said.

"I didn't. He came to the door. I didn't know who he was."

"Where's your mum?"

She must have heard the commotion because suddenly she was there.

"Where were you?" Dad said.

"What's the matter?"

"This daft boy of ours was about to reveal all of our bloody secrets to some soppy reporter. Bloody ghoul."

"No I wasn't," I said. What did he mean by ghoul? I wanted to ask, but with him, it was impossible.

"You were standing in the doorway talking to him."

"I was trying to close the door. He had his foot in it."

"You shouldn't have opened it in the first place."

There was no way to win an argument with him. I turned away and headed upstairs.

"Go on, then—run off," I heard him say, "Go and cry up in your room." And as soon as he said that I couldn't help but do anything else. I felt pathetic, exactly as everyone saw me. Like Edmund, I would betray the family. If anything, it only made the reporter's offer more tempting.

From the window, I saw Dad trundle off in the tractor, with Will sitting beside him. I watched them go along the drove until they were out of sight behind the elderberry bushes. As I was about to move away from the window, I spotted something else. Walking along the drove that ran closest to the house, near to the place where I'd found John, a man lurked. Was it Joseph Price? Would he dare? I leaned in closer to the window. It wasn't Price. Peering into the ditches and looking for something near the police tape was Shaky Jake.

I ran downstairs and grabbed Chappie's lead. The dog clambered out of his basket. "I'm taking Chappie for a walk," I yelled, but I don't know if Mum heard.

I moved as fast as Chappie would allow. We followed the path from the farm onto the drove–the same way that Dad had taken the tractor, but when we hit the drove, we turned the other way, towards the spot where I'd found John.

Shaky Jake stood there wearing some horrible, faded, green trousers, and he kept rubbing his hands on the side of them, as if they were covered in some disgusting sticky substance that he couldn't get rid of. Even though it was hot, he had on a navy-blue jumper. When he turned to look at me, I realised that he wore nothing beneath the jumper, as a load of curly, black hairs sprouted out of the gap in the V-shaped neck.

"'ello," he said, wiping his hands again on his trouser leg.

"What are you doing?" I asked.

He shrugged his shoulders. "Going for a walk. I like going for walks 'round here."

"What are you looking for?" I said. I let a little of Chappie's lead out, intending for the dog to take a step closer to Shaky Jake to scare him, but Chappie remained still.

"I heard about that poor boy." Jake's head bobbed forward as he said it. It was like he was trying to swallow a boiled sweet whole.

I shook Chappie's lead, trying to urge some action from him. He rolled onto his side and gasped.

"I wis jus' lookin' for clues," said Shaky. "I want to help."

"Do it somewhere else," I said. "Before people start thinking you had something to do with it."

He shook his head, and then jerked into a new pose, leaning forward with his feet shoulder-width apart. One hand moved towards his face and the forefinger straightened, vertical, in front of his rounded lips. "Shush," he said in a dramatic manner before putting his hands on his hips. "There ain't be no need to go tellin' tales," he said, and then he thrust a hand into his pocket with such force I thought his hand was going to burst through it.

From the pocket, he pulled a small white packet. "Wanna sweet?" he asked.

Fisherman's Friend. No way. "Get out of here," I said– with Chappie offering no aggression whatsoever.

First, he took a step towards me and then turned back the other way. He turned again as if he wanted to walk past me before deciding to stride off in the other direction.

I watched him meander to the end of the drove where it met the bypass. There, he pondered over which way to go before he clambered up the bank and walked along the new road.

In the evening we had a welcome visitor, one I'd hoped to see earlier. Granddad looked much older when he walked in, and needed to use his stick, rather than carrying it around as a prop.

"It were awful sad to hear you found your friend like that," Granddad said, putting his hand on top of mine.

I nodded.

"I thought he'd be okay," he said.

I looked Granddad in the eye, and could tell he felt bad about it.

"Don't get the boy worked up," Dad said. "He'll be crying his eyes out again if you keep that up."

Crap. I could feel the tears welling.

"Well, maybe he should cry. He found the body of his best friend a couple of hundred yards from his house. If that ain't worth crying over, I don't know what is." Granddad pulled me to him, burying my face into his shoulder.

I cried, but he was hiding it for me. There was no way Dad could see.

Dad sighed. "I'm gonna go check on them chickens and shut 'em up for the night."

After Dad left, Granddad let me go and urged me to sit next to him. "It's okay to be upset," he said.

By then I'd stopped sobbing, but I could still feel the silent tears creeping down my face. "It's not fair," I said.

"What is?" asked Granddad. "There ain't no such thing as fair; we jus' have to deal with whatever hand it is we've been dealt and hope we come out of it better."

"Dad makes me feel worse."

"Don't you worry about him. Tell him if he upsets you, he's not too big to have his ears boxed."

I smiled. I could never imagine saying that to Dad, but the thought of Granddad telling him off and clipping his ear made me smile. It felt like time to dob him in. "Earlier a man from the newspaper came," I said, "and Dad told me off and said I was going to tell him our secrets."

"Well, you've got to be careful around folk like that."

"I didn't tell him anything. I tried to get rid of him."

"Fly off the handle, did he?"

"He threw him off the doorstep."

"Did he? Well, I imagine he deserved it. Plus, your Dad's sensitive when it comes to reporters and the like."

Dad? Sensitive? I couldn't see it.

Granddad read the doubt on my face. "It goes back to when he were young. Uncle Rodney... he did something amazing. But there was this one reporter who wanted to twist it into something else. I reckon the experience of going through that stuck with your dad."

I nodded, but I struggled to picture Dad as a child. "Have you got any old pictures of Dad?" I asked. "From when he was around my age?"

"Reckon I do. Swing by after school one day and I'll see what I can dig out."

A few seconds later Dad came back in. He had about six eggs in one hand. "They're some good layers Rodney found us."

I took that as my cue to disappear to my room for the night.

Monday 25th June 1990

"You don't have to go to school today," Mum said. "Not if you don't feel like it." The smell of lard melting in the frying pan made me feel sick and the sizzling seemed to be too loud and the sound buzzed around inside my head like an angry wasp. I couldn't think of anything worse than sitting around at home all day.

"I want to go," I said.

"Well, you've got to get a good breakfast inside you," Mum said. Dad was already out, so I didn't have him hassling me.

"Can't I have toast?"

"Nonsense," Mum said, "I'm doing eggs and bacon, beans and fried bread. That'll set you up for the day."

Because stuffing myself with food was going to get the picture of John's face out of my mind. The purple blotches on his neck had spread like diseased fingers on his cheeks and he had dark black circles around his eyes. In one of my dreams, he leaned against the tree trunk and branches twisted towards him and twigs had grown and stretched out around his neck and got tighter and tighter until his eyes exploded out of his skull.

Will rubbed his stomach at the breakfast table and already had hold of his knife and fork, ready to tuck in. As soon as his plate hit the table, he shovelled food into his mouth. I cut a tiny bit of egg white and put it in my mouth. When I tried to swallow, I imagined purple fingers around my neck and coughed it back up onto the plate.

Will grinned at me.

I took a sip of orange juice and after that, I ate a few forkfuls of beans and a little bacon. I cut the corner off the fried bread, but when fat oozed out of its centre, I put it back down again.

"Thanks for breakfast," I said and took my plate over to the sink, "but we've got to get going."

"You've got plenty of time. Your Aunt Anne's picking you up, so you can finish your breakfast."

I took the plate back to the table and spent a few minutes pushing food around, managing a little more of the egg and most of the bacon. I wondered if I would be better off at home, but I could hear Mum singing to herself quietly as she was wiping down the already clean sink and I wanted to be at school where everything might be normal.

In the car, Liam was quiet. He kept leaning forward, looking at me, opening his mouth and then sitting back again.

Andy had a lot of questions. "What did he look like?" "Did he smell bad?" "Was his face gooey?"

But every time he got one of these questions out, Aunt Anne shushed him and he went back to having to think about it for himself. I tried to ignore the sounds inside the car as I gazed out of the window, watching the people emerge from their houses all through the village. It seemed much smaller—maybe because we passed by so quickly in the car compared to when we walked. There were a lot of cars on the roads, parents dropping off their children, and so many parents walking kids to school.

Aunt Anne leant round from the driver's seat and took hold of my hand after she pulled up outside the school. She let Will, Andy and Liam get out and then said, "If anyone says anything that upsets you and you want to go home, then go to the office and get them to call me."

Liam waited outside the car for me, but he said nothing. I couldn't read the look on his face. I'd forgotten how badly he'd taken it when his alien transition idea fell to pieces, and how he'd elbowed me in the stomach. Surely, he couldn't still be angry, not with John being found like that.

Mrs Palmer stood at the entrance to the school sending everyone straight to the hall for an assembly. We never had assemblies on a Monday, but I knew what this one would be about.

Mr Inglehart stood at the front of the hall with a solemn look on his face. Other teachers kept urging their pupils to remain silent as we sat down on the floor in our class rows. Once we were seated, Inglehart cleared his throat. "Many of you will have heard about the disappearance of John Glover, a pupil in Mrs Palmer's class. It is with deep sorrow that I have to tell you that John is dead."

Gasps filled the room and teachers peered down their class rows to quieten their pupils.

"John's body was discovered on Friday, and police investigations are continuing. If anyone has any information they need to share, please come to my office, or come along even if you just want to talk." I swear Inglehart was staring at me.

"We will plan a memorial service for John, and I encourage you to share any ideas you may have with your teacher. Now if you could put your hands together and join me as we say the Lord's Prayer."

I'd never paid attention to the words of the Lord's Prayer before; it was a chant we did without paying any attention, but this time the line 'Deliver us from evil', stood out. Surely John hadn't been delivered from evil? Whatever had killed him must have been evil? Or was the fact that his body came back his delivery from evil?

Mrs Palmer tapped me on the shoulder. Everyone had already got up and was in a line to go back to class. I stood and joined the line, looking only at the floor. I went to class, but, other than Mrs Palmer asking if I was okay every five minutes, I don't remember what we did. I kept staring at John's drawer and thinking he'd never be back to clear it out. His pencil case would never be opened again. His books would never be written in again. When it came to break, people headed out onto the pitch as if everything was the same as before, as if he'd left school and we were supposed to continue as if everything was normal.

As soon as we got onto the playing field, Andy found me and asked me if I was okay. "So, what's next?" he said.

"Next?"

"What are we going to do about it?"

I hadn't thought about next. In the last week, I'd always thought that we'd find John, or if we didn't, then he'd be back at school with no explanation and everything would be okay. Finding him seemed like the end—I didn't get the concept of a next.

"Don't we have to find out what happened to him?" Andy said.

At least we'd be doing something. "Yeah," I said, "We should do that." I remembered Shaky Jake snooping around the drove.

Liam had been loitering nearby. He'd still not said much to me. "Come on, Andy," he said and led him away.

I needed another look at those Top Trumps. I was thinking about the cards but got distracted by Will coming towards me. He followed Chris, from his class, and he kept grabbing his arm to stop him from walking towards us. When they were close, I heard Will say, "Chris, leave it." But Chris shrugged him off and came over to me.

"You saw his body," said Chris.

I nodded.

"What did it look like?"

"Like John."

"Was there blood or anything?"

"I don't want to talk about it."

"Were there worms crawling around his face?"

"Chris, he said he doesn't want to talk about it," Will said, coming between Chris and me.

"How come he was found on your land?" said Chris, going up on tip-toes to peer over Will. "Maybe your dad ran him over on his tractor."

Chris kept talking, and I put my hands over my ears. I could see his mouth moving and the little flecks of spittle forming at the sides of his mouth made him look rabid. And then Will, like Peter Pevensie in battle, swung back his arm and thumped Chris in the face. Chris was his friend, maybe even his best friend, but he wasn't going to let him upset me like that. I think Will would have punched him again, but Mr Inglehart called out and Chris ran away.

"Violence will not be tolerated in this school," Mr Inglehart said when he got closer. He told Will to go with him to his office.

Laura skipped over, her pigtails bouncing, with Becky trotting behind her. "Did your brother punch Chris in the face?"

"Yes." I felt proud of the way he'd stuck up for me.
"Why?"
"He was saying some horrible stuff about John."
"That's mean. He deserved it then. You found his body?"

I didn't want to talk about it with Laura. I didn't want to cry in front of her. A shrug was all I could manage.

"That's so terrible. Do you feel okay?"

I nodded and tried to smile. No doubt it looked forced and goofy, and when the bell rang, I was glad to go back into hiding in the classroom.

After break Mrs Palmer had us doing literacy work. She came over to me and said, "So have you had any thoughts about John's memorial?"

I shrugged my shoulders, "I don't know."

"We were thinking of planting a tree and putting up a plaque by it. How would you feel about that?"

John wasn't into trees other than climbing them to retrieve stuck footballs. He did that quite a lot. Then I had an idea. "You know they have that trophy they give out at the end of the year to the person who does best at sports day?" I said, "Could you name that after John?"

Mrs Palmer nodded. "That's a lovely idea. I'll tell Mr Inglehart. How are you coping, Thomas?"

I shrugged again.

"It can't have been very pleasant."

"So what's... next?" I said.

"After lunch we're going to do some painting, but if you don't feel up to it, you can read on your own if you'd prefer?"

"Sorry, Miss, I meant what's next, with John?"

"In what way?"

"What happens to his body?"

"There will be a funeral, and I don't know if John's parents have decided if they will bury or cremate him..."

"But before that, won't they need to look at the body to work out what happened?"

"I imagine so."

"Will they have to cut him open?"

"I don't know, Tom, why?"

"I don't like the idea of him being cut open. He's been through enough."

"I agree."

"Who did it to him?"

"That's for the police to investigate," said Mrs Palmer. She got a tissue from her sleeve and handed it to me. I didn't even realise I'd been crying.

At home, the kitchen shone. The tiles on the floor and the kitchen worktops gleamed and the whole place smelled like cleaning products.

"How was your day?" Mum said.

"Good," we both said and then Will took the letter out of his bag and slid it across the table where Mum was arranging some flowers.

"What's this?" she said.

"Letter."

"Haven't you got one, Tom?"

She looked at the letter then at Will. "Fighting? Whatever is your dad going to say when he sees this?"

"Chris deserved it," I said.

"I thought Chris was your friend," Mum said, bending down to look Will in the eye.

"He was upsetting Tom."

"He asked horrible questions about John," I said, and then went to the sink to pour myself a glass of water.

"I see," Mum said. "But still, we didn't bring you up to go around thumping boys on the playground."

"He said Dad ran John over on his tractor," Will said.

"That's ridiculous! Why would he say something like that? What a horrible child. I've got a good mind to have words with his mother."

"He was just being stupid, Mum," Will said. "Don't worry about it."

"It's not right, people making up stories like that. He'll get someone into trouble."

There was a noise from outside. Will glanced towards the window. "Where's Dad?"

"Outside, with the police."

"Can we go see what they're doing?"

"I suppose so, but don't interfere."

I didn't want to go out there, but Will practically dragged me. "Don't you want to find out what happened?" I wasn't sure if I did. I wasn't sure if what had happened even mattered anymore. It was only fun trying to solve a mystery when there was going to be a positive outcome. There wasn't going to be anything good from finding out who had killed him—or what.

There were loads of them out there. Dad stood with a group at the point where the drove led to the field entrance. We walked close enough to see they had tape measures. At the top of the bypass, more policemen swarmed around. Some explored the bank, others paced out how far it was to the markers they'd placed where the body was found.

"They must be working on how the body got into the ditch," Will said.

I glanced at the tree and shuddered. "There was blood near the tree."

"Maybe he was running away from someone."

"What about the tree? Do you think that had anything to do with it?"

"Don't be silly, that can't do anything."

"It stole Granddad's eye. And don't you remember the wasps?"

It was a few years ago, and we must have felt brave. We'd been out there in the morning helping Dad as he tinkered with a tractor that had broken down (that mostly involved Will running to get tools at Dad's command) when we heard the tree groaning. Normally that would have scared us to death, but Will had got into reading the Hardy Boys books which they had in the school library and he wanted to investigate everything like it was a mystery. So, after lunch, when Dad had finished with the tractor and was busy in another field, we went back. The closer we got to the tree, the louder the rumble became. There was a deep crack in the tree that got wider at the top. Will had shone his torch in at the bottom of the crack, but it was too narrow to see anything. He'd asked for a boost up, and using my fingers as a step, he shone the light in higher up. With his other hand, he poked away with his penknife, and then he jumped off my hand and told me to run. His voice was quivering, and I knew it was serious. I heard a violent buzz and looked up to see wasps flying out of the top of the tree trunk. We both sprinted straight for the bank opposite. We jumped over the ditch and clambered up the other side and didn't turn around until we were on the drove, which Granddad had told us was called Black Fen Drove, and would later become the bypass. The wasps hadn't followed, but it only made me more suspicious of that tree.

Will shook his head, "We've got to think about real possibilities, not trees and monsters and all that bullshit." He walked towards the group of policemen standing in the drove, and I walked back to the house.

NOW

It smells exactly the same: a mix of ancient engine oil and wasted grain. Billy points at the tractor's engine, and Charlie nods, feigning keenness.

"Thought you would've gone straight up to see your Dad," says Liam as we approach our sons.

No. Not yet. Being this close is hard enough. I'm not sure I can bring myself to look at him. I don't know what I expect to see—a man or a monster.

When I get to the tractor, I make the mistake of asking what they've been up to, and Billy goes into great detail about their progress. He seems a smart, young lad, and he's enthusiastic about working with his Dad, so Liam must be doing something right. But then I remember how close Dad was with Will, and how that turned out and the bitterness builds up inside me again at being allowed to live in a fantasy land for so long.

As Charlie is showing interest, I don't want to drag him away. Maybe it's seeing Liam again. I may have shut him out after that summer, but what we had meant something, until we found John, and Charlie has never had that experience of playing with a cousin. Cruel of me, I suppose some would say, but I have my ways of protecting him.

I glance around the shed and my eyes fall upon an old, metal bin lid which reminds me of Andy's Michelangelo costume. "How's Andy?" I ask.

Liam shakes his head. "Same," he says.

Same as what? I want to ask, but then wonder about how many cans of worms I might be opening.

"What about your Mum and Dad?"

"Well, Dad's fine, but... don't you know?"

"Don't I know what?"

Liam takes out the handkerchief again and squeezes it in one hand.

"She's dead. Cancer. Three years back."

My mouth falls open and I don't know what to say.

"I thought your mum would have told you," says Liam.

And I stand there, flabbergasted, feeling a loss I should have felt long ago; it hits me harder for the delay. That's what my stupid rules get me.

It was Anne that helped me get away all those years ago. She understood that it wouldn't be healthy for me to come back. First, her letters got me into college and later she helped me get into the hostel so I wouldn't have to come home. Now I can never thank her for what she did.

I want to run into the house and yell at Mum for keeping this from me, but then my own voice plays back in my head, telling her that I didn't want to know about anything that was going on in Little Mosswick.

When you've been in the dark too long, a little light is blinding.

Tuesday 26th June 1990

Word had spread around school that I'd found John. Everyone stared or pointed at me. Kids who wouldn't have bothered to speak to me before started conversations: "Got any swaps?" "See the football last night?" The answer was "No," in both cases and I walked away before they asked what they really wanted to. Would I have been the same if I wasn't the one to find him? Would I chase someone around asking what a dead body looked like? I can't say it was ever on my list of things to do, but if the opportunity was presented to me, I might have been curious.

Liam trotted over with his hand half-shielding his mouth suggesting he wanted to whisper his hot breath into my ear.

I stepped away. "Just tell me, Liam."

He raised his eyebrows at me and jutted his head forward, his lips closed tight. He peered over his shoulder, turned back to me and blurted out, "They're talking about transition again."

I sighed and shook my head. "Liam, that had nothing to do with anything."

"How do you know?"

"Mrs Palmer told us what transition was."

Liam pushed his tongue into his lower lip and scrunched his eyes closed to suggest I was being stupid. "Of course, she'd say that. She's one of the alien creatures."

"If we hadn't spent so long on your stupid alien theories," I said through gritted teeth, "we might have found John alive."

I didn't see it coming. With both hands, Liam shoved me, and too slow to adjust my feet, I fell.

"You're such a stupid bighead," he said, his face reddening. "I wouldn't even be friends with you if we weren't cousins."

"Me neither," I shouted, but he'd already turned away.

People walked past me, going to line up for class, no one thinking to help me up or ask why I was on the ground. I saw the teachers emerge from the building, so I hurried to my feet, dusted myself off, and joined my line.

After lunch, another assembly. We never had them after lunch. The chatter of the infants echoed around the hall and made my head throb. The thought of spontaneous human combustion came into my head, and I imagined the mess I'd cause if I exploded in the middle of the hall.

Mr Inglehart came in and settled the infants. I was glad of the quiet until he started speaking. "We have contacted your parents in order to make arrangements for everyone to be collected after school. The police have suggested that a curfew is enforced, and stated that no children are allowed to play out after school, effective immediately, until further notice."

The hall gasped, and the chatter started again. I suppose it didn't make much difference to us, we'd been under a curfew for the last week anyway, with our parents watching us and telling us not to go out to play, but I thought they were being over-protective. If it was coming from the police, that meant there was something evil out there, and they were worried it would strike again.

At the end of the day, Mum was waiting on the playground. On our walk home we saw a few police cars about and police officers going door-to-door. A car parked outside Mrs Johnstone's house made me think about her TCP and soft biscuits. There weren't any police around the farm which made a change.

"Do you boys want to watch the football with Liam and Andy tonight?" asked Mum.

A confusing range of emotions hit me. With Liam? After what had happened earlier? I couldn't say anything because Mum would tell us off for falling out. With that was the excitement of the World Cup: England were playing Belgium for a place in the quarter-finals. When England made the second round, I was sure that it meant that John would be okay, but he wasn't. Why was everything going wrong? Did it mean England would lose?

Before I had a chance to say anything, Will had answered on my behalf, and a couple of hours later we arrived at their house.

Aunt Anne had made a cake with jam and cream and offered us each a slice.

"Can I take it to my room?" Liam said.

"No, you can watch the football down here," said Aunt Anne.

"But won't you want to watch your programmes?" Liam said.

"Missing them for one night won't do me any harm."

Andy held his plate with one hand and paid little attention as he tore off little mouthfuls. The cake slid towards the edge of the plate in slow motion. I wanted to say something, but I froze and it tumbled off the plate and plopped onto the kitchen floor.

I was sure he'd get told off. He looked at Aunt Anne, his eyes getting watery. Andy turned into a crybaby at home, even though he never cried when we were out, even that time he ran into a barbed-wire fence and tore his t-shirt open and had blood pouring down his arm.

"Pick it up," said Auntie Anne.

He put it back on his plate. He reached to break off another bit.

"Put it in the bin. I'll cut you another slice." The second slice of cake was bigger than the first. "Now hold it with both hands."

I followed Andy into the living room as he gripped the edges of his plate. Aunt Anne had plump cushions on her sofa. They were great for plonking onto and hearing the air whoosh out.

We had a little time before the game started.

"I'm going upstairs," said Liam. Will and Andy followed, but I stayed to watch the build-up to the game with Uncle

Alan. He was talking about strategies and how the Belgians would play and I nodded absently. I excused myself, saying I needed the loo and pushed myself off the sofa. I needed a moment's quiet. As I moved through the hall, I saw Liam's pile of Top Trumps wrapped in an elastic band on the telephone table. I checked over my shoulder and, seeing it clear, grabbed them and shoved them into my pocket.

When I returned to the living room, the teams were on the pitch.

"It's starting," shouted Alan, and I heard a stampede on the steps.

Once everyone was downstairs, Alan left. I thought he'd been looking forward to the game? I soon forgot about him when they kicked off.

Every time Belgium came forward, I was certain they'd score, but somehow they didn't. The commentator said England's goal must have been 'charmed', and maybe it was under special protection. There was magic in that England team; I could see it every time Gazza got the ball. Somehow, he ran with the ball glued to his foot, weaving it from one side to the other, leaving the defenders bedazzled. The only thing the Belgians could do to stop him was to kick him in the shins. They must have annoyed him, because one time, after they got the ball off him, he tried to get it back by kicking them, but the referee said that was a foul and gave him a yellow card.

Neither team scored. Extra time. Still, the Belgians kept kicking Gazza, and for once he was given a free kick. There were only a couple of minutes to go, and a penalty shootout seemed certain. Gazza took the free kick. He floated the ball into the air, and it hung there for ages before it dropped just right for David Platt to volley it into the goal.

We cheered and then cheered again a couple of minutes later when the referee blew the final whistle. England had won. They were in the quarter-finals.

We were jumping around on the sofas when Aunt Anne came in, her eyes wide.

"Whatever are you boys doing?"

Will and I dashed off the sofa and stood with our hands behind our backs. Together we said, "Sorry, Aunt Anne," while Andy and Liam laughed, and then Liam flared his nostrils at me. I ignored him.

"No need to apologise, boys; with all that noise I thought one of you had had an accident!"

"England won!" Andy said.

"Fantastic," said Anne. "That sounds like a good excuse for more cake."

After we finished our cake, Uncle Alan came back in, with Dad behind him.

Uncle Alan dashed over to Liam and Andy, picked one up in each arm and started jumping up and down. "We won!" he cried.

"Come on boys," Dad said. "Time to go." He had a weird smile on his reddened face.

As we put on our shoes Liam asked, "Where have you been?"

"Meeting at the village hall," said Alan.

"What did they say?"

Alan turned to face Dad and then back to Liam. "Nothing new. Don't worry about it. We have to drop you off and pick you up from school, and it'll be back to normal soon."

How could it ever be back to normal? John was gone, and he wasn't coming back. Something had taken him and killed him. The police were so worried they'd put a curfew in place to stop the thing from getting us too. How could we not worry?

Wednesday 27th June 1990

Chappie's bed was empty when I got up, and his dinner bowl was full. A quick scan of his usual spots didn't reveal his whereabouts, either.

"Have you seen Chappie?" I said to Mum and Dad, who were eating toast at the kitchen table.

"And good morning to you to," Dad said. "Sometimes, I reckon you care more about that daft dog than you do your mum and me."

He spoke in that half-teasing, half-serious way that I never knew how to react to. Maybe that's because the dog doesn't make me feel like a bag of crap, I thought to myself.

Dad flicked out his hand and caught me on the forearm with the tips of his fingers and smiled at me. "I'm only teasing. He's asleep by the doorstep."

Once outside I gave my arm a rub. It was surprising how much it felt like a burn.

Chappie lay in the shade, sleeping. His legs slowly paddled, and his tongue hung out of his mouth. He looked peaceful, so I left him there.

Aunt Anne arrived a few minutes later. I wasn't looking forward to the journey with Liam. Normally they waited in the car as we had to hurry to school, but Andy got out, and Aunt Anne followed him. She opened the boot, and he leant in so far that both of his feet were off the ground.

Andy walked towards me, holding something long and brown in both hands. He also had something tucked under his arm. "This is for you," he said, holding out the long brown stick, with masking tape around the middle. "I made it this morning."

"Thanks," I said, trying to sound grateful and disguise my confusion.

"You can be Donatello," he said, "I made you his staff, so you can fight off the baddies."

I smiled, then realised what he had under his arm. A piece of cardboard cut into the shape of a sword and covered in tin foil: Leonardo's katana blade for Will.

"Let me take it in," I said. I couldn't bear for Will to start another argument about whether we were the turtles or not. If Andy wanted us to be Turtles, I was happy to be a Turtle, and that gave me something to chat to Andy about, so I didn't have to think about Liam.

At school, most of the chatter was about the football. That's why Laura Matthews' and Becky Reid's conversation stood out—they were talking about something else. I heard Laura say she'd seen something weird, so I interrupted them. "What did you see?" I said.

Laura glared at me, probably because I don't often go up to girls and start chatting. Also, it was obvious I'd been eavesdropping on her conversation.

"Nothing," she said.

"But I heard you. 'You won't believe what I saw,' that's what you said."

"Well maybe you should have kept eavesdropping instead of interrupting us," said Becky. She tucked her arm around Laura's and pulled her away from me.

"Sorry," I said, after jogging to get back in front of them. "But what did you see?"

"It doesn't matter," she said and, grabbing Becky by the arm, walked off.

I wanted to rush over to Liam, to tell him we had a new lead, but then I saw him with Daniel Richardson, pointing over at me and laughing and figured that he wasn't going to let his annoyance with me go.

At lunch, it became clear that Liam had been spreading some kind of rumour as everyone kept walking away from me without saying a word. I wandered back to the classroom early where Mrs Palmer sat in front of a pile of books with a red pen in her hand.

"Is there any news on who killed John?" I asked.

"I'm sure the police are working their hardest on it," she said, looking at me with sympathy. When did the police ever solve anything like this? This kind of mystery only happened on TV with the likes of Captain Caveman and Scooby Doo sorting it out. The police only showed up at the end once the mystery was solved. Regular crimes were all theirs, but no way was this a regular crime.

Mum picked us up from school. She had to go to the Post Office, so we had to accompany her.

"Have the police been back again today?" Will asked.

"Yes, but they're gone now."

"Did they find anything?"

"Oh, I don't know, Will. They don't tell us every little development. How was school?"

Will muttered something about his teacher, and I wanted to say school was a mess because no one knew what was going on and we get distracted and can't concentrate on a single thing, but Mum wouldn't have wanted to hear that. Liam and Andy were with us too. Liam walked behind me and I could hear him making stupid comments, but I blanked him. Andy had run on a little ahead, but after being warned by Mum not to go out of sight, he stopped and waited further up the path for us. We'd reached Downham Close. The Post Office was a couple of houses further along Main Street. Andy stood on the path pointing across the road to the police car parked outside Shaky Jake's house.

There was no point in relying on anyone else. I ran across the road.

"Thomas!" shouted Mum, but I blocked her out. I was going to solve this—rise above my position of cowardly second sibling and solve the case.

The police car was unoccupied. I tiptoed across his lawn and peered into his front room. The TV was on, but no one was in there. He had a lacy white tablecloth, like an old lady's, on his coffee table. He'd tidied his magazines away.

"Tom, what are you doing?"

I turned around and Laura was on the pavement with her mum and her little brother.

My face felt hot. "Nothing," I said.

"Thomas, get back here, now," Mum shouted, and I wanted to hide.

"Well, I better go," Laura said, and I watched as she crossed Downham Close and headed towards her house.

I crossed the road, and Mum cuffed me on top of the head.

"Don't run away like that. That's the kind of behaviour I'd expect from a toddler, Thomas, not you."

Liam jabbed me in the ribs and made a face at me, so I moved away from him.

At the counter, Mum spoke to Sheila who runs the post office.

She was old. She had white hair and glasses with a blue rim, and her arms wobbled when she got something down from the top shelf. John and I once asked her to fetch loads of different sweets from the top shelf so we could see how much they wobbled. I ate so many Cola Cubes that my whole jaw ached for a week.

Will asked Mum for a Calippo, so I said I wanted one too. In the end we all had one. I took mine to the counter where I spotted a box of Fisherman's Friends.

"Excuse me," I said, staring at Sheila, "Who buys these?"

"Lots of people."

"Could you give me a list?"

"Sorry," Mum said, and pushed me away from the counter, "Ignore him, he's acting daft today."

I leaned to the other side of Mum, "No, a list of everyone that buys them would be fantastic."

"I couldn't do that anyway, love," said Sheila. "My customers don't want me keeping tabs on them."

"I'll take a pack," Mum said. She turned to me, "Your dad likes them. Now stop being silly."

Embarrassed, I shuffled towards the door where Liam stared at the top magazine shelf. He pointed at *Fiesta*. "Look," he said. "They sell it here."

Mum caught up with us. "Liam Carter, what are you gawping at?"

I couldn't help but smirk as Liam's face turned pink.

As we walked back towards our house, we could see the police cars had returned.

"How would you boys like to visit your Granddad?" Mum asked.

Andy sprinted off along the path, and Will joined in, calling out, "Race you to the telegraph pole."

Liam and I watched as Will overtook Andy, but then slowed at the last second to let Andy win.

Andy jumped up and down. "I'm the fastest!"

Liam laughed. "I can't believe you got beat by a year three."

Will smiled and ruffled Andy's hair.

Andy was so excited when we reached Granddad's cottage that he blurted out about his victory as he pushed the door open.

Granddad peered around the doorway from the kitchen. "Well done, little man," he said before looking up at the rest of us. "I wasn't expecting you lot today. Is it my birthday?"

"Sorry to turn up unannounced, Norman," Mum said. It sounded weird to hear his name.

"Always a pleasure," Granddad said. "Got... company at yours?"

"It looked busy, yes," Mum said.

"You boys don't want to sit and listen to us blather on," Granddad said. "Why don't you head into the garage and search for those old photographs I spoke to Tom about?"

I let Will, Andy and Liam leave first and hung back a little.

"Found owt?" I heard Granddad say.

"They might have done, but they've not told us anything. By the looks on their faces, they don't seem to be getting anywhere fast." Mum turned and saw me by the door. She nodded in my direction.

Granddad spun round, quicker than I thought he was able, and tilted his head so that he looked at me with his good eye (he had the green glass eye in, one of the least scary ones). "Try the cabinet—back corner—the one I keep my tackle box on top of."

I left and caught up with Liam, Andy and Will who were looking in a box in the opposite corner from where Granddad had suggested.

"Found anything?" I asked, knowing they wouldn't have.

"Nah, a load of rusty nails and screws," Will said. "Oh, your friends are still here." He pointed behind me.

I turned round. Two of the three pheasants still hung from hooks through their beaks, their foul smell developed into something much ranker. They'd lost most of their colour and the feathers were dark and greasy. Their necks had stretched as if the weight of their bodies had pulled them out of shape. I turned away and covered my nose with the sleeve of my jumper. "We should check over here," I said, my voice muffled by my clothes. With my other hand, I pointed to the cabinet in the corner.

Liam was first over there. He opened the tackle box and pulled out the pot Granddad had got from Teddy Barnham. "Hey Andy, wanna play with the maggots?" As he held it in the air, he must have heard something, as he said, "Shush," and held the tub to his ear. He stared at us, his eyes wide and his mouth open. "It's buzzing!"

"Open it," Will said.

"No, Liam. Don't," Andy said, shaking his head and backing out of the garage.

"Go on!" Will said. "Don't be chicken."

I wanted to see what was inside, but I didn't want to stay on Liam's bad side. "You don't have to if you don't want," I said.

"Why, are you scared?" Liam asked, and he placed the tub on the cabinet and gripped the lid. Will smiled, as he stared at the tub. I was apprehensive, fearing the worst, but knew it couldn't be anything too bad in so small a box. Andy loitered by the doorframe, ready to run.

When Liam tore the lid off, two plump flies buzzed out and flew in opposite directions. One hit the dusty window and crashed to the floor, and the other headed for one of the pheasants and came to rest on its greasy feathers.

"Tom, catch!" shouted Liam, and tossed the pot towards me.

Instead, I moved away and let it hit the floor. It turned on its side, and the crispy carcasses of the remaining maggots fell to the floor.

"Out of the way," I said to Liam and brushed him aside.

He huffed and joined Andy by the door.

I opened the cabinet and inside were a couple of battered boxes. As I pulled the first out, it tore along an edge, and I could see that there were no photographs in there. I pulled it out anyway, but it was full of boring bits of material. The second box was much heavier. I placed my hand underneath it to help guide it out as the box felt damp, and I didn't want it to tear. Jackpot! I'd found the photographs. The dim light of the garage made it impossible to see them, but Will helped me to shuffle the box out into the daylight. We picked up the first photograph. With his slender figure, huge hands, and wild hair it was clearly Uncle Rodney. Although a child in the picture, he looked almost the same, a tall, thin child with comically large hands and clownish hair.

Andy and Liam dashed over to the box and plucked out the picture underneath. In it, a young boy and a girl stood under an apple tree. "Look," Andy said. "It's your dad."

I didn't believe it at first, but the shape of the eyes and the nose gave it away.

"He looks just like Will!" Liam said.

Will glanced at it. "Shut up," he said. "My hair's nothing like that."

But the rest of the face was similar.

"Who's that beside him?" asked Liam.

"Is it my mum?" asked Andy.

The gap-toothed girl with the pudding-bowl haircut was barely recognisable as Aunt Anne, but it had to be.

"Found 'em then," Granddad said, emerging from his cottage.

"You've still got pheasants in there," Will said.

"Oh, I'd darn well near forgot about them. They'll be jus' right for my dinner."

"Can I take them home?" I asked.

"The pheasants?" Granddad said.

"Urgh! No! the pictures."

Mum had also emerged from the house after Granddad. "They'll be too heavy to carry," she said.

"I'll tell you what," Granddad said. "Help me get them onto my kitchen table, and I'll bring them over to you another time. How's that sound?"

I picked up the box, on my own this time, and struggled into the cottage and through the hallway into the kitchen, dodging the various piles of junk on the way. As I popped the box down, I noticed that there was a piece of paper stuck to the bottom of it. I tilted the box forward and picked it off. It was an old newspaper. The headline read 'MISSING BOY FOUND BY LOCAL TEEN', and the picture beside it, though faded, looked much like young Uncle Rodney.

I heard people moving back into the house, so I jammed the paper back into the box to look at later.

NOW

I walk in through the back door, met by a blast of hot air. I breathe in, but there's no oxygen. Gasping at the thick air, my lungs work overtime to extract something worthwhile.

Charlie's behind me, and I go into a momentary panic thinking he won't be able to breathe either. I imagine myself on a plane, the pressure dropping as oxygen masks fall from overhead compartments. I want to pull one over Charlie's face to save him, but our masks didn't fall, and I'm struggling to gasp at the air before me.

Charlie tugs at my arm. I look around, expecting to see him suffocating, but, other than the concern on his face, he's fine.

Knowing he's okay allows me to breathe again. Yes, it's warm, and the aga is still firing away, but it's the shock of being here that I'm struggling with.

I look at where we used to keep Chappie's bed, and I smile. I take in the rest of the furniture which hasn't changed. There are still little squares of mismatched paint on one wall.

The one thing that's new to the house is an armchair in the corner. While the armchair itself looks ancient, the person sitting in it looks older than time.

He's asleep, so he hasn't seen me come in. Somehow, his white hair is thicker than ever. The skin on his face is so heavily wrinkled that it resembles the earth on the droves after a long dry spell. Granddad Norman will outlive all of his children and while that's tragic, I'm glad he's still living.

Charlie stares at his face in fascination.

"That's your great-grandfather," I whisper.

"What's wrong with his eye?" asks Charlie.

Grandad Norman doesn't have a glass in, leaving a gap where an eye should be, and I realise that I never told Charlie the story.

Our words make him stir in the chair, and his eye ebbs open.

"Will?" he says, his voice rattling through thick phlegm.

I can't help but sigh.

Granddad's eye opens a little further. The colour of the pupil has faded behind thick cataracts, and I wonder if he can see at all. "Thomas!" he says.

There is a flutter inside, a brief feeling of elation that I chase back down. I'm not here to rebuild the bridges I burned down; I'm here to make sure nothing rises from the ashes.

Granddad reaches for his cane, grabbing it on the second attempt. He leans forward, using the cane for balance, closer to Charlie who is captured in the cyclops' glare. "This your boy, then?" he asks.

"I'm Charlie." Charlie holds out a hand which Granddad swallows with his own.

"Well, aren't you a polite young man?"

"Where is everyone?" I ask.

"Your mum's taken some food up to your dad. He won't eat it."

"It's happening again," I say, thinking of that photograph of the girl, and picturing John's wounds on her.

"What is?"

"A kid's gone missing."

"Won't be the same."

"How do you know?"

"Can't be, can it, Tom? Not after how all that ended."

I pull a chair from under the table and sink into it. "I don't know," I say rubbing at my temples. "I really don't know."

Thursday 28th June 1990

Chappie hadn't eaten his food again, but his water bowl was empty. I filled a glass at the kitchen sink and poured it into his bowl. He didn't notice. He lay on his side, fast asleep, whimpering. Was he having a nightmare? I stroked him. He felt thinner, his ribs more prominent.

"Don't wake him, love."

I looked up and Mum stood over me.

"He hasn't eaten, Mum."

"He's probably not hungry. It has been hot."

"He's ever so thin."

"I could take him to the vet, but you know, Thomas, he is getting old…" Mum looked away, and then she made a show of looking at the clock. "Oh, is that the time? You'd better get your shoes on, and I'll walk with you and Will to school. Make sure he's ready."

As I was one of John's best friends, Mrs Palmer wanted me to dig the hole for John's memorial tree. I was taken out of class in the morning by Mr Inglehart and he walked me onto the school field, past the infants' play garden, to the spot where the tree was to be planted, a good spot, in view of the swimming pool and the football pitch, the kind of place that I could imagine myself and John sitting under on a hot day.

"We've already prepared the spot," said Mr Inglehart. "So, all we need you to do at the ceremony is to lift the top layer of turf out of the hole."

"What, just the grass?" I said.

"Yes, just there." He pointed.

"But that won't be deep enough for a whole tree."

"No, once you've taken the top layer off, Mr Jenkins will remove the rest of the loose soil."

Mr Jenkins was standing nearby leaning on a shovel. He gave me the slightest nod of his head.

"Would you like to see the tree?" asked Mr Inglehart.

I nodded, and he led me around to the side of the swimming pool where this puny-looking thing leaned against the fence. It was shorter than me.

"What do you think?"

He must have seen the disappointment on my face.

"It's a monkey puzzle tree."

I smiled.

"Yes, I thought you'd like that. They have to be planted while still quite young, but they're fast growers.

"John would have liked that," I said.

"That's one reason why we chose it."

"What happened to John?" I said.

The headmaster crouched and said, "I understand the police are still investigating."

"But it's been ages. Shouldn't they have found something by now?"

"Thomas, it's best you don't let such things concern you and try to strive on with your life."

"But we're not even allowed out after school. Why not?"

"Until the police have concluded their investigation, they believe that it is in your best interest to be under the constant care of an adult."

"Then how am I supposed to forget about the police and what happened when we can't even do the things we used to do?"

"I think it's time you went back to class, Thomas."

"But Sir, it's not fair."

"That's life, I'm afraid. You're sure you'll be okay with the ceremony this afternoon?"

John's parents were there. The school had invited them to come along, and they stood at the back, holding onto one another, watching. Our class sat on the grass and Mrs Palmer stood at the front with Mr Inglehart. He gave a speech first, telling everyone that John was a special child. He was my friend, and I loved him, but it felt funny only saying good things. It didn't seem true. He didn't find maths easy, and I always had to help him, and he could be a show-off, but I guess when someone dies people need to talk about the good stuff. I suppose if I were gone and people were talking about me I wouldn't want them bringing up that I was puny, and I couldn't lift a hay bale over my head. But there were great things they should have said about John that they didn't. He had the power to make me laugh when I was down, he was generous and would share anything without being asked, and he made me believe I could achieve anything.

"Thomas, can you come here?"

I hadn't been paying attention and didn't realise they were ready for me. I moved to the front, and Mr Inglehart handed me the spade. Mr Jenkins came along with a wheelbarrow and plonked it down beside me. I looked at John's parents. She was dressed much smarter than the other day when she'd come to the house. She was wearing this posh black dress, and her lipstick was bright red, but her eyes were black and she kept dabbing at them with a handkerchief. John's Dad was in a suit. I don't think I'd ever seen him before. He looked like he wore a suit every day for work. John said he had an important job 'in the city' and I don't think he meant Ely or even Cambridge.

I put the spade into the ground and then lifted the clump of grass into the wheelbarrow. People clapped, and then Mrs Palmer pointed back to where I was sitting before, so I sat down again. Mr Jenkins dug out enough earth and wheeled the barrow away. Mr Inglehart brought the tree out from round the back. I could tell everyone was looking at it the same way I did: it was too small and didn't do a good job of representing John. I whispered to Brian, who was sitting next to me, "It's a monkey puzzle tree, spread it." That made people giggle and I hoped John would have been happy with that.

After the ceremony, we were allowed to stay out on the field to "share memories of John," as Mr Inglehart put it. I was standing on my own, no doubt because of Liam's rumours, when Laura came over to me.

"I'm glad you're on your own," she said.

"Oh," was all I could mutter.

She must have seen I was hurt. "No, I don't mean it like that. I'm glad your friends aren't here because they can be a bit... silly."

I figured that she was talking about Liam. Could I tell her he wasn't really my friend?

"I wanted to tell you something, something that I've never told anyone."

"Not even Becky?"

"No, not even Becky."

Was she going to declare her love for me? If she did, I would say that I liked her too. I felt the hairs all over my body stand on end and I had to hold back a shudder.

"It's hard to say."

"Go on."

"I... I really liked John."

"Oh."

"I had a huge crush on him, and now he's gone, so there's nothing I can do about it. I'm telling you because you were his friend. Is that okay?"

I nodded. John was my best friend, and he was dead, and for a second I hated him because of what Laura had said. Guilt washed over me, and I felt this feeling of a great weight inside my chest and took back those terrible thoughts. Of course, Laura fancied John. He was the cool one. No one would ever fancy me. But it also made me realise something else about John. He was the only one that liked me for being me, not because we were related, not because of who my brother was, not because a teacher had made us work together. Now I'd lost him and was left with people in my life who tolerated me because they had to.

Aunt Anne dropped us at the end of the road, and as Will and I walked towards the house, I could see that it looked different. As we got closer, I knew why. Half of the ivy had been pulled off, and Mum was busy tackling the rest.

"Afternoon, boys," Mum said. She mopped at her forehead with the back of her hand and took a deep breath. "I don't suppose one of you would grab your mum a glass of water?"

With a puzzled expression on his face, Will went into the house.

"What are you doing?" I said.

"Taking down the ivy."

I looked up at the house. The ivy had been there as long as I could remember, and the brickwork appeared strange without it. Where the ivy had grown into the brick, it left a pink trail, like veins spreading across the face of the house.

Mum snipped again with the sheers and then set them down to grab the vines.

"Why?" I asked.

Mum pulled at the ivy and stepped back. As the ivy tore away from the wall, flakes of loose brick drifted towards us. Mum stepped back into a rose bush and grunted in annoyance. She stopped what she was doing and turned to face me. "It makes it look like we've got something to hide," she said before stepping aside, away from the rose bush.

I noticed that her dress had snagged on the thorns, and, seeing a couple of other small tears, I realised it wasn't the first time she'd stepped into it.

Mum tugged at the vines again, stepping back and yanking at them until they'd either come away from the house or snapped, leaving small worms of vine clinging to the house.

Will returned holding a glass of water. He handed it to Mum. "Do you need some help?" he asked.

"No thanks, love," she said before taking a gulp of the water. "You don't know how long I've wanted to do this." She put the half-empty glass on the ground, unfazed by the odd angle at which it sat, and picked up the sheers again, pretending we weren't even there.

    I went inside, through the scorching kitchen and upstairs to the bedroom. I picked up the *Secret of the Scythe*. The dice were kind; I had a good chance as long as I made sensible decisions. I ventured into the witch's house to explore, knowing I was strong enough to take on any surprises that the book offered. It was worth doing, too. Written on a scrap of paper, hidden behind a broomstick in the witch's kitchen cupboard, I discovered the secret of the path to the Underworld. You had to push on a tiny branch on the trunk of the tree that looked like a disgusting wart near its mouth. I thought of the tree in our field, visible from our window, sure that it had a similar knot. That damn thing was responsible in some way. That damn tree was covered in ivy, just like the house. But if the house could be freed from its dark influence, the tree could be defeated too.

Friday 29th June 1990

They'd taken the name from John's peg, and his P.E. bag was gone. It left a gap between Steven Farley and Brian Harper. For the first time since he'd gone missing, Mrs Palmer also completed the register, flowing from Steven to Brian, not even stumbling at the point where John used to be. They'd had their memorial, and they'd moved on. Even his name sticker had been torn from his tray, leaving jagged white fragments and sticky patches. Was that also the influence of the Underworld? Was the tree sending out brainwaves to erase John from people's memories? Were we supposed to forget that he ever existed, that he'd been a child, like us, and he'd been taken away and murdered? How could we forget when none of us understood why this had happened?

"We can't let it go," I said after finding Will at break time.

"What else can we do?" he said.

"Keep an eye on the tree. See if anyone else is visiting it. Follow Shaky Jake."

"Shouldn't we let the police get on with it?"

"They've done nothing."

"We're stuck, though. We're not allowed out after school, so we can't follow anyone. You can sit around watching a tree if you want, but I've got better things to do with my time."

"He was your friend too," I called out as he started to walk away.

"And I can't bring him back. What do you expect from me?"

To be the hero. That's all.

A surprise waited for us on the playground after school: Uncle Alan.

"Hey boys," he said as Liam and I came out of school, me following several paces behind him. Andy was already with him.

"What are you doing here?" Liam asked.

"The car has been serviced. Got to pick it up from the garage."

Once Will came out (almost last) we made our way to the garage. It was next to the Post Office, and we were following Laura and her family. We were also much quicker than them as her little brother was on a tricycle which made him slower than walking pace. I desperately didn't want to pass them or talk to Laura. I'd done such a good job of avoiding her during the day. Andy marched in front of them, and then they came to a stop, ready to cross the road. I was going to have to pass them. Laura didn't even look back. She crossed beside her mum, who held her brother's tricycle in one hand, and his hand in the other. If Laura knew I was there, she didn't care enough to even look at me.

We sat on the low wall outside the garage while Uncle Alan collected the car. I was still gazing at Laura's house, having watched her and her family go in a minute ago. I should have said something.

"Look who's coming," said Liam, nudging Will.

Shaky Jake was crossing the road opposite us. Andy leant back, hiding behind Will, who stared at Jake. Shaky hadn't noticed us until he reached the middle of the road, and when he did, he snaked back the other way to walk down the middle of the road in the direction of the Post Office.

"Shit, look," said Will.

A car had come around the corner and was heading straight for Jake. It blared its horn and came to an abrupt stop. Jake hurried onto the pavement and shrunk into himself as the driver shouted abuse out of the window.

"At least we're not the only ones who think he's a freak," I said, which Liam mimicked.

A few minutes later Uncle Alan pulled up in his car, which shone in the sun having been washed and polished. "Hop in," he called.

As he was about to pull off the man with the Fu-Manchu moustache came running out of the garage.

210 DEAD BRANCHES

"Mr Carter," he cried. "Don't forget your receipt."

As Uncle Alan was thanking him, I saw Shaky Jake walk by, having left the Post Office. Under his arm, he held a copy of *Fiesta*. It had to have been him that was spying on kids outside the school.

When we got home Will was in no mood to talk, so I picked up my notebook and took it downstairs. I was sitting at the kitchen table drawing a map of the farm, marking out the drove and the tree and the bypass and the spot where I found John's body when someone knocked on the door.

Mum stared at the wall. A series of coloured squares had been painted on it, and a number of tiny pots of paint sat by the sink. Was she literally watching paint dry? I don't think she'd noticed me come down and sit at the table, but she rested her hand on my shoulder as she passed to get the door. I looked around. John's mum. I closed the book.

"Hello Mrs Tilbrook," she said, "I wanted to pop over to let you know that John's funeral will be on Monday."

"Thank you for letting us know."

Barbara Glover leaned around Mum to look at me.

"Thanks for what you did at the school, Tom," she said.

I didn't know what to say, so I smiled, and she looked back at my mum.

"If Tom wants to come along to the service, it'll be fine. I know they did their own thing at the school, but he was John's best friend."

"We'll see," Mum said.

"Okay, goodbye. Bye, Tom," she said, but before I could say goodbye, Mum pushed the door closed.

"Can I, Mum?"

"Can I what?" she said as she headed back towards the sink.

"Go to the funeral?"

"I don't know, Tom. Funerals are difficult things, and you've already had the memorial service at school as Mrs Glover said."

"She also said I was his best friend."

"Let me speak to your dad about it," she said.

"I know it's a sad thing, but I want to be there."

"See what Dad thinks," she said before turning her back on me and prying the lid off another tiny pot of paint.

Saturday 30th June 1990

Dad had said I could go to the funeral, but I needed a suit. Dad knew a tailor in Ely, someone he'd gone to school with, though you wouldn't have thought that from looking at him. Half the size of Dad, the only hair he had on top of his head was a thin comb-over. He had little, round glasses which sat at the tip of his long nose, a tape measure hanging around his neck, and a pencil tucked behind his ear.

"Do my eyes deceive me, or is that Trevor Tilbrook?" said the tailor as he came over to Dad and shook his hand.

"Hello, Fred, how's business?"

"We have thin days and fat ones. I prefer the thin ones; they use less material."

He was odd.

"Still at Little Mosswick?" he said, and he rubbed his hands together.

"Yep, we don't go far."

"I drove through a week or two back—I won't be doing that much longer, what with the bypass opening soon."

Dad cleared his throat.

"So what can I do for you today? New suit?"

"It's for my son."

"Ah, is this one your eldest? Will, is it?"

I shook my head.

"No, this is my young'un. Thomas."

"And what's the occasion?"

"It's for my friend's..." I muttered, but Dad cut in.

"Funeral."

"Ah," said Fred. "Not that young lad that was killed in your village?"

"Yep, that's the one," Dad said with a sigh.

"Terrible business that. Has anyone been arrested?"

"Not as far as I know. Police are struggling. They keep combing over my land, looking for clues, but they ain't getting nowhere."

"Of course, it was on your farm that the body was found. Terrible."

"It was Tom who found him."

I looked up at Fred and he stared down at me. I was worried his glasses were going to fall off and hit me in the face.

"A friend of yours?"

"Yes, Sir."

He sighed, shook his head, and then took the tape measure from around his neck. "Let me measure you up and we'll see what we can do."

He measured my leg and scrawled something on a pad of paper with the pencil he took from behind his ear. Then he asked me to hold out my arms. "Like this," he said and put his arms out in an aeroplane pose. When he did so his shirt rode up his arms on both sides and I was amazed by how hairy his arms were. It was like he had a hairy sweater beneath his shirt. I glanced at his hands as he pulled the tape around me. No wonder he didn't wear a watch, it would forever be getting snagged in his arm hair.

As he worked, he breathed onto my face; his breath smelled like the tubs of maggots in Granddad's garage. It made me think of The Maggot from the Top Trumps cards, but other than the smell, Fred was nothing like him. He didn't look like any of the cards I could think of, but those arms made me think of the werewolf. The Top Trump werewolf wore a fancy blue suit. I made a mental note to check if it was a full moon when John went missing.

Fred inspected the measurements he'd taken.

"Yes, we should have something in black in your size, young man. You're lucky; we have a limited stock of junior-sized suits."

He fetched a pair of trousers, a jacket and a shirt from the back room and handed them to me. "Would you like to try them on?"

I had to hold them up to stop them from trailing on the floor. I went into the changing room and stripped off. I could hear Dad talking to Fred.

"It must have been hard on the young man, finding the body of his friend like that."

"He could do with some toughening up."

I started to hum to myself to drown out the rest of the conversation. Hearing Dad's opinion of me was the last thing I needed. No good, I heard every word.

"Yes, but I wouldn't wish a sight like that on one so young."

Distracted, I got in a muddle and buttoned the shirt lopsided. I undid them and tried again, taking more care.

"Was the young boy interfered with in any way?" said Fred.

"Police aren't saying, but there's some weird fuckers about."

I pulled on the trousers.

"A beastly business," said Fred. "There are some real monsters out there."

I heard a rustle from behind me and stepped out of the changing room, straight through the curtain without lifting it. The trousers were long, and I stepped on the back of them when I walked.

"Ah," said Fred, "Yes they'll need turning up a touch, come here."

He had me lift my arms again, and he tugged at the shirt. He put a finger between the collar and my neck which caused me to bend my neck over to that side so he had to struggle to get his finger out.

"Jacket and shirt fit fine," he said.

Then he put his finger into the front of my trousers.

"Not too tight?" he said and took his finger out again. I could feel his wiry hand hair scratching at my skin.

"No, they're okay, just a bit long," I said.

"Are you happy with that, Trevor?"

"Looks fine to me."

"When is the funeral?"

"Monday."

"Ah," said Fred. "Well, I have to make the alterations. How long are you going to be in town for?"

"Wasn't planning on stopping."

"Could you pick them up on Monday, first thing?"

Dad sighed. "I should think so. We'll come back then."

"Okay, thank you, Trevor. Good to see you again. Send my regards to the missus."

We left and Dad shook his head. "Monday? All that time to turn up a pair of trousers. He'll charge the earth too."

"Did you know him, Dad?" I said, trying to change the subject.

"We went to secondary school together. He was a twat then, and he hasn't changed."

"Oh," I said.

"Come on, boy, let's get home."

But before we got to the car park, he stopped. He put out his hand and stopped me too.

"Wait here," he said, and then he turned around, and he was gone.

He'd left me outside the haberdashery. Mum sometimes went in there. It always took ages because she'd get speaking to the woman behind the counter. I think they knew each other from school, too. I guess no one moves far from Little Mosswick.

It seemed like forever before Dad returned. He was carrying a bag from the tailor shop. When he caught up with me, he pushed the bag into my chest and I had to grab it before it fell to the ground. It was my suit. Dad's face was red. He put two fingers into his collar, and you could almost see the steam bursting out.

"I thought it wouldn't be ready until Monday," I said.

"I had another word with him to see if he could speed it along."

When we were on the way out of Ely, Dad had me get a sweet out of his glove box for him. They were those horrible Fisherman's Friends.

"You can have one if you like," he said as I fished into the packet and took one out.

"They're yucky," I said.

"Suit yourself. You won't get nothing else."

They reminded me of the time we found the empty packet of them and that magazine. I peered into Dad's glove box as I put the sweets away. If that was where he'd shoved the magazine, he'd moved it later. I poked about among the oily rags in the footwell with my feet. It wasn't down there either.

On the way home, after navigating the new roundabout that would lead onto the bypass, Dad took a detour. I daren't ask where. We left the village, and a minute or so later, he turned off the road, and I realised where we were going: Greater Mosswick. I had no idea why we'd want to go there. Dad took the turn that led to the river and pulled over by the pub, The Merry Maidens.

"Wait here," he said and left me in the car.

Two minutes later he was back.

"Thought Rodney might be here," he said. "I needed to have a word with him."

"The man in the suit shop said there are real monsters," I said to Will who was busy filling out his Italia 90 World Cup wall chart. We didn't buy *TV Times*, Mum and Dad watched the same programmes every week, so there was no point, but Will had seen that this one had the chart included and had asked Mum to buy it for him. He had to forfeit his ice cream that day, but he said it was worth it.

He'd not filled it in since the end of the group stage, but now he'd put all the results in and was writing in the teams for the quarter-finals.

"You've made me smudge it," Will said.

He was filling in the quarter-finalists. He'd smudged ENGLAND.

"If they don't win," he said, "it's your fault."

"Real monsters, Will. That's what he said."

"He can't have meant real monsters, can he? That's made up to scare kids."

"Or is it?"

"Why don't you go ask Mum what she thinks."

As I was heading for the door Will said, "And pass the Tip-Ex."

Mum was sitting outside on one of the patio chairs. We didn't have a patio, just patio furniture on the lawn. She gazed across the fields. I thought she was staring at the tree.

"Mum," I said.

She kept staring dead ahead. It was like it was hypnotising her.

"Mum," I said again.

She turned and looked at me.

"Are you okay?" I said.

"Do you think the bypass will ruin the view?"

I looked out, past the tree. I could see two policemen out there, walking on the new road.

"Listen to how quiet it is."

I listened. I could make out a lorry rumbling down Main Street.

"It'll never be this quiet again once that road opens."

It had been noisy for months as they'd been working on the road, and I figured it would be the same amount of traffic that used to go through the village. But that was distracting me from the reason I'd come down to talk to Mum in the first place.

"Mum, do you believe in monsters?"

"No, don't be daft."

"It's just, Dad was talking to the tailor, Fred, and he said there were some real monsters out there."

Mum stared at me. "Did he say that to you?"

"No. I was getting changed. I overheard him and Dad talking about John."

"What he meant, honey, was that some people could be monsters."

"So, there aren't real monsters, but people can be monsters? That doesn't make sense."

"Don't worry about that. How's your suit? Can I see it on?"

"Okay," I said and ran back upstairs to change. When I returned, Mum wasn't sitting outside anymore.

I wandered into the yard to see if she was out there anywhere, maybe talking to Dad. He was out there; she wasn't.

"What the fuck are you doing out here in that?"

I looked at my suit.

He marched towards me. "You've not had it five minutes. Do you want to get it covered in dust and dirt? Do you want to get grease, oil, and slub slarred all over it?"

He grabbed me by the head. His hands were so big that he could do that. They could wrap around my entire skull and crush it in an instant if he wanted to. He turned me around and guided me back into the house. "Now what in God's name are you playing at?"

"Mum wanted to see."

"And what made you think she'd be standing in the middle of the yard?"

"She was outside before."

"Before what?"

"Before I got changed."

"Get out of that suit before it gets wrecked. I don't want to see you in it again till the funeral."

As I slinked back through the kitchen towards the stairs, Mum popped her head out of the utility room. "That's nice, dear."

I remained upstairs for the rest of the afternoon not wanting to speak to either my mum or my dad. I picked up *The Secret of the Scythe* and remembered where I'd left it, having discovered the secret way to enter the Underworld. I read on and was making good progress through the book until a series of poor dice rolls left me weak after a battle with a creature called a dead-eyed wanderer. It was intense, and when I put the book down Will was fiddling with the TV. I checked my watch. It was time for the first quarter-final match and another excuse not to leave the room. Argentina versus Yugoslavia wasn't a brilliant match; there were no goals in normal time or extra time, so it went to penalties. Then something weird and unexplainable happened: Maradona, one of the best players in the world, one of the footballing magicians, one of the superstars of the game, the man who claimed to have God on his side, missed. His penalty didn't go in. I looked at Will and he looked as puzzled as me. It was more proof, if more proof were needed, that something was wrong with the balance of the world, and I was convinced that it was because of the evil emerging from the tree I could see from my bedroom window.

Sunday 1st July 1990

The more I read of *The Secret of the Scythe,* the more convinced I became that our oak tree was linked to the Underworld. The description matched, though I was going from memory, as I didn't make a habit of studying the tree.

"Will," I called. He was still under the covers, but I knew he was awake.

"What?" he groaned.

"Wanna come for a walk with me?"

"No."

"Why not?"

"We won't be allowed to go anywhere."

I could barely hear him as his mouth was muffled by his blankets. I got off my bed and moved over towards his. "Come outside with me. I need to look at the tree."

"Why?"

"I need to check something."

Will pushed the covers away from his mouth. "What do you need me for?"

"This is going to sound stupid..."

"What else is new?"

"Listen, Will. Something's wrong with the tree. I think it might be a pathway to the Underworld."

"You're right, it does sound stupid."

"It's all linked: Granddad's eye, the wasps, John, the thing that chased me."

"If I go along with this, what's in it for me?"

"Don't you want to be the hero? Don't you want to solve the mystery?"

"No, I want gold and riches." Will jumped out of bed.

"I don't have any of those."

"Okay, but if I come with you will you stop this fantasy crap?"

"If you see what I think you'll see, will you believe me?"

"Tom, I..." Will rubbed his forehead. "I don't think this is going to turn out as some great fantasy. There's no secret passage to Narnia."

"I'm not talking about Narnia, I'm talking about a pathway to the Underworld, a place worse than anyone's idea of Hell."

"It won't be that, either, Tom."

"What do you think then?"

"Someone kidnapped John. They kidnapped him and tortured him. Somehow, he got away, and he ran, but he couldn't make it. Some evil bastard killed him. That's what I think, Tom."

"What just a man?"

"Just a man."

"A madman?"

"Maybe."

"Like Shaky Jake..?"

"Maybe."

"So maybe it was just a man, but maybe he's involved in the Underworld..."

Will sighed. He selected a pair of shorts and a t-shirt from the clothes he'd strewn around his half of the room.

I found the page with the description of the demon tree and slid a bookmark in place. If this was the same tree, what would we do? And who would believe me if I couldn't even convince Will?

"Take Chappie," Mum said, when we told her where we were going. "And don't go any further than that field, you hear me?"

Chappie barely raised his head when I picked up his lead. He used to go crazy the second he heard the metal hoops rattling, but if anything, he buried his head further into his basket to avoid coming with us. He perked up when Will started to stroke him, and he arched his neck to lick Will's wrist, and when the lead was around his neck he did hop out of his basket, but by the time we got to the door, we were practically dragging him.

The fresh air seemed to do him good, and he took advantage of the opportunity to pee on a few weeds, but when we got close to that awful tree, he stopped. He didn't want to go near it any more than I did.

"What did you need to show me?" asked Will.

I fumbled with the book, but I didn't dare look at the page in case the tree attacked while my guard was down. I passed Will the book.

Will looked at the passage.

"Read it out," I said.

Will held the book in both hands and read the entry I knew so well.

159

After emerging from the thick brambles, you see a tree in front of you, and a feeling of intense dread surges through your body. Its thick trunk is scarred by a great scorch mark which runs from one side to the other and looks like a cruel mouth. Above it, two sunken knot holes which appear to have no end make eyes, and on one side, between the eyes and mouth is a tiny broken branch sticking out like a wart on a witch's chin. Will you:

Wait in the bushes	Turn to **359**
Put your finger in an eye hole	Turn to **24**
Stick your knife in the mouth	Turn to **234**
Twist the wart	Turn to **112**

"It's the same," I said.

Will glanced from the book to the tree. A wrinkle formed on his brow. "I don't see it."

"What do you mean you don't see it? It's exactly the same!"

"If you squint, maybe."

"It's close enough."

"Close enough for what?"

"In the book, the tree is a gateway to the Underworld."

"So?"

"Maybe that's why it's going wrong. We have to find a way to block it."

"That's ridiculous."

"No, it isn't. Don't you see that it makes sense?"

"Why can't you see this for what it is? Someone killed John because they're crazy."

"What's inside the tree made them crazy. Ever since it first tasted blood, maybe when it took Granddad's eye, its power has been building. We have to stop it."

Will shook his head. "You have to stop it, Tom."

"I can't by myself."

"No Tom, you don't have to stop the tree–you have to stop talking like that. It's time you grew up and stopped telling silly stories."

"That's not you talking. That's Dad. That's what he'd say."

"Maybe Dad's right. I'm going back."

I didn't have the power to convince him to stay, so I stared at the tree. The upper branches shook though there was no wind. I stared into the eyes, long and hard. Chappie whined and pulled away, but I remained fixed on the tree, a single tear running down my cheek. Crybaby. That's what Dad would say.

I wasn't going to have that. I wasn't going to be the baby. I stepped towards the tree, bent down and grabbed a handful of ivy. If Mum could strip the house, I could do the same to the tree.

Chappie whimpered, and, as I pulled, I turned to shush him. With a good yank, the ivy came away, but I wasn't paying attention. What a fool. I turned back to see a lump of bark flying towards me. Trying to avoid it, I turned my head, but the bark smacked into the side of my face. I let the ivy fall from my hands and it fell onto the chunk of bark I'd yanked off. I touched the side of my face, which felt tender, and there was a little smear of blood. If I'd not turned my head, it could have had my eye.

Chappie growled and took a step closer to the tree. He barked.

I touched my face again and saw more blood on my hand. I screamed and stepped towards the tree, slamming my fists into the trunk, shouting the worst words I could think of.

Chappie came towards me and closed his teeth around the leg of my trousers trying to pull me away.

I looked down at him, and he was shaking.

He kept looking away, urging me to follow him from the tree. I'd never heard him make such panicked noises.

I turned to walk away but found the tree had a hold on me. It pulled me back. I could feel panic rising but chased it back down. I was going to be the hero. I looked down and saw that I'd got my foot wrapped in the vines. I gave my foot a wiggle, freed myself, and walked away with Chappie glad to be hurrying away. A figure walked along the drove turning his head from side to side. Shaky Jake. I wanted to confront him, to stop him from getting near the tree to get more orders from the Underworld, but then he'd see my face, and he'd know I was injured, he'd know I'd been crying, he'd know I was weak, and he'd use it against me. I couldn't have that.

Instead, when I got in, I watched him from the bedroom window. There was a moment where I swear that he looked up at me, and I'm sure he was laughing.

I avoided Will for the rest of the morning and afternoon by reading *The Secret of the Scythe.* It took a couple of playthroughs, but I reached the end. There were monsters in the Underworld worse than in any of the other books I had played. I solved the mystery of the dead-eyed wanderers, who were said to slip through from the Underworld and possess the bodies of the living, their purpose being to bring fresh souls to the Underworld for the demons to feast upon. The book also featured the cruellest trick in the series. Often you would meet a fellow traveller who would help you overcome obstacles, such as Sym in *The Crypt of the Sorcerer*, but Kyle, the traveller you meet in *The Secret of the Scythe,* turns out to be possessed by the dead-eyed wanderers, and if you trust him, when you are confronted by another dead-eyed wanderer, he stabs you in the back. Literally. There are no friends to be found in the Underworld, and no one you can trust.

Eventually, I made it through to the end and gambled for the life of my master, but the game doesn't end there. The Grim Reaper honours the deal but sets the rest of his demons on you. First, I was forced to fight the chief demon who is one of the strongest enemies in the series, and the only one I've ever found with the ability to heal by sapping stamina. After beating him, his skin peels off and he turns into a fire demon, an even stronger enemy, and I used all of my provisions to get my health up enough to beat him. After that I had to flee the underworld, testing my luck to avoid being consumed by a fast-spreading fire, which the fire demon summons with the last of his strength. But I was lucky, and I escaped. The fire chased me back through the entrance to the Underworld and then, after I burst through, the tree is engulfed in flame, and burns to ashes, closing the door to the Underworld forever.

I turned towards the window and stared out at the tree, picturing it being consumed by fire.

That was the world I wanted to remain in. I wanted to remain in my cost bubble, in my room, away from everyone and everything. I didn't want to watch the football with the rest of them, but Dad made me. "Waste of bloody electricity," he said, "you sitting up here on your own, like a demented hermit, when we're watching it downstairs."

I was tempted to say that I didn't want to watch it at all, but I did, so I joined them. On TV, one of the reporters spoke to a man standing outside a mud hut. He was wearing a grass skirt and had a long mask over his face.

"That's a witch doctor from Cameroon," Will said.

I stared at the TV as he said, "Cameroon will win, 2-1."

"Bloody mumbo jumbo," Dad said.

Part of me wanted the witch doctor to be right, so I could rub it in Dad's face (in my head), but only for a second. I needed England to win the game. They had Gazza, and his magic was surely more powerful.

Cameroon started well, but after about twenty-five minutes England had a run with the ball. It got crossed into the box and David Platt was there again. It was like he'd teleported into the box to arrive just in time to head the ball into the goal, and England were winning. Even Dad gave a little cheer. Everything would be okay.

In the second half, Cameroon brought on Roger Milla, and I was worried. I looked at Will, and he was worried too. Milla had been amazing in the tournament so far, and there was every chance it was about to get tough. Milla won a penalty. Gazza, of all people, brought him down in the box. I know he was only trying to get the ball back, but Dad doesn't understand football, and said, "Daft prick."

I clenched my hands into fists and hoped Cameroon would miss. At least Milla wasn't taking the penalty. I thought that maybe they were giving England a chance, but they weren't. Shilton dived the wrong way. 1-1.

As the game continued, Roger Milla danced around the England players. It was like his feet had been enchanted, and I thought of the witch doctor and the spell he said he was putting on the team, and I could see it was true. Milla beat Gazza, he beat Wright, and he beat Platt to be through on goal. There was no way he could get it past England's giant of a goalkeeper, Shilton, and he knew it. Instead, he passed the ball across the goal to another one of Cameroon's substitutes who kicked the ball into the net. 2-1. The witch doctor knew.

When England got the ball up the other end and Wright slotted a perfect ball through to Lineker, I knew he wouldn't score. He didn't even have the chance to because one of Cameroon's defenders slid in and took his legs away. The referee pointed to the spot, but it didn't matter. England weren't going to score. Lineker took the penalty himself. He was good, but he was going to miss this one. He ran up to the ball, and he kicked it high, and I knew it was going to go over the bar and sail off into orbit, but then the net bulged, and I didn't understand what had happened. It was 2-2. "The witch doctor was wrong!" I cried out as I stood up.

Dad turned to look at me and frowned.

I sat back on the sofa, with my heart pounding. What did this mean? Was it more proof that magic wasn't working? Or was there a stronger force working for England? I didn't know what to think anymore, and the football became interesting again. It was no longer a foregone conclusion.

Cameroon had a couple of good chances, but Shilton wouldn't let them by. Eventually, England started to pass the ball better, and Gazza looked like magic again. He slid a perfect ball into Lineker, but he never got to it because two of Cameroon's players squished him like a piece of meat in a sandwich. Another penalty. Lineker must have been scared of missing this one, because instead of kicking it high up where the goalkeeper couldn't reach it, he hit it hard straight down the middle. The keeper dived to the side where he shot last time, and England were back in front. The Cameroon players were exhausted. It was like the spell had worn off them, and they couldn't get the ball back. England had won. We were in the semi-final of the World Cup.

"You boys had better get to bed," Dad said before they'd even cut away from the pitch and gone back to the studio. He stared at me. "You've got a big day tomorrow."

Of course. John's funeral. How had I forgotten about that?

NOW

When Mum comes downstairs, I'm drinking tea with Granddad, having a safe conversation about how I've been over the last few years. I came in defenceless but managed to put the barrier up in time to stop the sadness that hangs on his face from affecting me. He recounted my dad's steps in the years since I last saw him, so I know when he got out of prison, and the terrible condition that his lungs were in at the time. He doesn't tell me what caused it.

Charlie runs at Mum and hugs her around the midriff, and she nearly drops the tray of untouched food she's carrying. However hard I tried to keep them apart, there's a bond between them. I get up and take the tray from her, allowing her to put her arms around Charlie and give him a proper hug. She's aged in the months since I saw her last. The skin is loose around her face, and her hair is thin and lacking colour.

"Let me make you a tea," I say.

At first, she refuses and insists upon doing it herself, and I realise that, in this house, I never once made her a cup of tea.

Charlie convinces her by saying, "Dad makes nice tea," and she sits. Charlie pulls his chair close to hers.

"There's cake in the cupboard, too, if you want some."

I open it, unsurprised to find the layout as it ever was, and grab the half-eaten Victoria sponge cake from the shelf and place it on the table. The knives are still in the same place. Yesterday, had you asked me to draw this kitchen, I doubt I would have been able to do so with any accuracy. Now, I could tell you the home of every utensil.

"I saw Liam outside," I say.

"He's done a great job keeping this place ticking over."

"How's Andy?"

"He's not so good."

"I figured. Liam said he was the same, but I didn't ask the same as what."

"He didn't take his mum's death too well."

"Why didn't you tell me about that?" I ask, and a pang of guilt hits me when I see Mum's face strain to breaking point. "Sorry," I say, hoping I've caught it before it's too late. "That's my fault. They were my stupid rules."

"That boy can't see sense no more," Granddad says. "He's thrown away the sense he had. Poor bugger."

"Drugs," Mum says.

It wouldn't just have been his Mum's death that damaged him. I'd broken him before that with my stupid beliefs and what we'd suffered that night because of me.

"Alan does his best," Mum says.

Charlie finishes his cake and starts fishing around inside his mouth.

"Charlie," I say, and give him the look.

"What you got going on in there?" Granddad asks.

"Wobbly tooth."

"Come here, and I'll give it a yank."

Charlie shakes his head, and Granddad laughs.

"If you don't let it come out naturally, the tooth fairy won't come," Mum says.

"I don't believe in the tooth fairy," Charlie says.

"Then what happens to your teeth when they fall out?" asks Granddad.

"Dad throws them in the bin and gives me a pound."

"Oh."

Mum gives me a look, but I don't feel guilty. Leading Charlie to believe in the tooth fairy would only lead to him eventually realising I had lied to him. What good would that do?

Monday 2nd July 1990

The last time I had a day off school and Will didn't, he had a tantrum and insisted it wasn't fair. Not this time. He didn't say anything; he just put his hand on my shoulder before he left the house.

Mum was already in her dress, but Dad was absent.

"Where's Dad?" I asked.

"Out tinkering with something. He'll have work to do when he gets back."

"But haven't we got to get going?"

"We've got hours yet, love."

"But we've got to get to the other side of Cambridge."

John was being cremated. They were going to burn his body. I didn't understand why.

"Your dad knows what he's doing."

"Why isn't he being buried?"

"Well..." Mum came over and sat at the table beside me. "Some people prefer cremation. They don't like the idea of burying the people they love in the ground. I imagine they want to spread his ashes somewhere special."

"His what?"

"Ashes."

"Where do they come from?"

"Oh, dear, I don't want you to worry. After the body is burned, they collect the ashes and put them in an urn."

"Why isn't he being buried in a graveyard?"

"I don't know, Thomas. Maybe his mum and dad aren't religious. They might want to do it in their own way. Why don't you sit and watch some telly until we leave?"

Dad didn't come in for ages, and when he did, he stood at the sink scrubbing away at his hands for an eternity. I stood in the kitchen glancing at my watch, but I kept my mouth shut. When he stepped away from the sink, I could see that his hands still had dark smears on them in the creases. "Don't worry, boy," he said. "We've got plenty of time." He went upstairs to change.

When he came down, he was in his smart suit. His hands were pink, with slight spiderwebs of grease marking them. His face was red, and though he hadn't shaved for days, the beard looked deliberate and tidy. He might have even combed it. His suit was the same colour as mine. It was the smartest I'd ever seen him, apart from the picture of him and Mum on their wedding day. "Ready, boy?" he asked, and then he came over and adjusted my lapels. "Very smart," he said.

I was waiting for the 'but', or for some kind of criticism, but it never came. Mum came down the stairs a second later. She glanced at the clock, but neither of us dared say anything about how late we were running.

Whether Dad knew time was against him, or if it was for some other reason, he drove like a loony. He overtook cars on the approach to bends and was lucky nothing was coming the other way, apart from one time when the car flashed its lights at us, and had to swerve into a layby. Mum held on to the door handle, and I could see beads of sweat on Dad's forehead.

I kept looking at my watch. Dad must have seen me in the rear-view mirror.

"Take that bloody thing off." He turned to glare at me.

Concentrate on the road, I kept thinking, but he wouldn't turn back. I pulled the watch off, tearing the strap in the process. Once it was off, he turned around and then tugged at the steering wheel to pull us back into the lane. The horn of the car we'd almost hit, without any of us having seen it, blared.

"Spend a bloody fortune on a nice suit, and he's wearing a cheap plastic watch."

It wasn't a cheap plastic watch. It was a Casio calculator watch, a birthday present from Mum and Dad though I doubt Dad had much to do with it. I'd torn the strap between two of the holes. I could still wear it, but it would either be too loose and fall off or too tight and uncomfortable.

Where Dad had been sweating his hair at the front had darkened, and it had become scruffy where he'd mopped at his brow. He dug his fingers into his collar and breathed heavily.

As we pulled into the car park, Mum turned to him. "Let me sort you out." She reached towards him with her hankie.

Dad batted her hand away. "Leave it."

When we got out of the car, a group of people came towards us, some holding cameras. Among them was the man who'd come to my door before, Joseph Price. "Thomas!" he said. "Have you got anything to say?"

Dad glared at him, and he stopped.

Inside the chapel, soft music played, music that John wouldn't have liked at all. Most of the pews were already filled and we had to sit near the back. There were a few people from the village who I recognised, but mostly it was full of strangers that I assumed were John's family. The dark wood of the pews and the old brick made the place look gloomy. At the front was a podium which looked wonky because the wood on one side bowed. Small, round stained-glass windows on either side of the building were split into blocks of colour, red and yellow on one side, green and blue on the other. It wasn't like the stained glass at church: no sign of Jesus, and no cross. You could take a church being dark and dingy, because it was a church, and it was hundreds of years old, but the newest and brightest thing in the chapel was the red curtain behind the coffin.

Until then I'd not thought about the coffin. John was in there. My friend, John, who let me borrow his imported Gameboy before anyone else, who knew all the words to John Barnes rap from 'World in Motion' and could sing it perfectly, who'd picked me first in the football on days when I was feeling down, even though I was crap, was inside that wooden box with his body twisted and broken, with horrible red marks around his neck, with the hole in his head which got bigger, darker, and angrier every time I thought of it. John was inside that coffin because something had killed him, and I hadn't even got around to finding out what or why. Thinking about John, in that tiny box, I felt the roof of the chapel drop. The walls started to close in. I couldn't breathe. I wanted to get up and run, and Dad must have felt me fidgeting because he put a heavy hand on my leg and stared at me.

The sun must have come out from behind the clouds, because, as Dad was staring at me, his face went red. I looked up at the beam of light that shone on him through the red stained-glass panel. A slight yellow hue coloured the wall behind him, but it was nowhere near as prominent as the red on his face. It was getting hot in there, and my suit felt too tight and Dad's hand felt like a claw digging into my leg.

I looked around the room, seeking an escape route. A man emerged from behind a pillar, perhaps having come from a back room, and took his place on the podium. He cleared his voice, and he had everyone's attention. His words didn't sink in, but I started to calm down. I watched John's parents. His dad's arm was around his mum, who dabbed at her eyes with a handkerchief. Occasionally I looked at Dad, whose face was still illuminated in red light, giving him the appearance of a demon, and I had to turn away.

When the man at the front stepped down, I realised I'd missed his whole speech. John wouldn't have been able to sit through it either. Then he must have pushed a button, because the curtain opened, and two men helped guide the coffin through the hatch behind the curtain. I could imagine it opening up into a giant furnace which would swallow up the coffin whole, and spit out the ashes. For some reason, when the coffin had gone through and the curtains closed the Mario death tune played in my head. But John can't play on; he doesn't have another life.

As soon as we emerged from the chapel, Joseph Price approached. "How do you feel, Tom, that whoever did this to your friend is still out there?"

I'd never seen Dad move so fast. He had the front of Joseph's shirt balled up in his fists, and he lifted him off the ground. "I told you to leave my boy alone," he said, and he threw Joseph to the ground. Dad then loosened his tie, opened the top button of his shirt, and stomped towards the car.

Dad diverted on the route home to stop by Uncle Rodney's house in Greater Mosswick. He knocked on the door, and a few seconds later, he peered through the pane of glass beside the door. After that, he moved to the next window along (I think it was the living room; it had been a long time since we'd been over to Uncle Rodney's house) and peered in.

"Not home," he said as he got back into the car. He drove off and again stopped by the Merry Maidens.

While waiting for Dad, I caught a glimpse of the pub's sign. I'd never noticed that the three women dancing on the sign (presumably maidens) were topless. I felt uncomfortable and looked away so that when Dad opened the door, it made me jump.

"Well, I don't know where he is," he said shaking his head. "It's like he's disappeared off the face of the Earth."

Had the Underworld taken him too? He was an adult. He was tall and strong. If it had grown powerful enough to take Uncle Rodney, then it wouldn't be long before it was too powerful to be stopped.

We were back in Little Mosswick before the end of the school day. Dad dropped me and Mum off outside the post office, and we were going to walk down to the school so we could walk home with Will. We left the post office (armed with a Sherbet DibDab for me, and a Sherbet Fountain for Will) and headed for the school. As we passed Downham Close, I saw a police car outside Shaky Jake's house. He had to be a major suspect.

"My shoelace is untied," I said to Mum, and crouched down, staring across the road the whole time. Had they discovered that he was possessed by a dead-eyed wanderer? Had they made connections with the Underworld? The front door opened, and two police officers came out. Shaky was standing at the door, looking shakier than ever.

"Come on," Mum said. "Your brother will be out in a minute."

"The other one needs re-tying too," I said and watched the police officers get into their car, leaving Jake at his door. He closed it, and before the police had even started their engines, I could see his living room curtains twitch.

"Why didn't the police arrest him?" I said as we started walking again.

"How do you know he did anything wrong? The police have questioned a lot of people."

"But Mum, he's a weirdo!"

Mum stopped walking and put her hands on my shoulders. "Thomas Tilbrook, you do not speak about people in such a way. Jacob Radford may have his problems, but you can't go around accusing him of being a child murderer without any kind of evidence."

"But Mum...!" I didn't have an argument, but I knew there was something wrong with him. He was an agent of evil, and all I needed was proof.

I tried to figure out some kind of plan, but a few minutes later, we'd reached the school, and the hum of conversation broke my concentration. Aunt Anne was already waiting on the playground for Liam and Andy. I moved over to the door to Andy's classroom in order to catch him first. When he came out, I said to him, "Don't you think it would be a good idea to go see Granddad today?"

"Brilliant!" he said. "Let's go."

"You have to ask your mum. She'll say yes."

Andy dashed over to Aunt Anne while I strolled back with an innocent look on my face.

"Andy wants to go over to see Granddad. Do you want to join them?" Mum said.

Perfect. We could talk through some of our ideas with him, and he could help us come up with a plan to get rid of the portal to the Underworld, and bring Shaky Jake to justice.

Granddad was in his garden on his knees, wielding a trowel.

"Hi Dad," said Aunt Anne. "The boys wanted to come over and say hello."

"Hello boys, you can go now," Granddad said.

"No!" cried Andy, and Granddad laughed and opened his arms for Andy to run into.

"You can leave us here, if you like. Granddad will walk us home later," Liam said.

"Oh, will I?" Granddad said.

"If that's okay, I mean," Liam said.

"Of course, that's okay."

"Well if you're dropping them back, why not come in for dinner?" asked Mum.

"That's an offer I can't refuse," Granddad said. He struggled to his feet and waved off Mum and Aunt Anne.

Will started prodding around in the ground with the trowel Granddad had left on the ground, and Liam and Andy were peering into the holes he made, looking for worms.

"Now," Granddad said, as I bent over the border, "that's not your school uniform. You better step away from the dirt or your mum will have me hung, drawn and quartered."

I stepped back as Andy spotted a fat worm and plunged his fingers into the black mud to grab it.

I glanced down at my suit. "It was John's funeral today."

"I see. Well, you scrub up pretty well."

I moved closer to Granddad. "Why do some people get cremated?"

"Some folk prefer it that way."

"It seems wrong to burn the body."

"No, there's nothing wrong with that. He's at peace now, and they can scatter his ashes someplace nice."

"Will you be cremated when you die?"

"When I die? What makes you think I'm going to die?"

"You're not... but."

"I've already got a spot in the graveyard. Next to your nan. Couldn't leave her by herself."

"I saw the police today. Outside Jake's place. How come they didn't arrest him?"

"Why should they?"

I sighed. I was going to have to explain the whole thing. "You know that tree that took your eye?"

"Of course, I know it. Damned thing."

"It's a portal to the Underworld. Maybe when it took your eye it got this thirst for blood, or it might have been before. Do you know about anything else that happened with the tree before that?"

"Well, this is a tall tale," Granddad said. He straightened his back and then bent down to my height again. "Nothing before that I know of, but it was a fair old tree then, and I don't know its entire history. Tell us the rest of this tale."

"It's not a tale, Granddad, It's true."

"That may be so, but let me hear it."

I told him about the dead-eyed wanderers, and how they possess regular people and force them to bring healthy souls into the Underworld for the demons to feed on. Will, Liam and Andy had stopped playing with worms and were listening to my story. Liam folded his arms and shook his head.

"And that's why that poor boy's body was found not far from the tree?"

"Exactly," I said. "He escaped and was coming to me for help. So how do we stop it?"

"You've got a good imagination, and that's normally a healthy thing, but you're getting yourself tied up in knots. There's nothing so complicated going on here. There's no Underworld. Someone killed that boy, and we might never know why. It was a nasty, evil thing that was done, and we've got to live with that."

"But the evil's got to come from somewhere. People don't murder for no reason, do they?"

Granddad couldn't answer. "Let's rewind a bit. You said something about old Jakey, what's he got to do with this?"

"I think it was him that took John."

"You can't go around accusing people of things like that. That's up to the police to do."

"The police were at his today."

"That don't mean a great deal. They've spoken to Teddy a couple of times, too. They've been back here more than once. Jake's got enough to worry about without more rumours."

"So, what can we do?"

"You don't need to do nothing. Soon enough, the police will work it out, and things will go back to the way they were."

"But the tree, there's something wrong there."

"You've got some imagination, I'll give you that."

"There's more. I think it's taken Uncle Rodney."

"Rodney? What's he got to do with this?" Granddad appeared to be shaking.

"Dad was looking for him, and couldn't find him anywhere. Said he might have disappeared off the face of the Earth."

"I think it's time I walked you boys home." He turned to Andy. "Go wash your hands under the tap before you go, or your mum will have me strung up."

Granddad walked beside his pushbike, the box of photographs in the basket at the front. "You have a look through these," he'd said, nodding his head towards them. "That'll take your mind off the bleedin' Underworld and murderous trees."

The road was quiet as Granddad first dropped off Liam and Andy and then walked up to ours. When our house was in view, we realised why.

We arrived home to find Mum and Dad sitting outside, looking at the traffic passing on the horizon.

"Bypass is open then," Granddad said, as we watched the stream of traffic on the new road. It was far enough away to not be able to hear it well unless you tried.

"Bloody glad I stood my ground about my land," Dad said when he saw Granddad. "Any bleeding closer and we'd be choking on the fumes."

I couldn't even see any exhaust smoke from the cars, they were that far away. They never sat out here anyway and were only doing it to have something to complain about. I wished it was closer. I wished Dad had sold the land. They would have flattened the tree and closed the portal. John would still be alive. Or when they tore it open the creatures inside might have flown out and consumed us all.

Granddad stopped outside with Mum and Dad, the three of them watching the road, and Will urged me to follow him up to our bedroom.

"Look, Tom," he said. "You have to stop this talk about the Underworld. People are going to start thinking you're weird."

"Will, I don't care if you don't believe me. There are two ways you can see this. Either someone killed John because that's what people do; they go around killing each other when they feel like it, or people do bad things because some kind of evil overtakes them, but it's something you can stop. I know what I'd rather believe."

"But we're not going to bring John back."

"Don't you think I know that? I saw his coffin go through the curtain. His body was in there, and it was going to be burned into ashes. I know more than anyone he's not coming back, but shouldn't we be doing all we can to make sure the person who did this to him gets caught?"

"What can we do?"

"Nobody's going to suspect we're investigating this. I've seen Shaky Jake come backwards and forward to the tree. We might be able to see something that no one else has seen yet."

"Okay," Will said. "We'll do something, but please, give it a rest for tonight. You're driving me crazy. Go have a look at those photographs. Take your mind off it."

Will had agreed to help. That's all I needed. Maybe the distraction would be good for me. I went back to the box, and the newspaper article I'd glanced at the other day was still tucked down the side where I'd left it. I read the headline again, 'MISSING BOY FOUND BY LOCAL TEEN', and stared at the picture. It was definitely Uncle Rodney.

It was hard to make out all the words on the paper as it was badly faded, but it turned out that the boy had been missing for a couple of weeks. I moved it closer to my face as I tried to make out the name. There was a rot hole in the middle of it, but it left 'Jac   ord'. The boy was found close to death, with heavy bruises on his neck. Later in the article, his forename was repeated. Jacob. Could it have been Jacob Radford? Shaky Jake? Skimming through the rest of the article as best I could I saw words like 'deeply traumatised', and 'hasn't spoken since the incident'. The article finished with the phrase, 'police are still investigating.' Was this the moment that Shaky Jake was enlisted by the Underworld? He had to be stopped.

Tuesday 3rd July 1990

We had a plan. We'd needed Liam and Andy to help out, so I needed Will to speak to Liam for me. We wouldn't have long to pull it off, but it was a chance to start checking things out. Before school, I had another flick through my investigation notes. So many ideas had been ruled out. All the possibilities where John was still alive had been crossed out. Anything that involved his body being destroyed (such as spontaneous human combustion) was gone. We'd put the idea about alien transition to bed. There were a couple of persons of interest listed, but most of those were based on the fact that they looked like the creatures on the Top Trumps. Only one idea added up: the Underworld. Only one suspect stood out: Shaky Jake. I stuffed my notebook into my bag and set off for school.

The plan was simple. Liam, Will, and I had to sneak out of school after lunch and go snoop around Shaky Jake's until we found evidence proving him a psycho-killer. We'd be back in school before the end of the day, or close enough for Andy to blag us enough extra minutes. It was a perfectly constructed plan.

After lunch, once Mrs Palmer had got us started on some maths problems, Liam grunted.

"What is it, Liam?" said Mrs Palmer, annoyed to be distracted from working with the kids on the blue table.

"My stomach, Miss," Liam said. He scrunched up his face in feigned agony.

"I suppose you'd best go to the office and report to Miss Harding," she said. Miss Harding was secretary, school nurse, and occasional dinner lady all rolled into one.

"I feel so dizzy," Liam said. "I'm not sure I can stand."

"Oh Liam, that doesn't sound good." Mrs Palmer hurried over to him. She put a hand on his forehead. "Oh, you do feel hot."

Liam groaned.

He was overdoing it. She wouldn't trust me with him if she thought he was seriously ill. "Do you want me to take him to Mrs Harding?" I blurted out.

"No, I think it's best if he gets some air." She moved over to the window and pushed it open. "Come sit here, Liam."

"I think I'm going to be sick," Liam said, clutching his stomach.

"He's been like this before, Miss," I said. "He'll projectile vomit."

"You better go," she said and ushered him towards the door. "Are you sure you'll be okay with him, Thomas?"

"Oh, I'm used to it Miss. I've been on holiday with him when he's eaten too many donuts." This wasn't a lie. It was gross.

"Okay, but you hurry back to class once he's at medical."

Once outside and a little way down the corridor, Liam straightened up. He pulled the prepared note out of his pocket and then knocked on Will's classroom door. He opened the door, peered in, and then looked at the note. "Sorry, Miss, but Mr Inglehart needs to see Will Tilbrook in his office, please."

Seconds later the three of us were in the corridor together where we found Mr Jenkins exactly where we hoped to find him.

"What are you boys doing out of class?"

"We were sent to find you, Mr Jenkins," Will said.

"Whatever for?"

"There's a small boy stuck in the toilets by Mrs Harding's office."

Mr Jenkins shook his head and went marching off, leaving the path to Andy's class clear. There was an exit down to the field and the swimming pool beside it. The trouble was that Andy's teacher, Miss Norris, would see us if we went across the field. We were waiting on Andy.

I checked my watch and started to panic. Surely, he wasn't still pretending to be stuck in the toilet? Jenkins must have opened it from the outside? But what if he had broken the lock while pretending to be stuck and had become stuck for real? Before I panicked too much, I heard his cough. He was about to make his dramatic entrance to his classroom that would create our diversion.

We heard Andy open his class door and say, "You won't believe what happened to me, Miss…"

We went through the door, ducked down past the classroom window and hurried along, as best we could, to the fence that surrounded the swimming pool. We took a moment to catch our breath, knowing we were out of sight, and then continued along the edge of the field. If we were caught, we'd be in huge trouble. They'd phone home, for sure, and that would be worse than any punishment the school could come up with. I gazed back over my shoulder at John's memorial monkey puzzle tree. That was why we were doing this. The risk had to be taken.

At the bottom of the field, we scrambled into the ditch between the two elderberry bushes and jumped across the trickle of water to emerge on the drove, close to where we'd found the sweet wrapper and the magazine. If we followed that round, we'd come out by Downham Close, and Shaky Jake's house.

The road was clear. That was one advantage of the bypass. We crossed over and approached the home of the dead-eyed wanderer. First, we went around the back. A five-foot tall fence surrounded his back garden, but a few knot holes in the wood allowed us to peer into his surprisingly tidy garden. A slab path ran across the middle and on either side, the grass had been recently cut. A shed stood in one corner and from the muttering inside we deduced that Jake was in there.

"If he's hiding something, it'll be in there," Liam said.

"Liam, go knock on his door. When he goes to answer it, I'll jump over the fence and see what's inside," Will said.

Seconds after the doorbell rang, Shaky Jake started muttering to himself and then closed the shed door. As soon as he was through the back door, I gave Will a boost up and he pulled himself up and over the fence. He dashed over to the shed and peered inside.

"How's he doing?"

I looked around, and Liam was beside me.

"Aren't you delaying Jake?" I said, infuriated.

"I did a knock door bunk 'cause I didn't want him to see me."

"Will, hide," I called out in a loud whisper.

He emerged from the shed and then slipped behind it.

"Go back and knock again. Give Will time to get out."

"You're not in charge."

"Do you want Will to get caught?"

Liam huffed and then returned to the front of the house.

Shaky Jake had come back outside and was approaching the shed. "Rotters!" he cried when the bell sounded again, but instead of going straight to the door he scurried to his grass pile and picked up a pair of shears from the top of it. "Bloody rotters," he said and disappeared into the house.

"Will, quick!" I said.

Will popped his head into the shed again and then pulled out a thick blue rope, and a dusty white t-shirt.

"I've got to warn Liam," I said, "Can you get back over?"

Will nodded. He dropped the rope on the floor but stuffed the t-shirt as far into his pocket as he could and hurried towards the fence.

I ran around the side of the house towards the front and almost bumped into Liam.

"Thank God," I said, "I didn't want you there when he opened the door."

"I saw him through the front panel. He was holding some kind of knife, so I scarpered."

"Bloody rotters. I'll have you. One day I'll have you!" we could hear him shouting at the front of the house. We made our way round to the back where Will dusted grass from his school uniform.

"What is it?" I said.

Will took the t-shirt and held it out. We could see the Little Mosswick Primary School logo and recognised it as a P.E. top.

"We better get back," I said.

"No," Will said. "Let's see what he does."

We peered through the knot holes when he returned to his back garden. He saw the rope on the floor, dashed over to it, and fell to his knees. He picked it up and cradled it in his arms. Then he got up and went to the shed. He threw the rope inside and looked from side to side. He checked behind the shed and then looked over his shoulder again. When he was convinced no one was watching, he went over to the grass pile. He grabbed his rake and pulled the whole pile to one side and dusted away the mud. He lifted the slab it had been hiding and pulled out a pair of gloves. Mopping the sweat from his forehead with the back of his hand he called out again, "Rotters. I didn't do nothing. Why do you punish me?" He buried the gloves again, pushed the grass pile back into place, and sat rocking on the ground.

The sky had darkened while we'd been out of school and with the sun hidden behind a thick layer of cloud, I felt a chill, part it no doubt from the thrill of finding evidence to catch a killer. As we returned to the drove, out of sight of any villagers that might be driving down Main Street, Will pulled out the P.E. top.

"We've got to phone the police," Liam said.

"We can't," I said.

"Why not?" asked Will.

"They'll know we bunked school and broke into his shed," I said.

"We can call anonymously," Will said. "We'll leave a note in a box, telling them what we saw, and where."

"We can draw them a map," Liam said.

"Good idea," Will said.

"We'll leave it somewhere they can find it, and then call from a phone box," I said.

It was dodgy that Jake had that school uniform, but what proof did we have that it was even John's? "Name tag!" I blurted out, and Liam and Will looked at me. "All of John's clothes had name tags. Check the t-shirt."

Will pulled the t-shirt back out of his pocket again and peered into the neck hole. "Torn out," he said and shrugged.

I snatched it from him and checked myself. A small tear in the back of the neck indicated where the little white label used to be.

The clouds could contain the rain no longer, and as we approached the school, it gushed down. Despite hugging the edge of the trees for cover, we were getting drenched. It had been so dry that most of the droves had become dusty, but the rain turned it into a thick paste that stuck to our trousers.

We got back into the school without being spotted but were leaving muddy footprints behind us. Jenkins would be furious.

I popped my head inside my classroom door. "Liam's still in the toilet, Miss," I said.

"Do you need some help?"

"It's okay, I've been to the office. Mrs Harding has called his Mum, and she's coming to get him."

"Well if he's waiting for his mum, you'd better come back to us."

"I can't."

"Why not?"

"He sicked on my leg. It smells. I better not come in."

Mrs Palmer sighed. "Don't bring it in here. Can you borrow anything from the lost property?"

"I rinsed most of it off... but it's wet. I don't think I can sit down."

"I suppose the best thing is to wait with Liam. You'll have to catch up with these maths problems tomorrow, Thomas."

"No problem. Thanks, Mrs Palmer."

Aunt Anne was waiting for us on the playground under a huge umbrella. All the parents had umbrellas open which made a huge covered canopy. "How did you three get so wet?" she said, looking at Liam, Will and me, and then at Andy, who was bone dry.

"Dodgy tap in the toilets," Will said.

"And trust you three to be there when it went wrong. I don't know. Anyway, Tom, Will, a bit of bad news, you'll have to come home with me."

I was pleased. This would give us the opportunity to put together our evidence box.

"Why, what's up?" Will said.

"The police are back at yours again. Your mum phoned and asked if I could feed you some tea. Let's get you out of the rain."

We huddled together under the umbrella until we made it back to Liam and Andy's house. While Aunt Anne found some of Liam's clothes for Will and me to wear, Liam found a suitable shoe box. Together, we constructed our note. We were honest, in as far as we said we climbed into his garden, and then we listed what we'd found. The t-shirt we put in the box, along with a map Liam drew which indicated the spot where the gloves were hidden.

"Should we sign it?" Andy said.

"We can't," Will said. "It's anonymous."

"But we could sign it as the Turtles?"

"We're not the Turtles."

"The Crusaders then?"

"All of that was a game, Andy. This isn't a game. We can't put our names to it."

So, it was done. Only facts, no fantasy. We revealed only what we'd seen, and none of the speculation running through our heads. Was the rope tied around John's neck? Did Shaky Jake wear the gloves when he strangled John? Why did he keep the t-shirt in his shed, and what other souvenirs was he hiding?

Once complete, we had to convince Aunt Anne to let us out. There was a phone box outside the house next door, so we didn't need long, and Liam had us kitted out in raincoats and old trousers so the rain wouldn't be an excuse, and Andy had readied a good reason.

"Can we go outside?" Liam asked.

"It's raining," Aunt Anne said.

"But I made a paper boat," Andy said, holding his recently folded piece of paper aloft.

"You'll get soaked."

"We've got our raincoats on, and it'll be so cool!" said Andy.

"Okay, but only five minutes."

We had so much energy, so much tension, so much adrenalin, that none of us felt the rain on that brief journey to the telephone box.

Liam had convinced Andy to give up the only ten-pence piece in his money box, and he held it proudly as we huddled inside the telephone box.

"Where should we leave our evidence?" Liam asked.

"Here," Will said.

"In the phone box?"

"It'll stay dry and be easy to find."

"What if someone else takes it?"

"They won't. The police will be here within minutes."

"Who's going to make the call?"

"I will," I said. I felt it was my duty.

I shuffled past the others, picked up the handset, put the money in, and dialled 999.

The operator asked what my emergency was, and I asked for the police. Within seconds I was put through and asked for my name.

"I can't tell you my name, but we have evidence for the murder of John Glover in Little Mosswick." They tried to cut in, but I kept talking. "I am leaving it in a shoe box in this telephone box on Main Street, near number twenty-six. The evidence shows that Jake, who lives at the corner of Downham

Lane and Main Street is hiding something. Please check it out as soon as possible." I clicked the phone back into place, and there was a tinkle as the ten-pence piece came back out again.

"Hey, I got my money back," Andy said.

We floated Andy's paper boat, which soon fell on its side and bobbed away before returning to the house, and though my legs were soaked, I couldn't feel a thing.

"What were they doing?" I asked Mum when we got home.

"Searching the whole field."

"I'll tell you what they were doing," Dad said. "They were cutting up the land and finding the sum total of bugger all. Waste of bloody time."

"What are they looking for?"

"A clue, because they haven't got one."

There was no way I was going to get any sense out of Dad. His hair stuck up in crazy tufts, and his beard was bushy and wild. I couldn't look at him, so I gazed into the corner. Chappie's basket caught my eye. It was empty. His food bowl was still full, and I'd put that food in there in the morning before I left for school.

"Where's Chappie?"

"How the fuck should I know? Maybe the police have taken him in for questioning. They need to eliminate him from their enquiries. Maybe they've promoted him to lead detective because the current lot are bloody clueless."

"Mum, have you seen him?"

"Sorry?" she'd tuned us out. Maybe that was the best way to cope with Dad.

"Have you seen Chappie?"

"Not since I let him out this morning. He'll be hiding away from the rain somewhere."

I grabbed my raincoat. "I'm going to look for him."

"Stay in sight," Mum yelled, panic in her voice as she followed me out the door and repeated the instruction that I had no intention of obeying.

The rain continued, but not with its earlier force. As soon as I left the house, my eyes locked on the tree. Chappie wouldn't have gone there, not after the way he froze in fear when close to it before. He knew better than that. He also knew the location of all of our hideouts. I went to them one by one. Narnia was flooded, which reminded me why we'd abandoned it in the first place. Moon Base One was deserted. We'd not been there for days because of the curfew. I walked around the edge of the field, peering into the overgrown ditches as I went. There were a couple of runs where animals had gone in and out, and I tried calling Chappie, but there was no response. I walked around the top of the field, with the bypass only metres away, at the top of the bank. The police had staked off a larger area of the field with tape, and they'd turned the ground over, leaving dark ridges and darker troughs over half of the field. I looked again at the tree, and then my eyes fell on Chappie.

The white tops of his ears stood out, but his coat was camouflaged by the mud that covered him. I struggled through the mangled earth over to Chappie. "Hey Chappie," I said. He didn't respond. The surrounding ground was soft and I could feel my feet sinking into the mud. "Chappie," I called again and reached out to stroke him. He was still. "Chappie?" I touched his rain-sodden head, and it flopped over, lifeless. "No, Chappie!" I said. "You can't be dead. Not here." I put my arms around him and tried to lift him up, but the mud was sucking him back in. Laughter made me look up. The tree shook its branches, drenching me with collected rainwater. I hugged Chappie again and tried to pull him to me. His lower half was caught among the ivy. I slid my arms down, so my face was on his cold, wet, body and worked him away from the tree's grip. I fell back as his body came free and he dropped on top of me. I lifted him to the side, away from the tree, where the ground was firmer. I shuffled back and could feel my shoe held by the ground. It was trying to pull me in. I was around the back of the tree; surely it couldn't pull me into its mouth from there? I imagined it spinning round to face me, the mouth opening, and the branches dropping behind me and pushing me towards the entrance. I could sense the dead-eyed wanderers inside, ready to pull me in, and despite being soaked through, I could feel my temperature rising due to the presence of the fire demon inside. I shook my head and banished the vision, refusing to let them inside my brain. With my free foot, I kicked at the tree again and again, and then I pushed that foot against it and pulled hard on my stuck foot. It came, but without the shoe. I reached forward and grabbed my shoe by the laces and gave it a good yank. They were going to snap. Somehow, they held. I put it back on and felt the mud inside squelch into all the gaps. Gross, but I had no time to worry about that. I picked up Chappie and took the safest path back to the house.

"They got him," I said when I bundled inside.

"Who?" Mum said before she turned to look at me.

I must have looked some sight: soaked through, covered in mud, and with Chappie in my arms.

"Don't bring him in here covered in muck," Dad said, getting up from his chair and putting the paper down on the table. Normally they were so careful to hide the news from me. On the front cover was a picture of John, and beside it a picture of the crematorium, with the headline, 'REST IN PEACE'. Under that, a related story. 'New lead in Mosswick Murder Case?'

"He's dead, Dad," I said and put Chappie on the table.

I didn't see his hand coming. A sideways swipe caught me on the side of the head and sent me flying to the floor. Then he must have realised what I'd said, and he stared at the dog.

Mum stepped away from the aga and looked at the table.

Will must have heard the commotion because I heard his feet on the stairs, and a few seconds later he peered at us too. I was on the floor, covered in mud, my face burning; Dad stood in the middle of the kitchen, his chest heaving; and on the table, the mud and water from his coat soaking into the table cloth and turning it from white into a murky grey, was my pet, my friend, my dog, Chappie. Dead.

Mum was first to move, and it was over to me.

"Come on, let's get you out of those filthy clothes. Will," she turned to him, "start a bath running for your brother."

Will turned and went up the stairs, and Mum helped me up.

"Trevor, take Chappie out to the barn. We can sort out cleaning him up and burying him later."

I let Mum help me up. She was in total control, watching Dad as he picked up Chappie and carried him out. I let her lead me into the utility room and whip off my clothes. She grabbed the picnic blanket and wrapped me in it. She rubbed my arms to get warmth back into them. "You poor thing," she said. "Finding your dog like that." And she stayed with me, saying sympathetic words until Will shouted out that the bath was ready. She led me upstairs and then left me alone to wash.

As I sat soaking in the tub, I played it through in my head. We were close to catching Shaky Jake, and the Underworld had responded by taking Chappie. Getting Jake arrested would not be the end of it. There would be repercussions. It was possible that the armies of the undead were gathering for an assault, or they could send more dead-eyed wanderers through. Leaving Chappie at the gateway to the Underworld was supposed to be a warning. It was the Underworld showing me they could get at me, and that I had to leave them alone. There was no way I was going to let them get away with it.

"Will," I said, wrapped in a towel and dripping onto our bedroom floor.

He paused his game.

"I know you don't believe me about the Underworld, but I want you to help me."

We spent the rest of the evening formulating our plan.

NOW

"Do you want to go up and see your Dad, then?" Mum asks. With the tea drank, the cake eaten, and the conversation stalled, I can think of no excuse. I want to say no. There's a certain level of comfort sitting here, but seeing Dad will spoil that.

"Come on," she says, and I'm obliged to follow orders.

Like when I was a child, she decides she's going with me. She opens the door and I peer up the stairs. They stretch out, endlessly. She glides up them, and, tentatively, I climb onto the bottom step. As soon as I place my foot on the first step, I shrink, making the next almost insurmountable. I use the handrail to pull myself up and stretch my leg up as far as possible to reach the next step. This one feels like it's made of marshmallow, and I'm sinking. In the extreme heat, it's melting. I grab onto the next step but part of it comes away in my hand.

"Close the door," calls Mum from the top.

I turn round to close the door at the bottom of the stairs. It slams like the door of the aga.

I clamber the rest of the way up the steps under her watchful eye.

"Sit down," she says.

I sit on the top step, and she sits next to me. "I suppose there's no Father Christmas in your house either?"

If I was at home, I would have told her it was none of her business. I would have threatened to stop her from seeing Charlie. But in my old home, I'm as powerless as I was when I was ten. I manage a nod.

"Don't you feel that Charlie is missing out?"

I shrug. I want to tell her he's not missing out. I want to tell her he's experiencing these things on a much higher level than other children, but I can't think how to get the words out. I'm tongue-tied again, like I so often was here.

"Look in here," Mum says. She pushes herself up from the step with difficulty. She opens the door to my old bedroom, the room I once shared with Will.

"See that poster on the wall?"

Bowser. I remember Will tearing it out of a magazine that John gave us.

"Does Charlie have any posters on his wall?"

"Yes," I say. He has a poster of the periodic table.

"Any kids' posters?" says Mum, seeing right through me.

I shake my head.

Mum goes into the cupboard and takes out a box while I wait at the door, afraid to cross the threshold.

"I kept these," she says as she struggles across the room with the box. She places it at my feet and pulls it open. The sun emerges from behind a cloud to shine through the window and illuminate the row of green spines. "I know that you wanted to throw them out, but I couldn't let you."

I scan the titles, *The Caverns of the Snow Witch, Appointment with F.E.A.R.* and of course, *The Secret of the Scythe.*

"Does Charlie have any books?"

"Of course he does!" I picture his bookshelf, the rows of encyclopaedias, *Horrible Histories,* and the collection of magazines about rocks.

"Does he have any stories, Thomas, real stories?"

"No, Mum!" I say, raising my voice at her for the first time in my life.

"You can't blame stories for what happened."

No. I blame myself. But before I can tell her that a booming voice comes from the room down the hall, a voice I've not heard for a long time, a voice that scares me as much as it always has. "Stay out of Will's room."

I run.

Wednesday 4th July 1990

At school, all anyone could talk about was the World Cup semi-final. Their excitement meant they weren't bothered by the drizzle. England were playing West Germany for the right to play Argentina in the final who had knocked out Italy the night before. We didn't watch that game. We didn't even think about it as we plotted against the encroaching evil. This game was different, though. An England win would keep the magic alive.

The West German team lacked magic. They played without flair. Their approach was to bore the opposition to sleep by passing the ball from side to side. England, on the other hand, had Gazza. He was a proper player. Plus, we had Waddle and Beardsley, and David Platt had turned up out of nowhere to become a goal-scoring wonder. All those players had the ability to get the ball to Lineker, and he was the best striker in the world, so he wouldn't miss. Even if the Germans did manage to lull England to sleep, they'd have to get past Shilton the giant.

The only person who didn't want to talk football was Liam. "Do you think they got our message?" he said as soon as he saw us on the playground.

"They must have done. They couldn't have ignored the call," Will said.

We'd talked last night about involving Liam and Andy in our plan but had decided to leave them out of it. Liam had never been behind the Underworld idea, being more convinced about an alien invasion, but now his thoughts were pinned on Shaky Jake.

"After school," Liam said, "we should find an excuse to walk down past his house. They might be digging up his whole garden." Liam must have noticed that I was unenthusiastic about his plan. "What's wrong with him?" he said to Will.

"Chappie died."

"Damn. Sorry about that."

Liam had been with us on some of the best times we'd had with Chappie, walking through the droves, making our own bows and arrows, and building bases. Chappie always loved a game of fetch, too. He was one of the gang. I felt myself welling up again, so I ran.

Tears clouded my eyes. I headed towards the toilets to wipe my face. Laura stood by the entrance. The closer I got to her, the more she smiled. I wasn't even embarrassed by the tears in my eyes. I could tell her about Chappie. She'd understand; she'd make me feel better.

But as I got closer, I realised that she wasn't making eye contact with me; she was looking over my shoulder. She was looking at someone else. Once inside I turned and looked back through the window. She hugged Chris Jackson, and they walked off holding hands. I lost sight of them as my eyes clouded with tears.

"We've had a thought," Mum said when she came to pick us up at the end of the day. "Wouldn't it be fun for Liam and Andy to stay over tonight so we could watch the football together?"

Andy jumped for joy, and Liam gave him a high-five. I looked at Will and he kind of shrugged. "Yeah, that would be cool."

"Ace," I said, with a new version of the plan already working itself out inside my head.

"We've got some business to deal with first," Mum said, "but if you come over for around six?"

That bit of business was putting Chappie to rest. The rain had stopped by the time we got home, but the sky was still dark and the clouds looked heavy.

Chappie was clean again, and Mum had tied a red handkerchief around his neck. He used to like to wear it when he was younger, but in the last few years, it seemed to irritate him. Dad had dug a hole in our garden under one of the bushes where Chappie often liked to lie.

"Am I okay to put him in?" asked Dad. He looked at Mum.

I nodded, and Mum nodded at Dad, and he eased Chappie from the blanket and into the hole.

"Well?" he said, and my first thought was that I'd done something wrong. "Have you got any last words for him?"

"Bye, Chappie." I said. "You were a good friend."

A raindrop fell on my face.

"Will?"

"We had fun together," Will said.

Dad held the shovel out for Will to take. He took a little of the dirt from the top of the pile and poured it on top of Chappie.

Will then passed the shovel to me. The rain started to fall harder. One drip landed in the gap between my hair and my collar and followed the path of my spine down my back. I looked down at Chappie for the last time as I tipped the earth onto his head.

"Leave it to me now, boys. Get inside before you get too wet."

We didn't mention the plan to Liam and Andy. We figured we'd fill them in after the game. The start was so hectic, that I almost forgot about the plan altogether, with England winning three corners, and coming close to scoring each time. Gazza was playing well, with the ball glued magically to his boot, and he forced the German keeper into a couple of good saves.

England were the better team; somehow Chris Waddle hit the bar from almost halfway, but there were no goals in the first half. England played better than they had done in the whole tournament, proving good still existed in the world.

In the second half, West Germany took the lead, and in the only way possible, with a deflection. Brehme hit a shot after a free kick, which Shilton was already diving to save, but the ball hit Parker and looped up in the air. Shilton was already flying the wrong way. There was no way back, and the ball fell into the net. It wasn't over. I believed in England, and they didn't let me down. They made chance after chance, but it looked like they weren't going to score. I didn't give up on them. When Waddle was brought down in the box, and the referee waved play on I still had a feeling that we were going to be okay. Paul Parker, no doubt trying to make up for the ball going off him for the German goal, ran up the field and smashed in a cross towards Lineker. It bounced off a German player's leg, but then Lineker controlled it with his knee and knocked the ball into the only bit of space in the penalty box which wasn't swarming with West German defenders. He swung back his foot and shot into the opposite corner of the goal, giving their keeper no chance. We had ten minutes to win it, and then we had more important business to deal with.

No further goals meant a much later night than planned. It was extra time for the third England match in a row. They'd scored in extra time in the last two games, so why should this be any different? When Klinsmann jumped to meet a cross and headed the ball towards the bottom corner of the goal, I didn't doubt that Shilton would save it, and when the ball dropped to the same player in the box, I knew he'd miss. But then Gazza went sliding into a tackle and it felt as if something had gone badly wrong with the world. It seemed to take an age for the referee to pull out the yellow card, but Gazza knew it was coming. You could see it on his face; he was going to miss the World Cup Final.

Until that moment I was certain England would do it, but that card caused doubt to flood over me. I could see the tree out there and knew that it would be laughing at us. Its powers were strong if it could influence events in Italy. I wanted the game to be over so I could put that damned tree to rest forever. Instead, I had to sit and watch the inevitable. Extra time passed with no winner, so it would end with a penalty shootout.

The first six penalties were all scored before Stuart Pearce stepped up. I hadn't been able to watch any of England's other penalties, and this one was no different. I closed my eyes and put my hand in front of them too for double cover. The blackness in front of me formed an image of shaking branches and a cruel mouth. Before Dad even cried out, "You bugger," I knew he'd missed. The Germans scored the next one. They had to miss one, or it was over. I made myself watch Waddle's penalty, afraid to close my eyes again, and I watched him kick the ball over the bar and into the crowd. England were out, and it was my fault for playing with forces I didn't understand.

I went straight up the stairs to prepare for the assault. The first part of that plan meant cleaning my teeth and putting on my pyjamas. Will wasn't far behind, and Liam and Andy were hurried upstairs by Mum minutes later. We had to go to bed, or at least pretend to. Everything had to seem normal until after Mum and Dad were asleep.

We filled Liam and Andy in on the plan. Earlier in the day Will had gone out to the barn and moved a can of petrol to near the back door. He'd swiped the keys for the tractor and put them under a rock. I'd taken a box of matches from the kitchen cupboard. All we had to do was go down to the tree, cover it in petrol, and set it alight, closing the door to the Underworld and trapping the evil beings inside. Will would drive the tractor onto the field and run down anything that emerged. Simple.

"Will, I was speaking to you the other day about this," Liam said, nodding his head towards me.

"We're doing this. I don't believe the Underworld theory, I don't believe in aliens, but I do believe that when that tree is gone, this will settle down."

"But why?"

Will pulled Liam to him and whispered something in his ear, and then, for the benefit of all of us, "I want my life back. In three weeks, it's the summer holidays, my last summer holidays before secondary school. We have to end this before then, or how can we enjoy it?"

We waited until we could hear Dad snoring. It didn't take long on those nights in which he'd had a can or two of beer, and he'd had a few while the football was on. Will went first and expertly took the stairs, missing the creakers. I waited in the corridor while Liam and Andy crept down. They weren't so familiar with the floorboards in the house, and a creak made the whole house gasp.

"That you, Thomas?" It was Mum's voice.

"Just getting a drink."

"Okay, love. Night."

"Night Mum," I said, and we continued on our way.

It had rained while the football was on, and while it had stopped, thick purplish clouds still hung in the sky. It was around eleven o'clock, and I felt like it should have been darker. I guess it was unusual for us to be up so late. I grabbed the petrol can, and Will recovered the keys. We edged towards the barn to get the tractor.

Will arrived first and huffed loudly.

"What?" I asked in a whisper, but when I arrived by his side, I saw the problem. Dad had moved the combine, blocking the tractor in the barn.

"You still wanna do this?" Will said.

We'd have to take down anything that emerged from the portal by hand. "We're doing this."

We traipsed around the edge of the field, with the ground soft under our feet. A couple of times Andy lost his balance. He was much shorter than us and had trouble picking his feet up high enough to stop them from getting stuck.

We paused in front of the tree. The light of the moon had crept between the clouds and shone on his twisted face.

"So, it has come to this," I heard the tree say in my head.

There was a rumble.

"He's hungry," Andy said and took a couple of steps back, but then the sky lit up with a flash of sheet lightning, and he froze.

He'd brought his nun-chucks with him. He was too young for this.

"You don't have what it takes to stop me," I heard the tree say.

"Splash it on," Will said.

I moved forward and unscrewed the lid of the petrol canister. I sniffed at the opening and reeled back.

"Death juice!" Liam said and held aloft a stick, which I'd not seen him pick up. I wondered what he intended to do with it.

I swung the can, sloshing a load of petrol around the base of the tree and up the trunk and back towards us.

The first spots of rain had started to fall, and another rumble made us jump back.

"You don't know what you're doing," said the tree.

With the flash of lightning, which was no more than two seconds later, the rain gushed down. With the moon lost behind the clouds, darkness had descended upon us.

"Is it done?" Will said.

"We're empty."

I dropped the petrol can, pulled the matches from my pocket, and lit the first one. It fizzled out as soon as it sparked up. I tried another and the same thing happened.

"You are doomed to failure, boy," said the tree.

"Liam, Andy, Will, come here."

They stumbled over. By the time the next flash of lightning came, we were huddled together.

"Shield me from the rain," I said.

Bunched together, we were able to keep a match lit. I threw it towards the tree, but a gust of wind blew it back at us, dead.

The tree laughed.

"We have to get closer." I had to shout as the wind howled around us.

We moved together, but I felt our group get smaller.

"Who's not with us?" I said.

"Andy," Liam said.

"Andy, come on!" cried Will. "Join us!"

"No. It'll get me."

A flash of lightning illuminated Andy's petrified face. Fear looked to have aged him beyond his seven years.

"Stay there, Andy. We'll be back in a second," I said.

We edged towards the tree.

"Come on... come closer."

Liam fell away from us.

"Liam!" I called.

"I tripped," he said. "I'm going back to Andy, he's too scared."

He was scared. We all were. I don't blame him for giving up on us.

We were close to the tree, almost within arms' reach.

"Okay, do it," Will said.

On the third attempt, I lit another match. I tossed it at the tree. It fizzed for a second and then went out.

"It's too wet," Will said. "It's not going to work."

He stepped back, and as he pulled my hand, I fell.

"I will consume you!" cried the tree.

Lightning flashed, and I saw its mouth creep open. Inside I could see a glimpse of the Underworld: a tree-lined pathway, chasms of fire, creatures shuffling towards me.

I tried to move, but my foot was stuck. It wasn't like when my shoe was stuck in the mud, this was a different kind of grip, more powerful. I tried to yank my foot away but felt something pulling the other way, grazing against my ankle. A root had grabbed my leg, pulling me in. The hordes of evil creatures waited, ready to feast on my soul.

I opened the soggy matchbox and pulled out a match. It didn't feel solid enough to light a match with, but when I brushed the match head against the side, it sparked. I shoved the match inside the box with the others, causing them all to light at once and tossed the box at the base of the tree. A wall of fire flared up, its heat washing over my body.

I wasn't sure if it was the fire roaring or the tree crying out in pain. Will had hold of one arm, and Liam grabbed the other. Together they pulled. Something was sticking into the side of my foot and I felt it tear at the flesh as they tugged me free.

"Run," shouted Liam, and he took off for the bank behind the tree. Andy followed. Will helped me towards the bank. It took me back to the time Will and I had fled from the wasps that lived inside the tree and we'd got up onto the drove and fallen flat on our backs. That was before they started the construction work. There was no drove anymore; the bypass had taken its place. Will laid me down about halfway up, a couple of metres from the road and then continued towards where Liam and Andy stood.

I turned to face the tree, hoping to see it dying, hoping to see it screaming in agony, but the flames weren't attacking it with the same vigour as before.

"Get off the road!" Will shouted. I looked around but dazzled by the lights, I saw nothing. Seconds later, I heard three things: a screech, a thud, and a scream.

"What were you doing on the road?" the driver said. He was older than Dad, but not nearly as old as Granddad. He stood in the road staring at Liam who, for the first time in his life, had gone white. "What did I hit? Oh God, what did I hit?"

Andy lay in the road. Liam dashed to him. By the time I hobbled over, Liam was kneeling by Andy.

"Is he okay?" said the man, he started towards Andy and then stopped when he saw headlights coming the other way, and something else in the road.

Andy sat up. "Will pushed me," he said. He rubbed his head. "Why'd he do that?"

The man walked down the road waving his arms at the oncoming car. "Oh God," I could hear him mutter again and again.

Another flash of lightning revealed the shape of a body and the colour of Will's pyjamas.

"No!" I said and started to follow the man. Every time my foot hit the road, pain shot through my body.

"What were you doing in the road!" cried the man. I waited for an answer from Will, for some kind of noise, but there was nothing to be heard over the lashing rain and the approaching car which stopped a few feet short of Will's body, where the man was standing, still waving his arms, still asking why, and praying to God.

"Get help," said the man. "For God's sake, there's a boy on the road. I hit him."

The car sped off, its lights briefly shining on a trainer a few feet from me. I hobbled over and picked it up. It was warm and wet, sticky with blood and mud, and it reeked of petrol.

I looked towards the farmhouse, and between me and home, the tree. The fire had extinguished itself, and I swear to God that bastard tree laughed.

PART THREE

Thursday 5th July 1990

So many questions. How and why over and again. I couldn't answer. It seemed too stupid. I played the whole thing over in my head on the way to the hospital. People sped around and at first, they ignored me. A nurse eventually led me into a room where my foot was cleaned and stitched up. I felt no pain; I felt nothing. The rest of my family left me alone until Uncle Alan popped his head around the curtain where I was waiting with a nurse.

"Are you this boy's father?" she asked.

"Uncle."

"Okay. He's free to go. Standard pain medication. Keep the wound clean."

Alan helped me off the bed and then sat with me in the waiting area. "Liam said it was your idea." He stared at me, waiting for an answer, but there was no anger in his eyes.

"Is Andy okay?" I said.

"Bump on the head, but he'll be fine."

There was no point in asking about Will. We knew he was dead long before the ambulance arrived.

"How's the foot?" said Uncle Alan.

I looked at the four stitches. "Itchy."

"I don't understand what you were doing out on the road at that hour."

I couldn't explain it. Maybe Will had been right, and bad stuff happens for no reason. In the back of my mind was this idea that Will had been killed by the powers of the Underworld. They'd planned to take Andy by putting the car on that road at that minute, but Will saw it coming and pushed him out of the way, leaving himself in its path. Will would have said that was ridiculous. If I'd listened to him and stopped going on about The Underworld, we never would have gone out there, and he'd still be alive. It was my fault. I felt empty—as if I'd vomited everything from inside me leaving a mass of aching muscles and nothingness.

Uncle Alan passed me a tissue.

"It was my fault," I said. "I had this stupid idea, and now Will's dead."

"No, no," said Alan. "It was an accident. You didn't make that car hit him. Whatever you did do, you can't blame yourself."

"Where's Mum?"

"They're with the police. You're going to come home with me once they give Andy the all-clear."

Liam wasn't speaking to me. He didn't make it obvious, but he didn't let himself get drawn into conversation. Andy was better. He made me feel the bump on his head, and he said he couldn't remember anything that had happened the previous night. I sat around feeling lousy and thinking of Will. But when I tried to speak, no words came. I opened my mouth and a low moan would come out which would then break into sobs, making my body quake, and I had to wait for it to pass.

At some point in the afternoon, P.C. Wade came to speak to me. He didn't have that chirpy grin on his face from the road safety awareness days. "How are you feeling, Thomas?" he said.

I shrugged. "Horrible."

"I need to ask you a few questions to get to the bottom of this."

I nodded. "It's my fault," I said. "It was my idea to go out there."

"Why were you on the bypass?"

"We weren't meant to be. It was the tree in the field."

"What about it?"

"We wanted to destroy it."

Wade held his pen close to his pad but wrote nothing. "Why did you want to destroy the tree?"

"I had this idea." I paused, realising how stupid I sounded. "The tree is evil."

"Go on."

"Chappie died there. It's near where I found John. It took Granddad's eye, and we'd seen Shaky Jake hanging around, looking at it…"

"And you thought these things were related."

"Yes," I said. I didn't want to talk about the portal.

"When you say Shaky Jake, you mean Jacob Radford?"

"Yes."

"And how is he involved in this? Been telling you boys stories?"

"He's the murderer."

"What proof do you have of that?"

"We sent you a box! It had John's P.E. kit in, and a map…"

"Ah, so that was you."

"It was. Did you arrest him?"

"I shouldn't be telling you this. We checked with Mrs Glover. John's P.E. kit was at home."

"So, it wasn't John's?"

"No. But let's get back to the events of last night. You arranged for your cousins to sleep over, so you could sneak out and attack the tree?"

"It was supposed to be Will and me," I said. "But when Liam and Andy stayed over to watch the football, we changed our plans."

"Why last night?"

"It was stupid. I was certain that if we didn't get rid of it, something else bad would happen."

"Something bad did happen. Why didn't you tell anyone about this?"

"I tried! People said I was being silly."

From the hall, the phone rang. Aunt Anne stood up but heard Uncle Alan answer.

"So, you didn't listen to them?" Wade said.

"They wouldn't tell me what was going on with John. They kept on saying that sometimes bad things happen. I was trying to find out why."

"I see," said Wade. "It's a terrible tragedy, and we've had too many in the village." He stood up, and as he got to the door, he turned back to look at me. "I'm sorry for your loss."

After seeing Wade out, Uncle Alan beckoned Aunt Anne out of the room. More whispered secrets.

Aunt Anne came back in and took my hand. "That was your Mum on the phone. She thinks it would be best if you stayed here tonight."

NOW

I practically run into Liam in the doorway. I push past him and suck in the clean air. It's a bright day, almost exactly as it was the last time I saw Dad.

"Hey Tom," Liam says, oblivious to the state I'm in. Some things, some people, never change. "Some parents are searching the area for Jessica."

What's the point? She's probably already dead.

Liam grins. "I figure, who knows these old droves better than you and me?"

For a second, he's ten again.

"It'll be like old times," he says.

Like those old times when we thought that we could make a difference? When we searched the droves like a bunch of idiots, led by some bullshit cards thinking we'd be heroes? Those old times when my stupid plan killed my brother? Still, it's a route away from the house. We start walking. I glance at the place I found John's body all those years ago, and then to where we found Chappie's body, but that field is covered by solar panels. Is the tree stump beneath them? I watch the stream of traffic on the bypass, and when it clears for a moment I see Will's trainer, the pool of blood, and his lifeless body. I think about what's beyond if you follow the drove far enough.

"Come on," I say. "I know where she'll be."

I hurry along the drove, with Liam following behind. I glance into the ditch and see discoloured crisp packets, crushed cans of beer, and sweet wrappers. There was no litter in my childhood, not in the version I remember.

We keep going until we pass the bridge. I gaze into the water, and what used to be a constant stream is a dirty trickle. I look further down to where the ditches used to drain into the river and see a couple of old tyres. On the other side, a stagnant pool is trapped by a wall of sludge. The bridge creaks beneath my feet. I kick at the posts at the edge of the bridge, and rotten wood flakes off and sinks into the dirty water below. It's tainted and rotten. I know I won't find any good here.

Friday 6th July 1990

When Aunt Anne took me home in the middle of the morning, Mum was waiting for me in the kitchen. "Hi, love," she said. "How are you feeling?" Her voice sounded forced, and she looked grey and had bags under her eyes.

I shrugged. The tears were coming again, and I tried to fight them back as I ran to meet her.

She pulled me to her. I could tell she was crying too by her jerky breaths. She let go of me and bent to my level. "We've had to... make some changes."

"What?"

"Your dad wanted to keep Will's bedroom the way it was."

"What do you mean?"

"We've made a bed up for you in the spare room. Your new room."

I went upstairs. My bedroom door was closed, the old bedroom I'd shared with Will, but the spare room, my new bedroom, was open. All the boxes had been stacked up on one side, uncovering the bed that had been in there, unoccupied, for years. As I went in, I sneezed. Dust hung in the room from where Granddad's boxes of junk had been moved after so long. There was room for nothing other than the bed the boxes, and a pile of my clothes. I was glad to get out of Liam's baggy clothes and into some that fit. On the bed was the box I'd recovered from Granddad's house that contained the photographs, and on top of that someone had placed a book from my bedroom, the only one of my possessions that had been recovered, *The Secret of the Scythe*.

I wanted to look at Will's things. I left my room and approached my old door. Inside I could hear sobbing. I pushed the door open a crack and saw Dad sitting on the floor. His clothes hung loose on him, and his hair and beard seemed thick, as if it was consuming his skin.

"Dad," I said.

"Keep out!" he cried.

I pulled the door closed, but not before I heard him mutter, "Why did it have to be you, Will? Why you?"

I wished it was me too. I couldn't cope with the awful knowledge that I was responsible for Will's death. Dad knew it and wished me dead in his place. Even the way Mum held me suggested that she didn't love me as much anymore.

I returned to my new bedroom and picked up *The Secret of the Scythe* wanting to tear it to pieces. That book introduced me to the Underworld. Without that book, and its stupid tree, I would never have come up with such a ridiculous story. I grabbed the book and tossed it onto the bed where it struck the box of photographs. I gave the box a shove, hoping to push it to the end of the bed, out of the way, but I failed at that too, and the box tipped over.

Pictures of Dad, Aunt Anne and Uncle Rodney spread over the bed. In some pictures, I could make out Granddad Norman, and I vaguely recognised Nanna Betty. Among the photographs were various news clippings. A single-column story headlined 'Hero teen runs away from home' told the story of Uncle Rodney leaving Little Mosswick to join a travelling theatre company, as Granddad had said. Another story told of the ongoing suffering of 'kidnapping victim, Jacob Radford', and I started to sympathise with him. Maybe what he'd been through as a youngster had made him the way he was.

Then I found a large sheet of paper, folded in two and yellow with age, and I feared it would tear as I unfolded it. An image of a tree had names elaborately written on each of the branches, with plenty of on it I recognised. At the top, someone had elaborately written 'Tilbrook Family Tree'. I didn't know many of the names on the top half, but Norman Tilbrook was written in the middle, and his children's names were beneath that. My name and Will's were on the bottom row. Enid Tilbrook was on there too, on the same level as Granddad. She was his cousin, then, but there was another name beneath hers that I recognised too: Jacob Radford. I was related to Shaky Jake? I remembered all the things I'd written about him in my book of investigation, and I remembered that my book was still in my old bedroom, next to where Dad wept. If he saw that, and realised it was all my fault, he'd surely kill me. I had to get it back, but I'd have to wait for an opportunity.

I delved deeper into the box. It was full of decades-old paperwork and letters. Enid Tilbrook, it seemed, had once had a relationship with a young man from Little Mosswick, who had later been called up to fight in the Korean War. There was a child, and Enid died giving birth to him. This child, born outside of marriage was taken into care and given up for adoption. His adoptive parents gave him their surname, Radford.

Looking at the family tree again, it struck me as odd how much death there was in it. Many of the branches had died, and few men with the Tilbrook name lived. Liam and Andy were Carters. Uncle Rodney didn't have children. That left a single line: Granddad, Dad and me. I was the only one of my generation.

"Thomas," Mum called from downstairs, her voice cold and lifeless.

I trudged downstairs, unsure whether I could bear her judgemental eyes on me again, but when I opened the door, there was a kind voice.

"How's Tom?" Granddad said. While he looked upset, he still had some of his old colour. He sat down and rested with one arm on his walking stick. His other arm was open and welcoming.

I shuffled over to him, and he pulled me to him. As we hugged, he exhaled and sounded in pain. I leant back and could see him grimacing.

"You okay, Granddad?"

"Finished off those pheasants yesterday. They might have been past best. How are you doing, anyway? Tough day?" he said. He was always the master of the understatement when he wanted to be. He knew when to play up a story, and when to play it down.

"I'll make some tea," Mum said, still struggling to stop her voice from breaking.

"Listen, Tom," Granddad said, quiet enough so that Mum wouldn't hear. "You mustn't blame yourself for this."

I tried to squirm away. I didn't want to hear it.

"You're a good lad."

I wriggled and tried to shrink into myself, covering my ears with my shoulders.

"But you're like me, Thomas. That's the problem."

I stopped struggling. I was ready to listen.

"You love a good story, and you want others to share it. You know how I lost my eye?"

"The tree. The tree tried to take it."

"Farming accident. That's all. An unfortunate incident."

I nodded.

"But what kind of story is that? No kind; that's what. You get caught up in stories because it's in your blood. If that's anyone's fault, it's mine."

"No, Granddad, you weren't there."

"But I've been planting seeds in your head all your life. No wonder you got caught up in your own fantasy."

"I'm sorry."

"Never be sorry for that, Thomas. Your Dad don't understand you. He was never one for stories and he don't understand how they work. But I understand, and I say don't ever change. Okay?"

He let me go, and a little of the shell around me broke.

"I think your Dad needs me. He's been in Will's room all night." He pushed himself up using his stick, and then made his way up the stairs, grunting as he took each step.

Later, Granddad managed to talk Dad downstairs. He convinced him he needed some fresh air. It was my chance to

278   DEAD BRANCHES

nip into my old room and destroy my evidence. This story had gone far enough.

"Thomas," Mum said, as I was about to go up the stairs. "We do love you, you know." She opened her arms.

We cried. We spoke, but I doubt either of us can remember what about, and eventually, the book went out of my mind, and a tremendous tiredness spread through my body.

"I need a nap, Mum," I said, and we parted. When I got to the top of the stairs, I saw my old bedroom door open and remembered what I had to do. I went inside, picked the book off the bedside table, and started to flick through it. It was a story. Fiction. Full of ideas we'd come up with together. Crazy theories. As I was going to take it to my new room a shadow fell in front of me. The hulking form of my father blocked the light from the hall.

"Stay out of Will's room," Dad said. He grabbed the book out of my hand. "What's this?"

"It's nothing."

"Where did it come from?"

"My table…"

"In Will's room?"

"It was mine."

"It stays in his room." He turned a few pages. "John's killer? What's this?"

"Don't look, Dad."

"I asked you a question. What is this?"

"We had ideas about who killed John, and how his body ended up where it did…"

Dad continued to flick through the book. "You blamed a tree? That's what you were doing out there?"

"It's stupid. It was a stupid idea."

"What this tells me, is that if you weren't fooling around, Will would never have died." His face reddened and I could feel the heat radiating from him as his anger grew.

"I'm sorry. It wasn't supposed to happen."

He turned back another page. "What's this about Shaky Jake?"

"If it was him, the police would have arrested him."

Dad froze. He was staring over my shoulder. "The bastard. Returning to the scene of the crime. I'll show him." He darted down the stairs.

I turned around and looked out the window. Walking along the drove, peering into the ditches, was Shaky Jake.

"Thomas?" called Mum, and I followed down the stairs. "Where's your Dad going?"

"Call the police," I said. "Quick."

―――❦―――

Dad dragged Jake across the field by his hair. Over his shoulder, he'd coiled a rope, and in his other hand, he held the red petrol canister he kept in the Land Rover.

Granddad Norman started out across the field after him, with Mum behind, and me following. After the recent rain, the sun had returned with a vengeance.

"Trevor," Granddad said. "Come back inside."

Ignoring him, Dad continued to pull Jake across the field, dragging him over divots to keep him stumbling along.

The whole time Jake whined like something inhuman. He gripped Dad's hand; whether he was trying to free his hair from Dad's grasp or trying to stop his scalp from being torn off, I don't know.

Granddad Norman stopped moving and leant on his stick, gasping for breath. Mum reached him and placed a hand on his back to support him. He let the stick go and put both hands on his stomach before collapsing onto his knees.

I kept moving beyond them as Dad hurled Jake towards the tree. Air rushed from his body and he turned around. "No," he said. "I never... I never..." but he couldn't get the words out. Even from a distance, I could see he was shaking worse than ever.

Dad wrapped the rope around Jake and the tree.

"Dad, don't!" I said as I continued across the field.

"This is what you wanted, boy," Dad said.

"It's not," I said, as Jake kept muttering garbled nonsense.

"It ends here."

"We were only messing around!" I said. "Let the police decide."

"It's too late for that, boy." Dad's eyes were glassy, and his brown irises had become so dark they were almost black. He untwisted the cap from the petrol canister and started splashing petrol over Jake.

Police sirens sounded in the distance. "The police are coming. They'll know what to do."

"If they knew, they would have done it already. You and Will would never have got such crazy ideas."

I looked around for help. Granddad lay on his side with Mum over him. "Something's wrong with Granddad," I said. "Look."

Dad turned towards him. For a second the true colour returned to his eyes. The petrol canister dropped from his hands.

"I... never..." muttered Jake, his chin wet and shiny with drool.

The dead-eyed look returned to Dad's face. He put both hands to his head and scrunched his hair, making two wild tufts, like goat horns. His face was beaded with sweat, and his beard glistened with it. He reached into the deep pocket of his overalls and pulled out a box of matches.

"But he's family," I said. I ran towards him, thinking that I could knock the matchbox from his hand before he had the chance to light one. I reached out, got my fingers into the matchbox and got hold of a few matches. Pathetic.

With the hand that held the match, he struck me, the back of his hand catching me across the bridge of the nose, knocking me to the ground. He stared at me, his eyes scanning from my feet to my head, with a look of absolute disgust.

"Families make mistakes," he said. He struck a match and tossed it at Jake's feet.

Flames engulfed his shoes, licked at his trousers, climbed up his legs. Still, he protested, "I never. I never."

Dad focused on the flames, almost hypnotised by the way they danced. Fire reflected in his eyes. He'd been possessed. He couldn't take his eyes off the fire, and I couldn't take my eyes off him.

Jake's protests turned to screams. The flames covered him, and he was too bright to look at. The rope must have burned through because Jake fell forward. He rolled over in the mud until the fire was out, and then lay there twitching, smouldering.

The tree was alight. It had spread to the higher branches, and flaming debris dropped to the ground.

Dad still stared at the tree. The fire was so bright that his face was glowing orange; his eyes were almost entirely flame; his face was without emotion; his dry, cracked lips parted as he inhaled the smoke; and the horns of hair on his head solidified.

I felt something in my back pocket. Liam's Top Trumps. On top was the picture of the Fire Demon. I looked from the card to Dad. He looked more than human, as if he had the strength of a demon. I looked at the card again and the vision became clearer. It wasn't the flame that was making him appear orange, it was his skin. He was orange. Those were horns on his head, not tufts of hair. My father was the fire demon.

I ran, not up the bank and onto the bypass, I'd never do that ever again, but across one field and into another. I ran through the oilseed rape, no longer a bright yellow, having dropped its flowers, but green, tall and thick. Once I hit Catchwater Drove, I followed it towards the river. I could feel heat on my back, chasing me, closing in on me, daring me to turn around. When I reached the bridge, I turned to the left and followed the path of the river, past where it crossed under the new bypass. The old pumping station came into sight. I cast a glance behind me, fearing that it would be my last and the demon would be upon me, but he wasn't in sight. I didn't dare slow down, not until I was in the shade of the crumbling building.

Around the side was a door. I pushed it open and edged in only to be met by an almighty stench. Steps led down, and then there was space before it dropped down into a massive hole which had a low metal frame around it as an ineffective barrier. Whatever machinery used to be in there had been recovered, and inside was an empty shell. I took the steps, slowly and carefully, with one hand over my nose. The steps were slimy and slippery, and I had to hold on to avoid falling. At the bottom, as I stepped on something, I heard a rustle. Looking down, I saw some familiar sweet wrappers: Bamse Mums and Stratos. Not the typical sweets that you could buy at Little Mosswick Post Office.

I crept towards the pit, not knowing what to expect. It was too dark to make much out. I couldn't see the bottom. I felt around on the ground and found a stone. I dropped it in, and a couple of seconds later heard a plop. There was water, but it wasn't deep. My eyes started to adjust to the lack of light, and I thought I could make out chains hanging down the opposite side.

Light flowed into the chamber, and I looked to the door to see a tall silhouette with enormous hands and wild hair.

"Uncle Rodney!" I cried.

"Shush, Thomas, dear boy," he said. "Your father will hear you. He's gone crazy." He came down the steps towards me.

"How did you know where to find me?"

"I saw the fire across the fields from where I was having a quick drink and saw you running off. I ran as fast as I could and thought I might find you somewhere near here."

"Is Dad out there?"

"Keep your voice down. He's wild." Uncle Rodney's eyes grew large as he reached the end of the sentence, and he continued to walk towards me. "Stay here with your Uncle

Rodney," he said in a comforting whisper, "I'll take care of you."

Rodney wrapped his arms around me. He was breathing heavily and reeked of alcohol. "There's a place in here you can hide. No one will know you're here." He led me around the pit where it was almost pitch black. He grabbed something, which sounded like a piece of thick board, and dragged it aside. "Through there," he said guiding me through a gap. I felt myself passing under an old sack, and then I found my way to the end. There were cushions to sit on, but little else.

"Wait there," Uncle Rodney said. "I'm going to check to see if your father is still on the rampage."

I heard the board slide back across the entrance to the hole, which shut out all light, and then there was another sound, as if something was pushed against the board.

I tried to open my eyes wider to see anything, but it was absolute darkness. I touched the walls, making out some kind of scratches, but nothing else. I leaned forward and pushed at the board in front of the entrance, but it wasn't moving. Dad would never find me in here. The cushions were flat, but I used them as best as I could to make myself comfortable. The awkward bulk of the Top Trumps made sitting awkward, so I reached into my pocket and tossed them in front of me. There was something else in my pockets too. Some matches I'd grabbed from Dad. If I could light one, I thought, I would be able to see my surroundings.

The first one I struck against the wall snapped in half. That was no good. I tried again with a second, and with a satisfying fizz it erupted into life. On either side were old-fashioned pink bricks, thick with years of grime and in front of me the piece of board. On the floor, the Top Trumps were scattered. The Beast, the creature with a horror rating of 98, the creature pictured on stage, was on top of the pile. I turned to look closer at the bricks. Something had been carved into them, but before I could see what, the flame touched my fingers, and I dropped the match which extinguished when it hit the ground. I lit another, and to keep my flame going, I grabbed a random card and set that alight. Looking again at the words scratched into the wall, I realised what they were: Lyrics. The words 'hold' and 'give' had been carved deeper, suggesting the need for emphasis. It was John Barnes' rap from New Order's England World Cup anthem, 'World in Motion'. There was only one person who knew and loved that song so well that he'd turn to it in his darkest hour: John. He'd been trapped here, and I was stuck in the same place.

Shocked, I dropped the lit card onto the cushions, and immediately they caught fire, too. I yelped.

"Quiet," cried Uncle Rodney from the other side. "He'll hear you."

I lay on my back and kicked at the board. It barely moved.

"Stop it," said Uncle Rodney, "Or I'll have to silence you."

"It was you!" I shouted. "You killed John."

"No one can prove that, dear boy."

Behind me, a second cushion flared up. I kicked at the board again and again with my head lifted as far away from the fire as possible. Pain arched down my leg, and I could feel bleeding from where my stitches had split open. As I tried to breathe, I choked on the smoke. A thickness developed inside my skull as smoke surrounded me. I wanted to close my eyes and drift off.

"It's no good. You don't have the strength, my boy."

I was sick of being told I was too weak. I held nothing back and gave one more almighty kick. It moved. I squirmed around so that I was facing forward, and I was able to push my arm out of the gap. I pushed forward, edging the board, and whatever was holding it in place, forward, millimetre by millimetre until I could get my head out. I gasped at the air. While tainted, it was fresher than the smoky air behind me. My legs felt hot as I wriggled forward, trying to force my body through.

"I told you it's no good," said Rodney, and he lurched towards me. He put a piece of cloth over my mouth and a sickly-sweet smell hit me. I tried to hold my breath, but then a slither of light appeared over by the door and I gasped.

"Rodney!" called a gruff voice.

He dropped the rag and stood.

I felt dizzy and struggled to keep my eyes open. The figure at the door was surrounded by a fiery glow.

"Turn around Trevor. The boy wants to be here with me."

"It was you, wasn't it?"

"I don't have the faintest idea what you're talking about."

"It's always been you." Dad dashed down the steps, and I could feel a wave of heat wash over me. "You never rescued Jacob Radford. You kidnapped him."

"Why don't you ask him, see what he says? Oh, that's right; you toasted him like a marshmallow."

"That boy, John. That was you too." Dad now stood beside Rodney. The Beast versus the Fire Demon. Every statistic was in The Beast's favour.

Rodney grabbed Dad by the wrist.

"Dad," I managed to murmur.

He looked down at me, and as he did so, he seemed to weaken. Rodney was taller, and bent Dad's hands back, making him look puny. Of course, he did. The Beast had 87 points for physical strength; the Fire Demon, only 71. Dad broke the grip by yanking his arm away and flew at Rodney head-first. They came together in a flurry of blows. I could no longer see my father and my uncle, but two monsters. They locked their massive hands together, grappling, trying to overpower one another. The Beast loomed over the Fire Demon, and pushed down hard, forcing him onto one knee. He was losing. He looked weaker. I was going to be left to be consumed by The Beast. The Fire Demon shrunk into himself, and then he was my dad again. He roared, "I've lost one of my boys. I won't let you take the other." He let go of The Beast's hands and threw his body forward, his shoulder crashing into its stomach, orange sparks flying from his body.

The Beast came forward again and kicked Dad in the ribs. The Beast took a step back and joined his hands into a mighty club. He ran towards Dad again, but Dad arched forward, under The Beast's blow, and flipped him over his shoulders, sending him crashing against the pit's metal barrier with a sickening crunch.

"You okay, boy?" called Dad.

I managed a feeble, "Yes."

The Beast had climbed back onto his knees, but it wasn't The Beast anymore. He was Rodney again, with his ridiculous clown hair. His back was twisted, and he couldn't straighten his body. Dad planted his foot on Uncle Rodney's chest and pushed. Rodney tumbled back over the low metal barrier and fell into the pit below, screaming until he hit the water with a splash.

Dad approached me, flames flickering in his eyes. He placed his hands on me, and the last thing I remember is intense heat washing over me.

NOW

We keep moving along Catchwater Drove, and, frantic, I begin to look around. This is the place. It doesn't make sense for it not to be here. This is where the girl was supposed to be.

"It's gone," says Liam.

I break into a run and stop where it should be. A brick scar remains, running up from the river to where the pumping station once stood. The huge pits have been filled with the bricks that once made up the building.

"They tore it down not long after what happened there."

There is a low fence around it, with barbed wire at the top, and a sign that warns of danger.

I stare at the place where Uncle Rodney held me and think back to what Dad did. I can't shake the vision of two monsters battling with all their might, but then I remember the condition I was in. I remember the reason Liam and I are here is because we're looking for a missing child. What would I do if Charlie was in danger? Would it give me superhuman strength? Would it allow me to kill?

I feel the heat of the sun on my back and think of the sickening heat radiating from Dad's orange demon skin. "Dad turned into a monster. He burned Jake to death and then killed Rodney."

"He did it for you, Tom."

I see those burning eyes coming towards me again.

"Do you remember what happened when you left the pumping station?"

I remembered waking in my bed. Everything was hazy. I had a feeling as if I'd been plucked from a nightmare by a guardian angel. When the sun shone through a window, I thought I was burning. I screamed. After that was the hospital.

"Your Dad carried you home. Three police officers tried to take you from him, but he refused to let you go until you were safe."

I shivered, feeling a cool breeze blowing from the river onto us. "Then what happened?"

"They took your Dad away."

"And I told everyone he was a monster."

Liam puts an arm on my shoulder.

"What did they tell you about me?"

"They said you'd be okay. They told me not to worry."

"More lies."

"I don't know. I look at you, and you're not doing so bad."

When I first saw Liam again, I couldn't see a change. He'd seemed like a giant version of the ten-year-old I'd known with a little Liam clone beside him, but maybe there's more to him than that. "What would you know?" I say, brushing Liam's arm off.

Liam moves around to look me in the eye. "You and Charlie are all your Mum ever talks about—once she's stopped bossing me around with what to do on the farm."

"Really?"

"Yeah. The solar farm was her idea. That got us out of a hole."

But some things don't change. Same old Liam, getting the wrong end of the stick. "No, I meant, does she often talk about us?"

"All the time. So does your dad."

I knew he'd lied. I start to walk back towards the house.

"He does. He says he always knew you were the smart one."

I move faster.

With the extra weight he's carrying, he can't keep up. "He says he's proud of you."

I leave Liam behind.

When I get back to the farmhouse, I'll grab Charlie, and go. I can't take the lies. I won't even have to go back into the house, I realise, as Charlie is sitting on the patio outside, drinking blackcurrant cordial with Billy.

"Where's Dad?" asks Billy.

"He's coming," I say, and suspect it's true.

"They found Jessica," he says.

In my head, I see the photograph the police officer had flashed in front of me, now stained with blood.

"Her Dad had taken her."

"She's okay?"

"See, Dad," says Charlie. "There wasn't anything to worry about."

Mum comes out of the house. She ruffles the hair of both boys and then places her hand on my wrist. "We thought you'd gone again."

"I'm going," I say.

"Your Dad was so upset when you ran off like that."

"Why was he shouting?"

"Shouting? He can barely whisper, Tom."

Mum is still sticking up for him. Or maybe it was another echo from the past.

"He won't want me to tell you this, but he wept when you went back downstairs. All he wants is to see you again."

"No, Mum."

"He talks about that day all the time."

I see his mud-smeared face, wild beard and fiery eyes, and can hear him boasting about killing two men.

"He blames himself. Says part of him always suspected Rodney, but he didn't want to believe it. Then, when he saw the fear on your face, he knew he had to save you."

I try to pull myself away from her, but her grip on my arm is strong.

"I saw you two coming down the drove. He was batting police officers away like flies. 'Leave my boy alone' he was saying. 'You can take me when he's safe.' When he placed you in my arms, what I saw on his face was pure relief."

I imagine Laura Matthews is feeling the same kind of relief, knowing Jessica is safe. I guess there was nothing to worry about. Almost every day there's nothing to worry about. There are monsters out there, but they're not on every street corner. They're not hiding behind every twitching curtain.

They're not upstairs, in a bedroom of your childhood home, waiting for you to return so they can finally devour you.

I gaze up at the house and into his bedroom window. It's time.

I climb the stairs alone. There's nothing sinister about them. I don't need Mum to hold my hand. I push open the door, and I'm unsurprised to be hit by a blast of heat. He doesn't take up as much space as I thought he would. It's as if he's shrunk, but maybe it's because I'm twice as big as when I last saw him, and the last time I saw him, he'd become a monster in order to save me.

His eyes open. What should I say? I'm sorry I haven't spoken to you in twenty-five years? I'm sorry you spent years in prison because I refused to tell my side of the story?

I'm sorry I thought you were a monster?

"Hey, Thomas, my boy." That's what he used to call me, 'my boy'.

We chat about everything. We chat about nothing. At some point, he says, "I hear you've got a boy of your own."

"Do you want to meet him?" I ask.

He smiles, and I remember that he used to do it all the time, before that summer when he was so worried about trying to protect Will and me.

"Charlie," I call, and he flies up the stairs.

"This is your Granddad," I say.

Charlie reaches out a hand and takes my father's. "Pleased to meet you," he says. He takes a second to assess my dad and then reaches across to hug him.

Moments later Mum comes in. She had to check that we were okay, like she always has. "Made you a tea," she says and rests a hand on my shoulder. I've missed that.

"We'll be back," I say to Dad.

When he tries to reply, a cough catches in his throat, and I don't know how many opportunities I'll have to make it right.

I take Charlie by the hand and lead him downstairs. I may not be able to make it right with Dad, but I can with Charlie. As we re-enter the kitchen, Granddad stirs in his chair.

"Granddad," I say, "why don't you tell Charlie how you lost your eye?"

"Farming accident," he says with a frown.

"No Granddad," I say, giving him an obvious wink, "tell him the real story."

THE END?

Not if you want to dive into more of Crystal Lake Publishing's Tales from the Darkest Depths!

Check out our amazing website and online store or download our latest catalog here:
https://geni.us/CLPCatalog

Looking for award-winning Dark Fiction?
Download our latest catalog.

Includes our anthologies, novels, novellas, collections, poetry, non-fiction, and specialty projects.

TALES FROM THE DARKEST DEPTHS

We always have great new projects and content on the website to dive into, as well as a newsletter, behind the scenes options, social media platforms, our own dark fiction shared-world series and our very own webstore. Our webstore even has categories specifically for KU books, non-fiction, anthologies, and of course more novels and novellas.

AUTHOR BIOGRAPHY

Benjamin Langley is a writer of quiet horror with a creeping dread. *Dead Branches* was his first novel which was followed by *Is She Dead in Your Dreams?* and *Normal*. His most recent work is the alternative history horror trilogy, *Guy Fawkes: Demon Hunter*.

Benjamin has been writing since he could hold a pen and has always been drawn to dark tales. He has had short stories published in over a dozen publications including *Crescendo of Darkness, Pandemic Unleashed,* and *The Manchester Review*. He has also written Sherlock Holmes adventures for a number of anthologies.

He lives, writes, and teaches in Cambridgeshire, UK, where he also studied at Anglia Ruskin University. He was awarded the prize for best Major Writing Project while studying for his BA in Writing and English. He completed his MA in Creative Writing in 2015. An earlier version of *Dead Branches* was part of Benjamin's final project.

Readers…

Thank you for reading *Dead Branches*. We hope you enjoyed this novel.

Help other readers by telling them why you enjoyed this book. No need to write an in-depth discussion. Even a single sentence will be greatly appreciated. Reviews go a long way to helping a book sell, and is great for an author's career. It'll also help us to continue publishing quality books.

Thank you again for taking the time to journey with Crystal Lake Publishing.

You will find links to all our social media platforms on our Linktree page:
https://linktr.ee/CrystalLakePublishing.

MISSION STATEMENT

Since its founding in August 2012, Crystal Lake Publishing has quickly become one of the world's leading publishers of Dark Fiction and Horror books in print, eBook, and audio formats.

While we strive to present only the highest quality fiction and entertainment, we also endeavour to support authors along their writing journey. We offer our time and experience in non-fiction projects, as well as author mentoring and services, at competitive prices.

With several Bram Stoker Award wins and many other wins and nominations (including the HWA's Specialty Press Award), Crystal Lake Publishing puts integrity, honor, and respect at the forefront of our publishing operations.

We strive for each book and outreach program we spearhead to not only entertain and touch or comment on issues that affect our readers, but also to strengthen and support the Dark Fiction field and its authors.

Not only do we find and publish authors we believe are destined for greatness, but we strive to work with men and woman who endeavour to be decent human beings who care more for others than themselves, while still being hard working, driven, and passionate artists and storytellers.

Crystal Lake Publishing is and will always be a beacon of what passion and dedication, combined with overwhelming teamwork and respect, can accomplish. We endeavour to know each and every one of our readers, while building personal relationships with our authors, reviewers, bloggers, podcasters, bookstores, and libraries.

We will be as trustworthy, forthright, and transparent as any business can be, while also keeping most of the headaches away from our authors, since it's our job to solve the problems so they can stay in a creative mind. Which of course also means paying our authors.

We do not just publish books, we present to you worlds within your world, doors within your mind, from talented authors who sacrifice so much for a moment of your time.

There are some amazing small presses out there, and through collaboration and open forums we will continue to support other presses in the goal of helping authors and showing the world what quality small presses are capable of accomplishing. No one wins when a small press goes down, so we will always be there to support hardworking, legitimate presses and their authors. We don't see Crystal Lake as the best press out there, but we will always strive to be the best, strive to be the most interactive and grateful, and even blessed press around. No matter what happens over time, we will also take our mission very seriously while appreciating where we are and enjoying the journey.

What do we offer our authors that they can't do for themselves through self-publishing?

We are big supporters of self-publishing (especially hybrid publishing), if done with care, patience, and planning. However, not every author has the time or inclination to do market research, advertise, and set up book launch strategies. Although a lot of authors are successful in doing it all, strong small presses will always be there for the authors who just want to do what they do best: write.

What we offer is experience, industry knowledge, contacts and trust built up over years. And due to our strong brand and trusting fanbase, every Crystal Lake Publishing book comes with weight of respect. In time our fans begin to trust our judgment and will try a new author purely based on our support of said author.

With each launch we strive to fine-tune our approach, learn from our mistakes, and increase our reach. We continue to assure our authors that we're here for them and that we'll carry the weight of the launch and dealing with third parties while they focus on their strengths—be it writing, interviews, blogs, signings, etc.

We also offer several mentoring packages to authors that include knowledge and skills they can use in both traditional and self-publishing endeavours.

We look forward to launching many new careers.

This is what we believe in. What we stand for. This will be our legacy.

Welcome to Crystal Lake Publishing—Tales from the Darkest Depths.

THANK YOU FOR PURCHASING THIS BOOK

Printed in Great Britain
by Amazon